Rise *of a* REBEL

NIGHTFLY · BOOK 2

CHRISTINE SCHULZ

Emma—
Be a rebel!
Christine Schulz

ISBN-13 // 978-1-7352474-5-8 // Paperback
Cover design by Manuela Serra

Printed in the United States of America

1

"RYKER DID *WHAT*?" Catilda's hands slammed down on the table, her hot pink nails digging into the scratched up wood. "I *knew* that little weasel was hiding something behind that stupid adorable smile of his. I can't believe he was working for your father this whole time. You should have said something before I risked my life to save him!" She snorted like an angry bull, her knuckles turning white as she pressed her fingers into the table.

"Keep it down, Catilda! People are staring at us," I murmured in a low voice. Awkwardly tilting my head, I scratched the buzzed sides of my head to survey the coffee shop around us.

Not more than a week ago, my good friend Briyan had died from an overdose on Bliss right here in this cafe. The image would forever leave a sour feeling in my stomach. For all the other customers, life went on as normal. A noisy queue of caffeine fiends formed right up to the door. Machines ground away to keep up with the morning demand, producing magic-infused brews that left a nutty mix of caramel and maple lingering in the air.

Unfortunately, despite all the noise, Catilda's outburst didn't go unnoticed. An elderly man a few tables away peered over his newspaper and shot us an unamused glower, while an impatient female in line snapped her gaze at us with raised eyebrows.

"Besides ..." My head dropped, letting the short green strains of hair fall across my forehead. "I ... I don't think he was faking his personality. Ryker really *does* care about people."

"Whatever you say, Zulli." Catilda took a sip of her tea, leaving behind a perfect outline of her rosy red lipstick on the plastic lid. She leaned over the table, her silver bangles scraping against the wood. She took my advice and lowered her voice. "I know Ryker is your friend, but don't you find all of this a little ... suspicious? He admits he worked for your father, the criminal mastermind behind the dangerous mind-altering drug known as Bliss. He's then held prisoner by Zavyr Taracula himself, and conveniently Ryker's memories are erased of everything he's ever done while working for your father? Are you sure you can trust him? I think you should cover your own ass and report him. This could all come back to blow up in your face."

She leaned back in her chair, crossed her arms, and stared daggers at me with those baby blue eyes of hers. Catilda may have looked like she belonged on the cover of a fashion magazine, with her perfectly spiraled copper hair and silky top that hugged her slim waistline, but behind her pale, freckled skin was a massive brain, stockpiled with more information than an encyclopedia. Her concern about Ryker was a valid one.

"What good would reporting him do? He doesn't remember working with my dad." I took a napkin and brushed the muffin crumbs off my gray t-shirt. "I don't know what to think, Catilda. I've seen Ryker put himself in harm's way more times than I can count. Not just for me or Kasra, but random strangers he's never even met. People don't do that if they don't genuinely care about others."

Catilda reached for her jean jacket draped over the back of the chair and shrugged it on. "All I'm saying is something doesn't sit well with me. Be careful, will you, hun? I told Ryker

2

once if he let anything happen to you, I'd use my claws to gouge out his eyes. Don't make me actually do it."

A smile curled my lips and a spirited laugh passed through. The last week had been a tortuous hell for me, but despite my world crumbling, I knew I could always count on Catilda to help me put the broken pieces back together.

"Oh, I almost forgot!" Catilda grabbed her oversized tote from the floor and started rummaging through it. "I found what you were asking for."

"Really? And … you're sure I can have it? I can pay you for it."

She nonchalantly shrugged her shoulders. "There are a million different spelled items that people use for protection. Finding a pretty necklace wasn't all that difficult. We already had about a dozen of them in the shop. I told my parents it was for you and they said it was on the house."

She pulled out a velvet pendant box and slid it across the table. I snapped it open, and inside was a shimmering ruby teardrop necklace. The jewel was a deep, intense red. When I rolled it in my palm, its incredible brilliance sparkled in the pale daylight filtering through the storefront window. It was simple, yet alluring. And Kasra was going to love it.

"You know you can't bribe her with jewelry to gain back her trust, hun. It's only been two days. Give her some time." Catilda gave me a dismissive wave of her hand.

"I know." I snapped the box shut and tucked it into the front pocket of my plaid button-down. "I'm not trying to bribe her. But she's extremely pissed off at me about the whole hunting down Davian thing without her and then nearly getting Ryker killed. She hasn't been answering my phone calls and pretends she's not home when I knock. I'm not looking for forgiveness. I just want to prove to her I can be trusted and I can't do that if she won't even give me a chance. She loves things that are both pretty and functional, so I thought maybe the necklace would help encourage her to open up to me."

"Right. Well, you have fun with that. I have to get going if I'm going to catch the next bus back to the shop for my afternoon shift."

Catilda and I both rose from our seats. I grabbed my backpack and strolled over to the garbage can to toss my trash. We both stopped and whirled around when a feral growl erupted from a disgruntled customer at the front counter.

"What do you mean you ran out of the Mystic Sunrise brew? I don't want whatever this crap is. I stood in this ridiculously long line for half an hour, watching you incompetent children scramble around like clueless idiots. You'd better go in the back and find me some or the entire city will hear about this sad excuse for a coffee shop and its lazy employees!"

The man snatched the paper cup in front of him and hurled the hot coffee at the female behind the counter. The pretty young barista, probably not much older than sixteen, turned her shoulder and winced. Bracing for the steaming hot liquid to burn her skin, she let out a terrified scream as the coffee splattered across her chest and dripped down her neck.

Another female employee rushed over, handing her a towel. "Tilly, are you okay?"

She nodded and kept her eyes shut, dabbing the liquid off her tender skin.

"Sir, I think you need to leave." Tilly's co-worker, a friend of mine named Ambyr, kept her voice calm but commanding. She was doing an excellent job of keeping her face in a neutral expression despite the angry twitch of her lips. She pointed toward the door, but when the man refused to budge, she stomped around the counter, her long brown ponytail swaying. With a gentle hand, she attempted to guide the disgruntled customer toward the exit.

He rolled his shoulder and shoved her out of the way. As Ambyr tripped on her feet, her hand barely brushed against the man's chest.

4

"Get off me! You're getting my suit dirty with your filthy hands, and I highly doubt you could afford to get it dry cleaned on your measly salary."

"Sir, if you don't leave, I'm going to have to call the cops." Ambyr stood her ground, keeping her purple clogs planted firmly in front of him, hands digging into her hips.

"Go ahead. Call the cops. Do you know who I am?" He stiffened his shoulders and thrust out his chin. "I'm Cullin Maddox. Face of the five o'clock news!"

My pulse spiked at the mention of his familiar name. This was bad. Very bad.

Cullin paused for dramatic effect, like he was waiting for a round of "ohs" and "ahs" and people dropping to their knees in reverence. Something seemed off about him. I didn't know the guy personally, but on the news he was always calm and professional. I'd bumped into him several times during my father's fundraising events and had a few pleasant conversations with him. Now, he was acting like a rabid dog, going after anyone who got in his way. His personality, the way he held himself ... it was wrong. It wasn't him.

Panic widened my eyes when the thought came to me. Bliss. It had to be. The memory warping drug would have explained his previously cheery personality. Something was troubling him, and he took the drugs to forget about it. That, or was someone was forcing him to do it. He must have been taking it long enough that it was scrambling his brain.

"It sounds like I have an interesting story to report on this evening," he continued, projecting his voice so everyone could hear. "The headline will read 'Local coffee shop employee assaults news anchor'!"

"Assault?" Ambyr retorted. "I did no such thing. Everyone here can attest to that."

Glancing around the cafe, Cullin wasn't receiving the round of celebrity ovation he was looking for. Instead, heads were buried in phones, sipping drinks, and awkwardly glaring away from the unfolding situation.

"Seriously?" Ambyr addressed the crowd. "You should all be ashamed of yourselves for letting this man storm in here like he owns the place."

"You know what?" Cullin cut in. "I have enough money that I *could* own this place. Maybe I'll give the building owner a call later on and make him a generous offer. Then I'll fire every employee here and tear this place down. Maybe turn it into a bank where I can store my fortune."

My gaze locked on the news anchor. Even from across the room, the scent of his skunky cologne was overpowering my keen sense of smell. His perfectly tailored dark suit jacket rested on his shoulders, the fabric forming a crisp line down his arms. His full head of dark blond hair, combed over to the side, along with the smug grin on his clean-shaven face, boasted nothing but pure arrogance. He raised his hand toward Ambyr. With no desire to wait and see what he would do with it, I dropped my bag and lunged at him.

My cat-like reflexes engaged and claws shot out of my fingertips. My hand snatched around his wrist. I squeezed so tight I could actually hear his joints grinding under the pressure.

"My friend here asked you to leave." I nodded toward the exit, through which most of the remaining guests inside the coffee shop had fled. Catilda backed away, staying well behind me. "I suggest you listen to the nice lady before things get out of control here."

Cullin studied me with a thoughtful gleam stirring in his light brown eyes.

I stared back at him head on, not loosening my grip on his wrist in the slightest. "I know who *you* are, Cullin Maddox, but do you know who *I* am?" My other hand hovered over my trusty belt, stocked with several spelled powders and liquids packed into color coded bullets. "Ah, that's too bad. Allow me to introduce myself. My name's Zulli. I'm a soldier in the Chitol military, and I have some friends in pretty high places who could make your life a living hell. But you know who you should *really* be afraid of? My father. He's the CEO of NightFly Technologies and has the power to completely destroy you. Does the name Zavyr Taracula ring a bell?"

It was a risk to even mention my father's name, given that I knew he was up to something shady with Bliss, but it paid off. A slight tremor of terror caused a muscle in Cullin's jaw to tick. Almost immediately, though, the fear vanished and his lips curled into a half smile.

"Why yes, I do know Zavyr very well." He dropped his voice to a low whisper and leaned toward my ear. "He has eyes everywhere!"

His unexpected words transported my mind down a dizzy, dark spiral of thoughts. My pulse spiked, and I trapped all the remaining air in my lungs. Was he threatening me? Was my *father* threatening me?

Overcome with shock, I let go of his wrist. Catilda's voice called to me, "Zulli! Look out!"

I snapped out of my trance to see a vibrant aqua marble drop from Cullin's hand.

"*Lapsus.*"

Catilda was too far away to intervene, but the full force of Ambyr's body weight crashed into me. We both careened sideways as magic exploded out of the small object. A shimmering powder fluttered in the air and rained down on us. My head cracked hard against the wooden floor, Ambyr's weight crushing my chest and forcing out the air in my lungs. She rolled off me, hands clutching the sides of her head as a dreadful scream tore from her throat.

"Ambyr …" I doubted she could hear me, because I could barely hear myself.

A weightless feeling overcame me, like my hands and legs had completely detached from my body. My ears felt clogged, the sound muffled inside my head. With my body unable to communicate with itself, I lay there on the floor in a helpless heap of panic. The room spun like a carousel, my head rolling on the ground as a nauseous bubble formed in my stomach. The ceiling blurred and the walls warped around me.

"Zulli ... Ambyr ..." I couldn't place the voice. Perhaps it was one of the other employees? But I could feel the vibration of the cautious footsteps coming toward me.

"Don't! Don't come any closer. It's a ... disorientation spell." I wasn't sure if my words made any sense, but the footsteps stopped.

Three blurry Cullins laughed nearby, and when they spoke, they all mocked me. "Your magic is nothing compared to your father's. You can't stop me, but I'd like to see you try."

And try I would. I closed my eyes, the eternal darkness in my mind still spinning. Engaging my half-spider shifter powers, I raised my fingertips into the air. The vibration of his menacing cackle rolled over my fingertips, oscillating like a pendulum as the wind reached me. With a quick sniff, I caught a whiff of that dreadful cologne.

Still lying on the floor, I ripped what I hoped was a yellow bullet from my belt and flicked it toward the vibrating sound and toxic fragrance cloud.

"*Fodio.*"

A yellow blur of magic erupted in my peripheral vision and a disturbing male growl followed. Feet shuffled across the floor, colliding with a chair that screeched as Cullin used it for balance. My aim must have been slightly off since the stun spell should have left him paralyzed.

"You have no idea what you're doing, Ms. Taracula!"

Erratic footsteps whizzed by me, the sound fading as he escaped out the front door.

"Zulli, are you okay?" Catilda slowly approached me. I inhaled a few deep breaths, counted to three, and pushed myself up. Catilda grabbed an arm, helping me into a chair.

"Totally fine," I assured her, holding onto the seat like my life depended on it. After a few rapid blinks, the world came back into focus. Ambyr was curled up on the floor, cradling her head. Tilly was by her side, comforting her.

A firm hand placed a cup of water and a towel in front of me. "Thanks for that, Zulli."

The eccentric male stood next to me wearing more jewelry than Catilda. Leather straps wrapped up his arms and piercings decorated every body part on his face. His chocolate curls spilled out from under his beanie. Thick black eyeliner accentuated his hazel eyes, and a rebellious five o'clock shadow covered his chubby jawline. I didn't recall having ever met the employee before, but the name tag on his apron said "Kid."

"Hi. Catilda Harper." Catilda stepped in front of me before I could respond. She held out her hand and beamed an enchanting smile at Kid. "Magic archeologist in training and Zulli's best friend. That's a fascinating leather strap on your wrist. The one with the blue embroidery. Looks like a design passed down from the ancient Kese civilization. Spelled for ... let me guess ... vitality?"

His eyes lit up and his mouth dropped open. "Uh, yeah. It is. The magic slowly absorbs into my skin throughout the day to give me a little extra energy boost. Not many people pick up on that. I'm Kidson." Shiny black fingernail polish flashed before me as he clasped Catilda's hand. "But everyone calls me Kid."

Catilda blushed and giggled playfully. The two continued chatting about whatever ancient magical folklore history buffs spoke about, while I left the comfort of my stable chair to test out my wobbly legs. A heavy coldness swept through me, exhaustion taking over like my mental battery had just been completely drained. My fingers reached for the pounding area right above my left eye. There was no blood, but definitely a nasty bump from hitting the floor.

"Ambyr. Tilly. Are you both okay?" I stared at the two women propped up against the wall.

Ambyr still had her face buried in her knees. Her hands covered her head and a muffled whimper barely broke through. Tilly was crouched next to her, trying to comfort her. She peered up at me, and relief cascaded through me when I realized that only a slight redness covered her neck.

"I'll live," Tilly answered. "Actually, the coffee wasn't even that hot. But Ambyr ... that magic stuff is still affecting her. How did you snap out of it, Zulli?"

"The military trains its soldiers to endure common magic spells like that." I flexed my fingers, staring down at my icy hands. "Hold on."

Canvasing the coffee shop, I found my black backpack over by the garbage bin where I had dropped it. Pulling out a sponge, I placed it in Ambyr's hand and activated the magic.

"*Devoro.*"

Her soft whimpers died, replaced with a steady breath. She released the tension in her shoulders and looked up to face me. "It's ... It's gone. I no longer feel like I'm free falling in an endless void."

"The sponge absorbs magic." I pulled a white bullet from my belt and handed it over to Tilly. "Take this. Healing ointment. Activate the magic to soothe the burn and heal it faster."

"Wow ... thanks, Zulli. Next time, breakfast is on me!"

I raised my eyebrows. "Really? Because I could devour everything in that display case in one sitting."

A frantic expression came over her as her gaze traveled over to the muffins and pastries on display. She'd seen me scoff down four muffins in one sitting, but when I started laughing, she knew I was only teasing.

"Sorry I can't stay to help clean up. I actually have to be somewhere. Will you be okay?"

Ambyr waved her hand at me, using the other one to push herself up from the floor. "Don't worry about it, Zulli. Thank you for your help."

"Well, you have my number. Call me if he comes back or if the police come questioning."

She nodded and, after assessing the minimal damage to the cafe, moved to grab the mop from behind the counter. Grabbing my backpack, I swung it over my shoulder and checked the time on my phone.

"Catilda! Come on. We gotta go. You're gonna miss the bus." It felt like I was wearing concrete blocks for shoes, and I exhaustedly dragged my heavy feet toward the exit.

There must have been an exchange of contact information, because Kid was smiling at a crumpled up white napkin with a very familiar red lipstick print on it. Catilda waved an enthusiastic goodbye, and she bounced out of the cafe behind me.

It was a gloomy spring day in the city of Chitol. Thick gray clouds loomed above the tall city skyscrapers, the warm sun refusing to make an appearance. A brisk wind slapped me in the face and sent a shiver down my arms. I wrapped them around my chest, trying to keep the cold from biting my skin. I hadn't worn a jacket this morning, but I had wished I did.

"So, who's your new friend?" I asked Catilda, both skeptical and a little nosy.

"Oh come on, hun. You know I'm a sucker for the bad boys, and it's not like *you* were going to ask him out." Catilda waited a whole three seconds before turning the questions to me. "You want to tell me what happened back there?"

"A crazy news anchor got pissed off that he didn't get his coffee and took it out on me. I'm not like that when I wake up in the morning, am I?"

Catilda jabbed me in the ribs. "Not funny, dummy. I saw you flinch back there. It was only a fraction of a second, but Cullin whispered something to you and it got you spooked. What did he say?"

I dug my trembling hands into my pockets, shrugging at Catilda's question and keeping my gaze focused ahead. "You remember that crumpled up list of names I found the night of the attack on NightFly Technologies?"

"Yeah, sure. Wait ... was Cullin ..." Catilda's fierce grip tightened around my arm.

"Yup. Although I'm still trying to figure out what that list was intended for. My best guess is that my dad is targeting them. Of the names I recognized, they were all authority figures." Catilda gasped, and I peered over to see a crinkle forming between her brow. "Cullin said my father has eyes everywhere. What's that even supposed to mean?"

Catilda wrapped her arms around mine and leaned her head against my shoulder. We continued to walk alongside each other down the street. "Sounds like a threat to me. I told you to be careful, Zulli. Do you think Zavyr is watching you?"

The second she mentioned it, the hairs on the back of my neck stood on end. Trying not to attract attention, I scratched my head and stretched around to see if anyone might be following. Busy pedestrians zoomed by us, walked into office buildings, or turned the corner of the street. No one was giving off stalker vibes.

"I wouldn't be surprised if he was." We approached the crowded bus stop just as the bus pulled up and passengers started piling on to grab a seat.

Catilda let go of me to give me a hug. She clasped my hands in hers and squeezed. "Call me later? After your big meeting with the colonel?"

"Sure."

Catilda started heading toward the bus, but stopped when I didn't let go of her hands. "What is it?"

"My father ... I don't think he'd hurt me, but he has no problem hurting my friends. If you have even the slightest worry that something might be wrong, please call me? Or your parents? Or ... anyone you can trust."

Her radiant smile lit up the dreary gray city around us. "Of course, Zulli. You're number one on my speed dial."

With that she skipped to the bus just as the doors were about to shut. I glimpsed her waving as the vehicle pulled out onto the road.

Raindrops started dotting the sidewalk as I began making my way back to my apartment. My body still felt disconnected, cold, and numb, with a foreboding feeling of emptiness settling over me. It wasn't Cullin's attack or frigid rain against my skin.

I knew exactly what was causing it. I had lost my magic.

2

---◈---

LOSING MY MAGIC wasn't anything that surprised me. It had been on the fritz, coming and going, ever since I had met that runt Adrian and sucked out his magic at the bar a couple days ago. I had no idea what triggered the change. Sometimes I felt invigorated, my body overflowing with more magic than I could handle. Other times, like now, I couldn't feel an ounce of magic left in my system. Once in a while, I could even *see* magic. That was a rare ability only a select few had and one I was certain didn't belong to either cat or spider shifters. I hadn't told anyone about this change. Doing so would sideline me from my job as a military soldier, and I had an important mission coming up that quite literally involved a life or death situation. I had made a bargain with my father to save Ryker's life, but the payment he demanded from me was to take the life of another.

I splayed out my hands in front of me, straining as I tried to force my claws to come out. Pointed nails started to form, my fingers trembling and aching from the struggle. With a defeated sigh, I let go and the magic vanished.

Raindrops now splattered heavily on the sidewalk. I looked up at the stormy clouds, letting the cold water hit my cheeks.

The fear that I would eventually lose all my magic weighed down on me like a pile of heavy bricks crushing my chest. Protecting *anyone* without my magic was nearly impossible. My only hope to figure out what was going on would be to find Adrian and ask him what the hell he had done to me. To do that, though, I'd have to go through Captain Myra Llama. On the outside, she may have seemed like a cuddly, lovable teddy bear, but I knew she was hiding something. I didn't trust her. If she felt threatened by anything I said, she'd head right for the colonel's office and rat me out.

A faint roll of thunder sounded in the distance. Pedestrians around me scrambled for shelter, and I figured I should start doing the same. Only a few blocks away from my apartment, I picked up my sluggish pace and began a brisk walk.

Water droplets dripped off the ends of my hair as my gaze constantly scanned the surrounding street. My senses widened as much as they could without my magic. I breathed in a deep breath of cold air through my nose, inhaling the scent of bus fumes and wet concrete. My ears twitched at the sound of car horns blaring down the street.

The hairs on the back of my neck prickled, and a shimmer of tension ran down my spine. The eerie feeling of being watched had never left, the unease triggering goosebumps on my arms. Was I being paranoid about what Cullin had said? Or was someone really following me?

As I rounded the corner, the busy crowds of the main road dispersed and my fingers hovered over a blue bullet on my belt. My neighborhood was a residential area, not heavily traveled during the day. It was the perfect place for someone to jump me, kidnap me, or—I gulped—kill me.

Something rattled to my right. I snatched the bullet, whirled around, and launched the projectile at a garbage bin next to a set of front steps. The sleep powder erupted in a colorful explosion. The metal bin swayed, falling over with a loud crash, and rolled across the sidewalk.

The tabby cat should have been taking a nice nap. Instead, the feline leaped over my feet, a slight wobble in her step but otherwise unaffected by the sleep spell. Since I lacked the ability to use my own magic effectively, spelled objects apparently didn't work very well either.

The rain washed the blue powder off her wet fur, revealing dark black and light gray stripes with thick curving bands that swirled around her torso. It reminded me of a marble cake, and although I'd just eaten, I was hungry again.

I scrubbed my hand through my hair, my thumping heartbeat slowly calming. "Get a grip, Zulli," I reassured myself. "It's just a stray cat."

The feline started licking the remaining powder off her paw, and the emerald glare of her eyes slashed toward me.

"Stupid cat. Stop judging me. If you'd gone through what I just did, you'd have done the same thing." I rubbed my temples and a sharp pain radiated through my skull where I'd accidentally grazed the bump above my eye.

Leaving behind my feline stalker, I trotted up the crumbling steps to the entrance of my apartment building. The inside of the complex echoed the poor state of the outside. It wasn't fancy enough to warrant an actual front desk attended by a staff member. In fact, the lobby was just a large room with paint-chipped walls and a single light fixture hanging overhead. A dying plant sat in a dusty pot on the floor next to a cluster of mailbox units built into the wall. While water dripped off my clothes, creating a puddle around my boots, I waited for the creaky elevator to open up and drop me off on the fifth floor.

The hallway that led to my apartment smelled like wet gym socks, my feet sinking into the squishy, puke-green carpet laden with stains. I jiggled my key into the lock, my other hand wrapping around the doorknob.

I sucked in a breath and held it. My back straightened and every muscle in my body went rigid. A deep, penetrating chill inside me felt like an icy fist clenching my throat. I peered up and down the hallway, but there was no sign of activity. Pressing my ear to the door, I closed my eyes and tried to concentrate on the sound of movement. Without my enhanced senses, I couldn't hear much, but the TV was definitely on. My heart thumped against my ribcage. Whoever it was inside my apartment had unlocked my door and let themselves into my home.

Kasra had a key, but since we weren't on speaking terms at the moment, I doubted it would have been her. Ryker would have called before stopping by, not to mention he would have portaled directly inside.

The odds of it being a random attack from a burglar were slim. The people who lived in this complex weren't exactly known for their lavish lifestyle, and I certainly owned little of anything valuable for anyone to steal. That left one remaining person.

Panic competed with my blank brain and the ability to think. Instinct told me to barge into the apartment, but without the ability to use magic, I would be at a severe disadvantage. I inhaled a deep breath and counted to ten, a simple technique my mother had once taught me to calm myself down whenever I was freaking out.

The most logical choice of action would be to find Kasra, who lived a few floors above me, and go in with backup. Surely she'd put our differences aside and still help me out if I was in danger.

When she didn't answer her phone, I had to prepare myself to go in alone. If I make a beeline toward the closet by the entrance, maybe I could grab my supply bag. I'd hidden other weapons throughout my home, but they were less accessible. Some popcorn kernels spelled with smoke screens were in a bowl on an end table. I kept a paralysis dagger hidden under the kitchen sink. A few other spelled objects, like the shoelace with the strength of an iron chain, were stuffed under my pillow. I adjusted my bullet belt around my waist. None of those items were of any use to me without my magic, but that didn't mean they couldn't be used against me.

Steeling my nerves, my hand slapped on the door and pushed. The flimsy piece of wood bounced open, wobbling on its hinges as it smashed against the wall with a loud bang. I pushed off on my feet, somersaulting on the floor over to the entryway closet. Reaching up, I grabbed the handle and yanked the closet door open, using it as a shield, and dove inside the cramped hole in the wall.

The closet was full of shoes and boxes of junk. With shaking hands, I unzipped the duffle bag and pulled out the first thing I touched. Paralysis daggers. At least the blades would still work.

The open closet door blocked my view of the rest of the apartment, so I kept my hand pointing at the wall directly in front of me. The deafening sound of an explosion caused my heart to jump into my throat. When I remained unharmed, I realized it was only the TV. With each passing second, my anxiety climbed into uncharted territory. I waited for a blast of magic to rip the door off its hinges. For some poisonous gas to consume my apartment and choke me. For … anything.

Why wasn't anything happening?

Perhaps the intruder was already gone. Or maybe I'd underestimated my stupidity in leaving the TV on and the door unlocked before I left. I fixated my gaze on the floor, looking for a shadow or any sign of movement. Something struck me as odd. My windows faced the side of another building. Not much light reached into my apartment, even on a sunny day. With the current stormy weather, it should have been pitch dark inside. So why was there a golden ray of sunshine stretching across the wooden planks of my entryway?

"What the hell …" I whispered to myself.

With steady feet, I pushed myself up into a crouch. Keeping the dagger in one hand, I pressed the other against the closet door. Peeking around the edge, a radiant glow of bright light blanketed my cold, wet skin in warmth. The intensity of it swallowed my vision. Squinting past it, I could barely make out a female figure stretched out on my sofa, the heels of her knee-high boots resting on my coffee table.

"For a cat shifter, you're not very subtle, are you, Zulli?" a high-pitched, whiny female voice announced. The light around her dimmed. My vision adjusted as I watched the woman put down a bowl of popcorn on the table and stand to face me. She flashed me two pieces of puffed up corn in between her slender fingers. "You need to do a better job of hiding these spelled objects if you don't want people to accidentally kill themselves by eating them." She tossed them over her shoulder, clearly confident that she wouldn't need them.

She swept about a dozen thick braids off her shoulder and let them dangle down her back. Glittery golden ribbons were woven into each one, accentuating the reddish auburn color of her hair. Her black crop top was a stark contrast to her white blazer, her high-waisted leather pants leaving only a strip of skin visible across her stomach. There was something both refined and fearsome about her. While her sunflower-colored eyes and polite smile made me want to believe she meant no harm, her stiff posture warned otherwise.

"Who are you?" I demanded, brandishing the dagger in front of her.

"Take a guess."

She held herself perfectly straight, like she had an invisible thread running through her spine, lifting her up. She moved her shoulders back, her chin dipping slightly as she looked down at me.

"I don't have time for games. How did you get into my apartment?"

She took a step toward me, and I took one back.

"Oh, with this of course." Her fingers slid into the pocket of her skin-tight pants and pulled out a key. "You should be more careful who you hand these out to. You never know who might stop by for an unannounced visit."

Her thin eyebrows raised in a perfect arch, the whites of her eyes brightening.

"You're with my father," I concluded. By process of elimination, if it wasn't Kasra or Ryker, I knew she had to have retrieved the key from someone in my family.

"Look at you, putting all the pieces together. You can call me Reeva. I've been given the distinguished responsibility of making sure you do nothing ... stupid." She slowly nodded at the dagger clenched in my fist. While she didn't seem too concerned that I would attack, her penetrating gaze was constantly assessing my movements in case I did.

"Good luck with that." I smirked, chuckling to myself. "You can go back to NightFly Technologies and tell my father I'm a grown woman. He made it very clear what he wanted me to do, and I can do this by myself without someone constantly breathing down my neck."

She sniffed at my comment. "You think I'm going to enjoy babysitting you? I am Zavyr Taracula's esteemed security advisor, and I have better things to do than follow *you* around because you can't be trusted. However, I am loyal to your father and take my job *very* seriously. Not to mention I was given permission to do whatever was necessary to ensure the success of your mission. I convinced myself it sounded like a fun challenge. Now, let's not make this any more difficult than it needs to be. We need to go. Your father requests your presence."

For a moment, I thought about complying with her request. My father had no issues hurting my friends, but so far he hadn't come directly after me. I believed her when she said she worked for my father, but I had also never met this woman before. If she was going to be sticking around, then I needed to know what she was capable of.

"No," I answered, defiance carrying my voice. "Not interested. I have to meet up with my teammates later, and I don't plan on spending my free time being lectured by my dad."

Reeva rolled her eyes. "Zavyr mentioned you'd be a stubborn brat about this. Sadly, even though I would love to make you mysteriously disappear and get on with my life, I can't. But your father approved all other means of apprehending you." She flashed me a candy-coated smile that was somehow both friendly and disturbing.

Without thinking, I lunged toward Reeva, the small paralysis dagger pointed directly at her delicate neck. She crossed her arms over her chest to block me, but slashed them down to her sides. A searing hot, blinding light emanated from her body and disoriented me. I stumbled backward and my boot kicked the coffee table. Dots danced in my vision, my skin burning like I had been lit on fire. I couldn't tell where I was falling, only that I was.

My chest smacked into the coffee table, the glass popcorn bowl rolling off the edge. I thrusted my hands out to brace for impact. Before I could let go of the dagger, my wrist collided with the couch and the sharp tip of the blade pierced my bicep.

Reeva's high-pitched squeal of a laugh mocked me. "I can't kill you, but I never thought you'd end up killing yourself!"

Thankfully, the paralyzing spell hadn't activated, but the radiating pain that traveled down my left arm wasn't much better. Warm blood soaked into my already sopping wet shirt, the liquid trickling down my arm and dripping off my fingertips. My whole left upper side was throbbing. I curled my fingers, ready to fight back, with or without magic.

I snatched the dagger from the floor and flicked it at Reeva.

"*Torpens*," I shouted, hoping that at least *some* of the magic might activate and slow her down. With lightning fast reflexes, she threw up a hand, her palm facing outward. A wall of light about half her size appeared, the dagger vanishing into the blistering abyss. The heat radiating off her shield was so hot that I could see the air rippling around her. When the light winked out, a molten hot puddle of melted metal had burned a hole through my rug.

Still on the ground, I frantically searched around me, my hands feeling for anything I could use against her. I came up with a dirty fork that had hidden itself under my couch.

"Are you ready to give up yet? This is very irritating." Reeva's hand reached for my injured arm as spears of white magical light escaped through her fingertips. It burned right through the fabric of my shirt as she clenched tightly around the wound. I wailed as she yanked me to my feet, her fingers like a hot iron branding my skin. The pain escalated to an incomprehensible level, so extreme that I could no longer think straight to register how bad it actually was. My eyes rolled into the back of my head, and my limbs numbed from adrenaline. The smell of my burning flesh left an unsettling feeling in my stomach that nearly made me vomit.

The magic started fading, and it took me a moment to gather my senses before I could reply to her.

"I'm not done yet," I snapped at her, my breath heavy with determination. With my uninjured arm, I raked the fork across her cheek. She pushed me away, swiveling her head and taking a step back. She gasped in horror at the thick red liquid coating her fingers. Before she could recover, my knee shot up into her stomach. A heavy exhale rasped from her lungs. As she bent forward, the elbow of my good arm striking right in the middle of her shoulder blades. She dropped flat on the floor.

I lifted my boot, ready to slam it down on her back to pin her in place. She rolled out of the way as I stomped on the ground. Reaching out her hand, she snatched the empty glass bowl and threw it square at my head.

A flash of light appeared before me. The thick glass didn't break. At least I didn't think it did. A persistent ringing in my ears dulled my senses. Stunned, I stared straight ahead at the living room wall, stars dancing in my vision.

"I win," I heard her muffled voice say, barely comprehending the words through my confusion. I dropped to my knees, then toppled over onto my side. My eyes fluttered closed when her next words reached me. "Now let's go before you do something else stupid."

3

———◈———

THE CONSTANT POUNDING inside my head woke me up. An unfamiliar woman hovered over me, dabbing some kind of gel on my forehead. The cool sensation turned into a mild warmth when the magic activated.

"Get off me!" I swatted her hand away and tried to stand up, but a wave of dizziness kept me in place. "Where am I?"

The woman, maybe in her late forties, put the tube of gel into the front pocket of her lab coat and scurried out of the room without answering my question. She didn't have to. As soon as the lab technician had stepped away, I knew exactly where I was. Rain pattered softly on the panel of windows that lined one side of the room. A cloudy haze reduced the majestic view of the city outside. Given that the sun was taking the day off, it was hard to tell how long I had been out, but I suspected an hour or two at the most.

My hands ran along the red and white houndstooth chair I was slouching in, two black leather sofas flanking me on either side. Next to me on an end table was a family photo—an old one that had been taken about twelve years ago before my mother went missing. It showed my two brothers, their innocent teenage faces trying to hide the discomfort of being forced into stuffy suits. My father stood in the back, prim and proper as always, with a hand placed on a chair where my mother sat. Unlike the rest of us, dressed elegantly for the occasion, she wore a simple sundress with red roses on it. The tips of her wild hair were dyed a violet orchid and swept over her shoulder in a loose ponytail. Her pale face glowed with laughter, and her vibrant green eyes sparkled in the camera's flash. She had her protective arms wrapped around me while I sat on her lap.

A deep pang hit the center of my stomach. My gaze pulled away from the photo and was drawn to an oversized desk in the center of the office. Behind it sat a man in an expensive navy suit. His jet-black hair was streaked through with an off-centered blaze of gray, slicked back and kept in place with gel that glistened against the sharp light from his desk lamp. Despite his immaculate appearance and the gentle movements of his hands, there was a hardness behind his eyes that belied his mild facade.

"My little spider." My father's chair rolled out from under him as he stood. He poured a cup of tea from a tray set on a table beside his desk, then sat down on one of the leather sofas next to me. "Here, drink this. There's a special magic powder mixed into it to speed up your metabolism and give you an energy boost. You'll need it to be in top shape for your next mission."

I sniffed the brown liquid, surprised to smell a delightful mix of orange and cedar. Lifting the cup to my mouth, I quickly took a sip to hide the excitement creeping up my lips. My magic was back.

My father's judgmental gaze assessed the missing sleeve of my button-down, then he made his way upwards toward my forehead. My fingers ran across the bumpy surface above my eyebrow where Reeva had whacked me with the glass bowl. It was the same area I'd hit on the floor at the cafe. While the healing ointment had helped close the cut, the pounding of my brain wasn't dulling.

"Reeva's light magic is often underestimated." A smooth smile crossed my father's lips as he looked at me. "Most people think light is harmless, but Reeva can make it deadly when she wants it to be. I'm glad to see you didn't sustain serious injuries in your squabble. Next time, perhaps you should listen to her and avoid conflict."

"Serious injuries?" I spat at him. "She—" My hand reached over to my left arm. I expected to see a mottled handprint, bloody and blistering, from where Reeva had seared through my skin. Instead, confusion racked my brain when my fingers pushed aside the frayed fabric to discover only a rough scab. Not even a bumpy rash from Reeva's burns were visible, and I felt none of her residual magic lingering.

"I had nothing to do with that, Mr. Taracula. That was all her own stupidity when she tripped over the coffee table and stabbed herself," Reeva's nasally voice came from behind me. I turned around to see her and another man dressed like a sleazy car sales-man guarding either side of the exit.

"No, that's—" I didn't have the words to explain it. Even with a magic healing ointment, it would have taken several days for a burn that severe to disappear completely. What had caused the burn to heal so quickly, but the stab wound to remain untouched?

"Regardless, I'm glad you're here, Zulli. We need to discuss something." My father's voice wasn't aggressive but com-manded my attention. After fifteen years of being the CEO at NightFly Technologies, the art of manipulating and persuading people was second nature to him.

He leaned toward me in his chair and maintained eye contact while continuing to speak. "As you are well aware, the Chitol military apprehended Davian Grymes so he is no longer an asset to me. I understand you are meeting with the colonel later today to discuss your next mission—a search and rescue of a young boy named Colton Meyers. You are to ensure that the rescue part of this mission doesn't happen. You need to kill him."

The way my dad so casually said the words, like killing someone was no big deal, made my throat tighten and my mouth go dry. My hands gripped the arms of the chair tightly, my claws slipping out and digging into the rough fabric.

"What could some teenager on Earth possibly have done to a powerful CEO on Iradel that resulted in the need for his death? I'm not going to kill an innocent kid. I'm not going to kill *anyone*." I crossed my arms and stared him down.

A low laugh came from my father. "It's not what he has done, but what he has the potential to do. He could destroy this family. This business. Do you want that to happen, Zulli?"

"Well, no, but—"

"Did you forget our deal? A life for a life. I gave you back that man you call your friend, Ryker, even though he lied to you and betrayed your trust. This was the deal, Zulli. You *will* do this." His chilling words sent shivers down my spine, and I shuddered at the fact that I knew he was right. I'd made a deal, and if I knew one thing about my dad, it was that he always got what he wanted.

"And what if I don't kill him? What are you gonna do about it? Keep going after my friends? Kill *me*?"

"I am appalled that you would ever think I'd hurt you, Zulli!" If my words actually offended him, he didn't show it. "But I am a powerful man with many powerful connections. I don't suggest you test me."

"Yeah, uh huh." I raised my eyebrows and threw up my hands, then slapped them down on my lap. "And how exactly am I supposed to do this without anyone noticing? Kasra and Ryker won't just stand by and watch me kill someone. My magic can be traced back to me. Is that your plan? To sabotage my career so I have no other choice than to rely on helping you?"

He rolled his eyes and leaned back on the couch, crossing his legs. "Of course not. As much as I wish you would, I know you will never join your family here at NightFly Technologies. But your skills are still valued. You will be my eyes and ears within the military."

"Woah, wait a minute." I jumped up from the chair and pointed my finger in his face. "You said a life for a life. Not the *rest* of my life."

A sly grin creased his lips. "Call it a contingency plan. I suspect you'll be needing my assistance again in the future."

A heavy knock resonated from the other side of the closed office door.

"Who is it?" the sleazy salesman asked. I heard a male voice reply, but wasn't paying attention to the name. A moment later, Reeva opened the door and allowed in our guest.

Ice slid through my veins and my entire body froze. A broad-shouldered man walked into the office wearing a white dress shirt and dark pants. His black hair was combed to the side, a rogue curl having fallen just above his silver eyes. He had the same assertiveness in his swagger that my father had, demanding that all eyes focus on him when he entered the room.

"Brodin?" I gasped. "What are you doing here?"

My oldest brother stopped by the couch next to my dad but didn't sit.

"Hi, Zulli." Despite his dominating presence, his voice still had a subtle gentleness to it. "I came to give you this. You'll be needing it for your next mission."

He pulled out a small plastic bag and placed it in the palm of my hand. A tight, sickening feeling centered in the pit of my stomach when I saw a syringe filled with a clear liquid.

"What is this?" I asked him guardedly.

"This is what you will inject into Colton. It's a simple poison, highly toxic and easy to find almost anywhere. You won't need to use any magic. Given that this poison is commonly used among many criminal organizations, the evidence will suggest someone else got to him right before you did."

"And what about Kasra and Ryker?" Dread crept down my spine at what Brodin's answer might be.

He pulled out another clear plastic bag from his shirt pocket, and I nearly fainted at the sight of it. Inside were two white pills, a small black crosshair stamped on the capsules.

"Bliss? You want me to drug my own teammates?" I turned my attention to my dad. "This is going *way* too far. Ryker nearly died from overdosing on Bliss, thanks to you. I will not be the one responsible for that happening again."

"Relax." My dad held out his hand and motioned for me to sit back down. When I remained standing, he rose to face me instead. "I assure you, this is a new and improved version of Bliss, and a very low dose. Slip it into a drink or knock them out and force it down their throats. I don't care what you do, Zulli, but with this you can command them to forget everything they saw you do, and, with this upgraded version, you can implant any replacement memory you desire. The effects aren't guaranteed to be permanent, but we can deal with that problem later if it arises. However, if you make the story convincing enough, they'll never suspect their memory is a lie."

Looking for assurance, I gave a wary glance to Brodin, but he kept his face etched in stone. Clenching my fist, I growled my defiance as I shoved the two bags into my front shirt pocket.

"If you tell anyone about this, Zulli, there will be consequences. I need you to promise me you will keep this a secret between only those in this room." My dad slipped me a threatening glower.

"Yeah, sure. Whatever." I plopped back down into the chair and took a big gulp of tea. Its warmth blossomed in my stomach and I hoped the magic would help soothe the aching in my head.

"Promise, Zulli. I need to hear you say it." He dipped his head and steeled his gaze. His lips pressed into a thin line.

"Fine. I promise not to tell anyone about the plan." As I said the words, the warmth inside my chest intensified, swelling until it felt like I had swallowed a ball of fire. I choked, coughing hoarsely as I pounded on my sternum with a fist.

"What did you do?" I wheezed out.

"Assurance." A satisfied grin crept up my dad's face. "I'm not a fool to think you won't try to tell your teammates, and while Reeva and Liahm will be there to observe, they can't be everywhere at all times. I may have mixed a little extra something into that tea."

"An oath spell." I coughed again. As the magic settled, the pain subsided until I could finally breathe again.

"Correct. I actually created it for the military. Quite literally prevents soldiers and informants from providing details that aren't meant to be provided. If you try to tell anyone, you'll experience that same burning pain but much more … excruciating."

I swallowed hard then rubbed my chest. For once, I had actually wished my magic hadn't returned. The spell wouldn't have worked, and I'd be free to tell Ryker and Kasra whatever I wanted to. Now, the only way to bypass the spell would be to wait until the magic wore off, and by that point, it would be too late.

"I should get going." I stood up from the chair, but before I could make my escape, my dad pulled me in for a tight hug and gave me a kiss on the forehead.

"Stay safe, my little spider. I am assigning both Reeva and Liahm, two of my most trusted security personnel, to watch over you. If anything goes wrong, I have instructed them to step in and protect you."

My gaze traveled over to my two new babysitters still guarding the door. Reeva was standing firmly on both feet, her hands on her hips, giving me a death stare. Her partner, Liahm, didn't quite fit the scary bodyguard persona, with his baggy dress pants and oversized blazer dangling from his narrow shoulders. His thin brown hair was combed back, hiding an obvious bald spot on the top of his head. While he was no longer in his youth, he held himself with the dignity of a man claiming experience.

My father may have tried to make me believe he was looking out for me, but it wasn't hard to figure out the true reason both

Reeva and Liahm would be following me around—to make sure I finished the job.

"Shall I walk her out, Mr. Taracula?" Liahm's gravelly voice sounded something like a strangled frog. With my heightened senses having returned, I could smell the tobacco rolling off his breath even from across the room.

"I've got this." Brodin pressed a firm hand between my shoulder blades and guided me out of the office. It was only after we were in the elevator and I was certain we were far enough away from prying ears that I spoke.

"You know what Dad's doing, right? He created Bliss, and he's using the Black Mark gang to distribute it throughout the city and mess with everyone's minds and take control of the authorities. People are dying, Brodin, and Colton is an innocent kid. How could you support this?"

Brodin kept his gaze straight ahead, tucking his hands into the pockets of his dress pants. "There's more to it than you realize, Zulli. I understand how this looks, but people overdose on all kinds of drugs every day. We can control that no more than we can control Bliss. There is a reason why mind-altering drugs like Bliss aren't standard medical treatment. Combining magic to treat the mind is a complex, delicate matter. Because of the risk, there is limited funding available to test it and an entire library full of rules and regulations we have to adhere to. It would take a hundred years to get to where we got to in six months. Yes, it's a shame people have died. But a far greater number are living more fulfilling, happier lives because of what Bliss has provided them."

"You really believe that? You know, there are rules for a reason, Brodin."

He glanced over at me with a laugh before returning his gaze forward. "Says the woman who breaks every rule she possibly can." His playful smile faded. "I'm sorry about what happened at Catilda's shop last week when I attacked you. It was my intention to frighten you, to stop you from snooping around. I never intended to hurt you."

The elevator door chimed open. I stepped out into the lobby, but Brodin remained where he was. He threw out his hand to keep the door from closing.

"I tried to keep you out of this, Zulli. I'm sorry, but your stubbornness made you a part of this. You can't blame that on me or Dad." He paused for a moment before dropping his hand to his side. "I'll see you when you get back. Good luck."

My judgmental gaze never left Brodin as the elevator doors rolled shut and he disappeared behind them.

I continued making my way through the lobby. The large reception area was full of business professionals wearing polished outfits I could sell for enough strawberry milkshakes to satisfy me for a lifetime. Or at least a solid year.

Keeping my head down, I stared at the marble floor as I left the lobby through the front doors and entered the plaza. The cloudy afternoon sky was still overcast, but the rain had let up. The light mist was a ghostly gray haze that limited my visibility, but I could still make out the colorful garden plot directly in front of me. Its lively flowers welcomed visitors to NightFly Technologies with a friendly greeting.

I slowly shuffled my way over to an empty bench but chose not to sit. A warm, fuzzy feeling in my stomach blossomed outwards and warmed the damp, brisk breeze that brushed against my skin. I marveled at the sight of the vibrant reds and pinks of the blooming rose bushes—my mother's favorite. Other rare and exotic flowers, like golden snowdrops, which only grew in arctic climates, and fireweed, a beautiful red vine impervious to fire, surrounded the square plot. Thanks to a special magic fertilizer, they could be kept alive all year long no matter the weather.

"Zulli? Is that you?" I tripped over my own two feet when I twirled around to see who was calling my name. Cold hands steadied me before I fell. "Careful. You okay?"

My other brother, Maeck, faced me wearing a checkered dress shirt that resembled a picnic blanket. Colorful striped socks peeked out from his khaki pants, which were about an inch too short. His short black hair was frizzy from the rain, but the glimmer in his stormy gray eyes was a welcoming ray of sunshine. Unlike Brodin and my father, Maeck didn't have an ounce of authority about him. He was more of a follower, which had me worried even more.

I raked a hand through my hair. "Yeah, I'm good. Thanks."

"What are you doing here, Sis? And what the hell happened to you? Out fighting bad guys again?" He hooked a thumb through his belt loop. A plastic bag swinging from his wrist rustled against his leg.

"Something like that. Just stopped by for some medications and stuff. Didn't feel like going back to the military for treatment."

Maeck scrunched his eyebrows. "Okay. Anyway, are you leaving? I just picked up some lunch. Probably not enough to satisfy your bottomless pit of a stomach, but I'm willing to share."

My nose caught a whiff of something that reminded me of roasted peanuts with a mix of aromatic spices. "Did you get Pad Fly for lunch?"

Excitement lit up Maeck's face. "Sure did! There's a new place that opened up down the street. Instead of peanuts, they actually mix in these seasoned black flies. It adds a unique salty taste and crunchy texture similar to a peanut, but *so* much better. Come on, let's go inside and grab a table in the cafeteria."

"Nah, can't. Got somewhere to be in a little while, and I need to go home and clean up."

"You sure?" Maeck sighed, finally taking notice of my disheveled appearance. "I'm working on this really cool new project that I'm dying to tell someone about. There's a chance it could actually prevent deadly illnesses before they even happen."

I pressed my lips together and frowned at him. "Maeck …"

"Yeah, I know. Dad wouldn't approve of actually *curing* people. Less money for business. I never actually told him what I was testing. You can't tell him anything about this, okay? It will probably never work, anyway. It's just a fun side project I've been messing with in my spare time."

"My lips are sealed." My fingers mimed zipping my lips. I was still pulling for Maeck to be one of the good guys. If he was going behind my father's back to test his own magic formulas, then maybe there was a chance he wasn't involved in this whole Bliss situation.

"Okay. I trust you, Sis. He can't find out!"

"He won't! I promise. That sounds really cool, though. I'd like to hear about it. Maybe some other time?" I wrapped my arms around my chest, the torn sleeves of my button-down letting the chilly air nip at my skin.

"You mean like maybe next week? You know what next week is, right, Zulli?" He widened his gaze at me, and I peered over to the rose bushes.

"Yeah, I know."

"Dad and Brodin are conveniently busy whenever I ask, but the two of us should get together and celebrate Mom's birthday. I'm sure she'd want us to have a drink on her behalf. Maybe at the Spicy Shark?"

A glint of hope sparked in Maeck's eyes as he awaited my answer.

"Mom disappeared eleven years ago on a business trip. You really think she's just gonna conveniently stroll into her favorite dumpy seafood restaurant on her birthday at the exact same time we're there?"

Maeck snorted. "Yeah, that place was never up to Dad's standards, but he always agreed to go every year for her birthday. You never know, though. Her body was never found. I can still dream of seeing her again one day. Please, Zulli? Don't make me go alone."

34

I let out a deep sigh. "Fine. I'll hit you up after my next mission is over."

"Awesome!" He punched me in the arm, right where my stab wound was. I bit down on my lip as a flash of pain traveled down to my fingertips. "Go do what you do best, Zulli. Take down the bad guys and make them pay for whatever they did."

Maeck waved at me and turned to head inside to get back to work.

My apartment was quite a long walk from NightFly Technologies, but I decided on taking it anyway. It gave me time to think about what I was really going to do about this mission. Death was something the military prepared soldiers for. I knew at some point I might have to take a life, but I couldn't go through with killing someone who was, as far as I was concerned, innocent. However, my father had already tried to kill both Ryker and Catilda. I didn't doubt he'd try it again or come up with something even worse if I backed out now.

This boy was a complete mystery to me. Just what was so dangerous about Colton Meyers that he might destroy my family? Destroy *how*? None of this made any sense, and I doubted I'd get any more clarification during my team meeting with Colonel Buckner.

I trudged up the steps to my apartment building, passed through the lobby, and pushed open my still unlocked apartment door. Grabbing some clean clothes, I headed for the shower. The rush of water felt refreshing until I turned off the faucet. Once I stepped out, coldness crept across my naked skin until I completely wrapped myself in a fluffy cotton bath towel.

"*Calor.*" Soft warmth tingled through me, the scent of lavender inviting and calming.

My apartment complex didn't have all the fancy amenities I'd had growing up in a wealthy household. There was no spelled paint on the walls for temperature control or curtains created with magical fabrics to let in the perfect amount of light. Although magic items were common, I never felt the need to spend my hard earned cash on such lavish items. While I owned a few things, like my gravity boots and rain-repelling umbrella, the one luxury item I could never live without was a bath towel spelled to be super soft and keep me warm when I got out of the shower.

Forcing myself to get changed, I removed my military uniform dangling from a hanger placed on a hook secured to the bathroom door. Believe it or not, the tan shirt and forest green pants had been recently laundered and ironed. My hair was so short there wasn't much I could do to style it, so I just raked my fingers through it to give it a quick comb. Before bandaging up my arm, I gave the wound a quick lick. My magic sizzled as the rough texture of my tongue glided over the damaged flesh, encouraging it to regenerate and heal. This ability was pretty weak when it came to the severity of injuries I could treat, but it was better than nothing.

The clock by my nightstand gave me two hours before my team meeting with the colonel. I took the remaining time to tidy up the place, scrubbing blood stains that had soaked into the rug and moving the coffee table to hide the burn from Reeva's magic that had melted the dagger. As I did, I noticed a small velvet box on the floor. Kasra's necklace must have fallen out of my pocket during my skirmish with Reeva. I picked it up and placed it on top of my dresser to give to Kasra later.

With under an hour to spare before I had to leave, my racing thoughts about my upcoming mission consumed me. My hands were shaking, my breath quickened. I dug out my phone from my pocket. Kasra was doing her best to avoid me. Catilda was working. And I was still unsure where I stood with Ryker. The past two days he'd been distant, not even bothering to call or check up on me like he normally would. He seemed to have recovered the memories that were taken from him—everything except the most critical ones. That included the entire time he'd betrayed me by working with my father.

Heaviness settled in my chest. I had never felt so alone.

I'd made the mistake of casting aside both Kasra and Ryker once before, and it didn't end well. I contemplated what to do now. Reeva and Liahm probably weren't far away, and with this magic preventing me from actually speaking about my mission, I couldn't exactly warn them even if I wanted to.

But Kasra and Ryker were my teammates—friends I needed to confide in and trust. I owed it to them to explain the truth. Even if the magic burned my stomach from the inside out, I had to tell them.

My finger was about to tap the screen of my phone to call Kasra when a knock sounded on my apartment door. I shoved my phone back into my pocket and went to investigate.

Peeking through a small slit in the open door, I saw a tall blonde staring back at me. "Kasra? I'm glad you're here. I have to tell you something."

Without a response, she pushed the door completely open and strode into my apartment, shoving me out of the way as she did. I was about to close it when a foot slipped through to prevent me.

A thin woman wearing a shiny pair of black boots strolled inside. The hardened gaze of her golden eyes was at odds with the charming smile that stretched across her face. The piercing sound of her whiny voice was like nails to a chalkboard. "Zulli! So good to see you again. May I come in?"

Dread tingled down my spine and my shoulders tensed. Reeva didn't wait for an invitation, already casually gazing around my apartment as if this were her first time encroaching on the place I called my home. She popped into the kitchen, proceeding to open drawers and cabinets until she found a half-empty bag of potato chips, then strolled over to my flat-cushioned couch and made herself comfortable.

"I met your friend Reeva in the elevator," Kasra enlightened me. She must have just finished an afternoon jog around the neighborhood, seeing as she was breathing heavily and sweat stains had soaked into her striped athletic top. A few loose strands of her wet hair escaped her ponytail and were plastered to her forehead. "She said she was trying to remember what apartment you lived in. I just came here to show her the way."

Reeva opened the bag of chips and slipped one into her mouth. She loudly crunched down on it, flashing me a flattering smile as she did. Unlike our previous meeting, she had a completely different aura about her. Gone were the leather pants and blazer, replaced with a casual t-shirt and a pair of tight jeans. Her stern posture was more relaxed, less threatening, and more inviting. She was almost as good as Kasra at playing to the whims of others. Almost. She was clearly trying to hide a mocking laugh when she chomped down on another chip.

"Hello, Reeva! I am beyond excited to see you again." I made no attempt to hide the sarcasm in my voice. "What are you doing here?"

She leaned forward to place the bag down on the coffee table, just slightly out of reach. She then stood to face me. "Sorry for barging in on you like this. I heard about what happened to your father last week. Such a shame his company was attacked. I was in the area, so I came to check up on you. See how you were doing."

"I'm fine. Can we catch up another time? There's somewhere I need to be." I attempted to guide her out of my apartment, but she turned around and paced the other way. Kasra was leaning against the entryway wall, watching with feigned disinterest as Reeva and I conversed. Her foot was tapping loudly on the wooden floor.

"Oh, come on, Zulli! I'm already here. At least give me a few minutes before you go galloping off to save the world." Ignoring me, Reeva picked up a picture I had on my end table. It had been taken the day I was introduced to my team. Ryker was in the middle, protecting the two lovely women on either side of him. Kasra stood to his right, chin up and fists pressed into her hips in a confident power pose. Then there was me, flashing an awkward half smile because the man who'd taken the photo had given no warning.

Reeva pressed a hand to her chest and inhaled a sharp breath. "Is this that Ryker fellow I've been told so much about? He sounds like such a kind boy."

Kasra grunted, shifting her gaze away from us.

"Oh, I've been told so much about you too, Kasra! You live three floors up, right? How are the amenities here? I've been looking for a new place to stay. Oh, and Zulli introduced me to that coffee shop you both frequent down the street. Their magic-infused coffee is the best in the area!"

"This place sucks," I spat at her. "Everything in this building is outdated and falling apart. I'm sure you can find a better place to live."

A slight smile creased Reeva's lips, and with a delicate hand, she placed the photo back on the end table. Kasra knitted her eyebrows at Reeva and pressed her lips into a thin line. She gave her a penetrating stare, almost as if she might be a little jealous of the completely fake friendship she thought I had with the security advisor.

Reeva clasped her hands together and peered over at Kasra. "The three of you sound like such an amazing team! Zulli tells me you all took down Ozcar Thorne's drug business by raiding a bakery? I'd love to hear all the details. And to think, you've only been working together for six months."

I ground my teeth, the pain radiating through my clenched jaw. Reeva had clearly stalked Kasra into the elevator. She knew where we all lived, what we did in our spare time, and all about our previous missions with the military. There was no hiding anything from her.

"I'm heading back upstairs." Kasra's hand was on the door-knob but she stopped turning it when Reeva spoke.

"Oh, how rude of me, Zulli! You said you had something to tell Kasra right before I walked in, didn't you?"

Kasra turned around to face me, crossing her arms and leaning on one foot. "Oh, yeah. What was it you wanted to say?"

"Uh ..." My gaze darted back and forth between Reeva and Kasra.

"Hurry up. I have a few things I need to do before our meeting." Her fingertips drummed across her biceps. Reeva tilted her head and raised her eyebrows, daring me to speak the words she knew I had been planning to say.

"I just ..." Fire roiled in my stomach at the very thought of telling Kasra the truth. I coughed violently, rubbing at the burning pain in my chest. "I just wanted to know if I could hitch a ride with you to base for the meeting?"

An eye roll accompanied Kasra's sigh. "Yeah, fine. Be ready in twenty minutes."

The door slammed shut behind her, leaving Reeva standing alongside me in the living room. As soon as Kasra was gone, she burst out laughing.

"Nice try, Zulli! You think I didn't know you'd try to find a way around Zavyr's orders? That magic oath spell is pretty solid. It'll melt your insides before you can even get out three words." She rolled back her shoulders and lowered her chin so that her gaze aligned with mine. Hostility returned to her posture and there was an abrasiveness to her stuffy voice. "I know everything about you and your friends, Zulli. When it comes to this mission, I will intervene to make sure it succeeds. That includes stepping in if your friends get in the way. I can't be held responsible if something unfortunate should happen to any of them."

My fist was shaking, and it took all the willpower I had not to punch her in the nose or rip one of those braids out of her hair.

She waved a hand in the air, not bothering to look back as she sauntered over to the front door. "Good luck with your mission, Zulli! I'll be rooting for you, because, frankly, I think it'd be rather exciting to sit back and watch the show."

She left the door open behind her.

4

———◈———

I WAS THANKFUL that Kasra didn't ignore me the entire ride over to the Chitol military base. She was naturally a curious person. A few days ago, Colonel Buckner had informed us of this new mission regarding Colton Mcyers. That our team had been authorized to travel to a different planet on a mission to save the mysterious boy was gnawing away at her need to know what was going on.

"This seems really odd to me. How did we get put in charge of this mission? This is like ... a job reserved for the best of the best. And, well, let's face it. We're still pretty new at this. Is there something else going on here that I should know about, Zulli?" Kasra raised an eyebrow at me as she pulled into a parking spot on base and shut off the car. Although she didn't know about my father's current concerns with Colton, I had told her everything else I knew about my father, my brothers, and the family business. She knew about Bliss and the truth about Davian. But there were still a lot of questions we didn't have the answers to, including why my father was so concerned about Colton.

"I really don't know." I shrugged as I shut the car door and started walking across the parking lot.

Kasra and I entered the main lobby of the Chitol military base, a bland welcome area with beige walls, beige floors, and a female soldier in uniform sitting behind a reception desk. She was quite busy, fielding multiple phone calls at a time. Thanks to her magical earpiece, the thoughts in her head were translated into words that would then enter into our computer database and be handed off to the appropriate people—or if she wasn't careful, inappropriate people. The last receptionist was relieved from her duties after a rather scandalous thought of her superior popped into her head and was relayed directly to him.

We passed by her and into the main hallway, where we had to dodge several more soldiers darting up and down the corridor and in and out of different rooms. So many conversations were going on at once that people had to yell over each other in order to be heard. A short male with mussed up hair and a frenzied expression rushed out of a room and collided with my shoulder.

"Watch it, bud. What's the hurry?" I glowered at him.

"I … I'm sorry! I have to get these reports over to Captain Myra Llama immediately!" He scrambled off ahead of us and rounded the corner out of sight.

"Did we miss a memo? What's going on?" I questioned Kasra. She bit her lip and grunted, just as lost as I was.

We continued on our way toward Colonel Buckner's office. We had about ten minutes before our meeting. I hadn't heard from Ryker, but he was likely already waiting for us.

My pace slowed when a cheery female soldier with strawberry blonde hair waved to me from down the hallway. A bright smile worked its way across her face and into her turquoise eyes the closer she came.

"Since when are you friends with Captain Myra Llama?" Kasra brushed a hand down her black shirt to smooth it out. She then adjusted her silver belt, the waist of her thick cargo pants falling low on her long torso. In the twenty minutes she took to get ready, she'd styled her hair into a slick, tight bun and apply a perfect amount of makeup to make her fierce eyes pop.

"Uh, I'm not." My gaze darted from side to side, searching for an office I could jump into and avoid Myra.

"Zulli! There you are." Myra tucked a folder under her armpit before turning her attention to Kasra. "Good evening, Kasra! How is your day going?"

Kasra's eyes blinked wildly and her lips parted. The two had never formally met as far as I was aware, but Myra knew exactly who she was. She always seemed to know who everyone was, not to mention everything about them.

"Oh, I'm fine, Captain. Thanks for asking. How are you doing?"

"I'm doing fantastic!" Myra clapped her hands together and her smile widened even further. "Would you mind if I borrowed Zulli for a moment? We need to have a quick chat."

Kasra was too awestruck to answer, so I did it for her. "Can it wait? I have a meeting with Colonel Buckner in ten minutes."

"All I need is five!" Her voice was a jolly ray of sunshine, but the grip she had on my elbow was strong enough to crush my bones.

"I'll meet you in Colonel Buckner's office," I assured Kasra. She stood in the middle of the hallway and stared at us with a dumbfounded look as Myra dragged me away.

Myra's palm pushed a metal bar. One of the double doors leading into the gymnasium clicked open and we strode inside. A few bleachers, used more for water bottles and dirty towels than for bodies to sit on, were scattered around the spacious facility. Sneakers squeaked on the glossy wooden floor and echoed loudly as a few soldiers teamed up to run training drills. As we passed by them, the raw, human smell of sweat forced me to gag. Above me, the clinking of exercise equipment came from the open second story that circled the perimeter of the gymnasium.

One soldier was bench pressing what had to be at least two hundred pounds of metal weights using nothing but two fingers and her magic.

"Why are we here?" I asked Myra as she stepped onto a cushioned mat in the far corner of the gym. She tossed the folder down on the ground.

"Fight me," she stated. "I want a rematch from last time."

"Excuse me?" I squeaked out. "You won last time. Are you trying to humiliate me in front of all your soldier friends? I'm really not interested in starting something with you. I thought we were good?"

"Just come at me. It'll be fun!" Myra crouched into a fighting stance and beckoned me with a curl of her hand. The determination flashing in her eyes showed no signs of humor.

"That's probably not a—"

Myra puckered her lips and a dense fog blew out of her mouth. The fresh cotton smell of her magic blasted me in the face as my surroundings disappeared in a smokey white cloud. Before I could engage my own magic to track her movements, my feet left the ground. My butt hit the hard padding of the mat. Myra jumped on top of me, using her forearm to crush my throat and cut off my air supply. I pushed against her hold, wishing I had the full strength of a spider shifter to counter.

She pulled back and bounced to her feet. "Again! This time I won't even use my magic."

"Are you insane? What the hell is wrong with you?" I rubbed my throat and swallowed hard. A few onlookers stopped to let out their mocking laughs directed right at me.

Myra giggled, almost as if she had taken my insult as a compliment. Enraged by her teasing and fueled by embarrassment, I balled my hands into fists and grunted. I squeezed my sweaty fingers so tight that my wrist throbbed. Fury bubbled and steamed inside me, and I couldn't contain it.

She charged at me, ready with a punch. As she did, I felt a sudden surge of power rise inside my chest and burst outward.

44

Adrenaline coursed through my veins, an unbelievable power beyond anything I had ever experienced before. I threw up my arm to block her, my limbs feather-light and moving with inhuman speed. She used her momentum to pivot sideways. The sharp point of her elbow rammed into my hip and knocked me off balance. The pain rippled through me in waves.

Another fist was inches away from shattering my jaw. Although Myra's reflexes were quick, mine were quicker. My human body transformed into a tiny arachnid, avoiding the sweeping motion of her arm. Silky webbing shot out of me and latched onto the sleeve of Myra's t-shirt. I reeled myself in and used my eight spindly legs to jump off her shoulder. Once behind her, my body reclaimed its human form.

My arm locked around her neck, and with my other hand, I clasped my wrist. My healing stab wound pulsed with an intense heat, but the overwhelming sensation of magic coursing through me pushed it aside. With my nose brushed up against the side of her head, a whoosh of fresh, sun-dappled airiness shot past my nostrils. The smell of her magic became more defined, with notes of leafy greens softening to powdery florals. A light pink sheen, like the color of bubble gum, glistened off her shiny hair as her magic became visible.

My forearm squeezed tighter against her slender neck. I was used to my magic coming and going, and the ability to sometimes see magic was completely new, but the dial had been turned up to eleven and I was going to take full advantage of it.

Myra's fingers bit into my skin. A hoarse cough ripped from her throat and she dipped her head back. Her turquoise eyes were wide, nearly popping out of their sockets. Her mouth dropped open, but no air was being sucked in. The porcelain color of her skin was nearly as white as the cotton that her magic smelled like.

Icy horror sloshed through my veins and I eased up on my grip. In that moment, a satisfying grin crept across Myra's face. She was much smaller than me, maybe about five feet tall, but a skilled fighter knew how to use that to her advantage. She hooked a boot around my ankle and my body pitched backward. Gravity took over, and Myra's body crashed on top of mine as I smacked onto the mat. The air wheezed out of my lungs, spittle flying everywhere. An intensely mind-numbing, dull ache spread outwards from my chest.

Myra pinned me to the mat, shifting to sit on top of me with a hand holding down each of my wrists. I unsuccessfully tried to wriggle out of her hold.

"Surrender," Myra demanded.

While both my magic and pride were pushing me for payback, a lingering gut feeling inside me warned me to stop. I knew there was no purpose in continuing the fight just to prove a point. My upcoming mission was too important to risk her accidentally breaking my arm or something worse.

"Fine. I'm done. Are you satisfied now? I get it. You're stronger than me."

She didn't move. The ferocity of her eyes locked onto me. "Your magic reeks of *him*." Her voice was a hushed whisper, filled with anger and flavored with a touch of her boisterous girliness at the same time.

"Him?" My thoughts scrambled to figure out who she might have meant. Ryker made no sense. Did she know about my father? No, she said my *magic* reeks of him. That could only be one person. "You mean … Adrian?" She squeezed my wrists tighter at the mention of his name.

"I sense *his* magic radiating off you. I don't know what you did, or what you plan to do, but I'm warning you to stay away from him. He's *mine*." Disgust dripped from her voice. The last I remembered, the two had been working together. What had Adrian done to get on her bad side, and what was Myra planning to do to the poor guy?

"Fine with me. You can have him. Now can I go? I have a meeting to get to."

Just like that, her personality snapped back into the sunny, girlish soldier adored by everyone at this base.

"That was fun!" She leaped off me and held out her hand to help me up. A round of applause came from the crowd that had gathered to watch us fight.

"Nice one, Myra!" a soldier cheered.

"You really got her!" Another male stepped forward to give her a fist bump.

Had I not loosened my grip, I would have had her. No one sang praises for my performance, though. The only thing I heard was an "eww" coming from a female hiding off to the side. She followed it up with, "Spiders are so disgusting!"

That was the very reason I hated transforming in front of others, even Ryker and Kasra, but I couldn't blame the woman. Spiders *were* gross. Even I hated them.

As I rolled my eyes, I glimpsed the clock hanging above the bleachers. "Crap! I'm late!"

Full speed ahead, I left Myra behind and dashed through the gym doors, straight down the hallway toward Colonel Buckner's office. With a heavy hand, I shoved open the colonel's door.

"Colonel Buckner!" I heaved, completely out of breath. Both adrenaline and fear were pumping through me.

Facing the colonel's metal desk were Kasra and Ryker, their spines stiff and faces void of expression. Colonel Buckner was leaning back in his office chair, his fingers tented in front of him. As the leader of this military base, he had a prestigious reputation to uphold. He kept his gray hair buzzed short, each strand evoking perfect uniformity. Every morning, without fail, he'd start off the day wearing pants and a field jacket that had been professionally cleaned and ironed. Because his magic allowed him to change the density of objects, including his own body, he sometimes walked around base with unnaturally large muscles just to intimidate others. And he was doing it at this very moment.

"You're late, Private Taracula." Colonel Buckner crossed his arms over his chest, his biceps threatening to rip the seams of his jacket. He lifted his chin to assess me, the veins in his neck popping out like worms wiggling under his skin. "I'm glad to see you're actually wearing your uniform today, but it looks like you just rolled out of bed. A proper soldier takes the utmost pride in their appearance."

My shirt was untucked and my boots were untied. A small blotch of red was seeping through the gauze wrapped around my upper arm. While I couldn't see my hair, I would have imagined after my skirmish with Myra that it was sticking out in all directions.

"My apologies, sir. It won't happen again." I bent down to tie my shoe, tucked in my shirt, and ran a hand through my mussed up hair.

"You said that the last five times." His cold gray eyes impaled me with an unblinking glare.

I could have blamed the whole thing on Myra, but seeing as the colonel's niece could do no wrong, it likely wouldn't have done much to help my cause. Falling in line beside Ryker, I let my breathing calm and my heart rate slow. He flashed me a quick smile before returning his attention to Colonel Buckner.

"As I was saying," the colonel continued, the tension heavy in his voice, "you are to travel to Earth to rescue a sixteen-year-old boy by the name of Colton Meyers. I recognize with your level of experience, this isn't a typical mission for a team such as yourselves, but the group I previously assigned to this mission was called away abruptly." He gave a frustrated sigh. "Given the last minute change, there weren't many available teams to choose from. Not to mention your names came across my desk as highly recommended replacements. With your combined abilities and limited experience, I know you can travel, sneak into places, and coax information out of people. I am trusting you three to be professionals in this matter and to get the job done."

Colonel Buckner stared straight at me. A ball of ice formed in my core, and I clenched my stomach. Who in their right mind would have recommended us for a mission this dangerous and why would Colonel Buckner even agree to it, even if we were his last resort? Did my father have control over someone in the military who could pull the strings on such a high level mission?

Kasra was bouncing on her heels and overjoyed with excitement. Ryker did his best to remain professional, but the faintest twitch of his lips told me he was looking forward to this mission as well. Unfortunately, I wasn't.

"Will there be anyone else joining us?" Kasra questioned.

The colonel dragged his hands down his face and grunted. I had never seen him so stressed about anything before. There must have been other missions that made him nervous, but he had always kept his emotions in check. "I contemplated sending Captain Myra Llama with you three, as she's been to Earth several times on previous missions. Unfortunately, she has another more important matter to deal with so you'll be on your own." His long exhale had a hint of worry in it. Was he more concerned for our safety or that we'd completely screw up the mission?

"What other information do we have on Colton? Do we know why he's being targeted?" Ryker's fitted t-shirt clung to his chest, barely moving as he reached for the folder the colonel handed him. His hair was neatly combed but damp, and a glossy sheen reflected off his rosy skin. Although Ryker wore the same standard issued military pants as everyone else, his were washed out and faded.

"Everything we know is in that file." The colonel nodded to the folder. "We believe Colton's parents fled Iradel for sanctuary on Earth when he was just a small child, but we know nothing about them because the name Meyers doesn't match any official records in our database. To our knowledge, his parents are no longer in the picture, but whatever they were caught up in seems to concern the boy. Some dangerous people have already attempted to take his life more than once, and it's your mission to bring him back here to Iradel, where he belongs, so we can protect him and figure out why."

Ryker opened the folder, and Kasra and I glanced over his shoulder to view its contents. There wasn't much information in the file—only one printed sheet of known information and a photo of the teen walking down a city street. He was lugging around a backpack that didn't fully zip closed and was carrying a stack of books in his arms. Peeking out over the top was a pale face with bottle blond waves bouncing just above his forehead. The picture wasn't the best quality, but it was impossible to miss those dramatic mismatched eyes. One was a striking ocean blue, while the other had a distinct milky, reddish color to it.

My hands started to shake, so I clasped them behind my back. Unless someone else was also after Colton, my dad had already attempted to end this boy's life and failed on multiple occasions.

"If Colton has escaped death several times already, someone must be protecting him, no?" I contemplated the thought to myself, although I said the words out loud. "People on Earth aren't as capable with magic as we are on Iradel. They would never see an attack from one of us coming. Colton must have someone on his side."

The colonel gave a thoughtful mumble. "Very astute observation, Private. I believe that is Private Klein's specialty, to infiltrate and gain valuable information. If at any point you feel you can't handle this mission yourselves, immediately call for backup."

I gulped loudly enough that it caught the colonel's attention.

"Is there something else you'd like to add, Private Taracula?"

"It's just … if someone else is going after Colton, what if we're too late? What happens if he's already … gone when we get there?"

The colonel drew in a deep breath and puffed out his chest. He let out the air with a sigh. "That is always a possibility, but not one that's very likely. The last attempt on his life was made not more than a week ago. Colton has since been relocated with

50

another foster family. Whoever is hiding him doesn't want him to be found. Just as the military had to search for him, it will take time for the people pursuing the boy to find his new location and come up with another plan of attack. Given the restrictions of using magic on Earth, anyone going after Colton would have to avoid being seen using any kind of magic. It's not as easy as it seems."

Guilt swelled inside my stomach. This poor kid had no family and no place to truly call his home. Every time someone discovered where he lived, he had to relocate somewhere else and start all over. I wondered if he even knew why people kept trying to kill him or if he just thought he was cursed.

"Private Stone. Private Klein. Private Taracula." The colonel nodded to each of us. "Go home and get some rest. First thing tomorrow morning, you are to leave for Earth. We've secured a safe house nearby Colton's last known location. This is an extraction mission. You are to scout the area, infiltrate, and bring him back here. Alive."

"Yes, sir!" the three of us responded in unison.

We filed out of the colonel's office. Kasra, the last one out, shut the door behind her then beamed a smile that stretched from ear-to-ear.

"I'm gonna go check out some supplies for tomorrow. Anyone coming with me?" Kasra spoke with enthusiastic urgency, bouncing on her heels and vibrating with excitement.

My stomach growled. "I'm gonna hit the cafeteria first. I'll meet up with you later."

"Hmm. I haven't eaten dinner either." Ryker tilted his head as if he had to think about it. "I'll go with Zulli. You want me to pick up something for you, Kasra?"

"Sure. Sounds good. See you in a bit." Kasra disappeared into a room at the end of the hallway, just as an older soldier with a shiny bald spot on top of his head came into view. He strolled toward me, his brown t-shirt falling loosely from his narrow shoulders and his cargo pants too baggy for his lanky frame.

Liahm gave me a nod, his dark brown eyes making strong contact with mine. As he passed by, he left the harsh smell of tobacco in his wake. He entered the same room as Kara.

My feet rooted to the spot I was standing in and my mouth slackened. I shook my head and blinked, as if I might have just experienced an illusion.

"Is everything okay, Zulli?" Ryker's eyebrows drew together as he looked at me. He reached out to touch my arm but I pulled it away to rub the back of my neck.

"Uh, yeah, I'm good. How have *you* been feeling?" Ryker's rosy cheeks and boyish dimples sent butterflies fluttering inside my stomach, his compassionate smile inviting me to smile back. I couldn't help but wonder if this was the same Ryker I had known for the past six months. A part of him had been lost, probably forever.

Ryker closed his eyes and massaged his temples with his fingertips. "I'm okay. These headaches, though … they're not getting any better. While I was in the infirmary, Lana gave me some pills to help with the constant pounding, but it's not really working. I feel like there's a ticking time bomb inside my head about to go off any minute."

"Oh …" My thoughts trailed off. I knew it likely had something to do with the antidote my father had given Ryker to return his memories, but asking my dad again for help was out of the question. "If there's anything I can do, just let me know."

"Thanks, Zulli, but I don't think there's much you *can* do. I wouldn't object to a batch of snickerdoodle cookies, though."

"You got it, Ryker." My lips twitched with a half smile.

"On that note, let's go get something to eat." Ryker started walking toward the cafeteria, but I didn't follow him. "What's wrong?"

I glanced at the doorway into the supply room. Liahm was here, pretending to be a military soldier, and he was in the supply room with Kasra. How many other people had my dad planted within the military? "Actually, I changed my mind. Let's join Kasra first."

Ryker frowned at me. He knew I was never one to turn down a free meal, but he didn't question my sudden change of plans.

We joined Kasra in the armory, stocking up on a few necessities, including tactical gear and some smaller weapons that wouldn't draw attention. All the while, Liahm casually strolled around, casting shifty glances my way when no one else was looking. Thankfully, he never approached us.

Once we had what we needed, we hit up the cafeteria and filled up on a hearty meal, courtesy of Ryker. Stuffed and exhausted, I leaned back in my chair and patted my stomach as I yawned.

Ryker stood up, holding his dirty tray in his trembling hands. Throughout the entire dinner, he had rubbed his forehead vigorously. He didn't even eat much, although he never usually did. "I'm going to head home. I'll see you two bright and early tomorrow morning?"

Before I could say anything, Kasra responded. "We'll be ready bright and early!"

The spicy scent of Ryker's cinnamon magic warmed my insides as he opened a portal and stepped through it. Kasra and I lugged our two oversized duffle bags out to the parking lot, then shoved them into the trunk of her car. We drove off in silence, Kasra bouncing with uncontrollable happiness in her seat while I sank deep into mine and let the icy cold of my nervousness solidify inside me.

5

———◈———

I HALF EXPECTED Reeva to be taking a nap in my bed when I arrived back at my apartment. Thankfully, wherever she and Liahm were, they weren't within my sight.

I spent most of the night packing clothes and other necessities. When I swiped a pair of jeans off the top of my dresser, a black velvet box tumbled to the floor. I slipped Kasra's necklace into a zippered pocket in my duffle bag, hoping I'd remember to give it to her before the mission. Once I was satisfied I had everything I needed, I tried to get some rest, but the unsettling thoughts of Colton and what I was going to do about my father's request had other plans for me. My skin was sweltering hot, my hands clammy and shaking despite the cold draft drifting through my dark apartment.

Giving up on sleep, I got up in the middle of the night to bake a batch of snickerdoodle cookies and take my mind off things. As I slid them off the cookie sheet and onto a wire rack, I smiled to myself, inhaling the warm scent of cinnamon that reminded me so much of Ryker's magic.

Even though we wouldn't be leaving for another few hours, I changed into a pair of black jeans and a baggy t-shirt so I'd be ready to go at a moment's notice. I rested on my bed, staring into the black void that was my ceiling. Eventually, my eyes fluttered shut, only to shoot wide open some time later when a loud knock startled me awake.

My heart pounded, my pulse spiked. I rolled over, getting tangled in my sheets and tripping as I scrambled to get out of my bed.

"Zulli, is everything okay in there?"

My heartbeat steadied at the sound of Ryker's voice. I glanced over to the clock on my nightstand, noticing the time was eight in the morning. The shadows of night that once swallowed my apartment had lifted, replaced with a dull light that filtered through the windows with a subtle orange glow.

"Hold on a minute!" My bare feet thumped against the cold wooden floor as I raced toward the front door and swung it open.

"Zulli, it's time to go. Get changed and—" Shock flashed across Kasra's face. "Oh. You're actually ready. That's a first."

Ryker, standing next to Kasra, entered my apartment and handed me a paper bag. The bottom was saturated with grease. "Figured you might want breakfast."

"Thanks."

Kasra followed behind him holding a similar paper bag of her own. She placed her duffle bag on the floor, her long braid swinging over her shoulder as she bent down. She adjusted a large overstuffed backpack on her shoulders when she straightened. Intending to blend in, she was dressed casually, with jeans and a light-weight turtleneck under her unzipped canvas jacket.

The smell wafting out of the paper bag hypnotized me. It was a fresh, slightly sweet, yeasty aroma, mingling with a rich nuttiness that warmed my nostrils. I unwrapped the magical creation—a round ball of crusty bread with magic flavor-enhancing crystals sprinkled on top. Taking a bite, I melted under the delectable taste of creamy cheese complimenting the velvety eggs and crispy bacon. Mixed inside was some kind of white sauce, the creamy magic infused in it typing the whole breakfast together.

"This tastes like a full breakfast rolled into one," I mused, taking another bite, then continuing to speak as I chewed. "What is it?"

He offered me a warm smile before responding. "I stopped by the artisanal breakfast place near my place. They specialize in innovative magic infusions. That one is the farmer's breakfast. Coffee, bagel, eggs, toast, and orange juice all rolled into one."

Having scoffed the entire thing down in a matter of seconds, I licked my fingers then eyed Kasra's bag with a hungry gaze. She pulled it closer to her.

"Let's get going. The sooner we get there, the more time we have to scope things out." Impatience and eagerness were twisted in her tone.

Ryker agreed. Drawing in a deep breath, he closed his eyes. Gently, he massaged a palm with the pad of his thumb. Ryker once explained to me that opening a large portal had felt like smashing his fist through a thick sheet of glass. There was nothing I could do to help him, since traveling through his portal was the most convenient way for us to get to Earth, but I hoped the bag of snickerdoodle cookies I had stashed in my backpack would at least let him know I appreciated what he was doing.

Reaching into his back pocket, he took out a picture of our destination. As he focused on it, a warm pocket of magic started forming in front of him and the invigorating scent of cinnamon filled my apartment. Kasra and I grabbed our bags. I stepped through the portal, the vibration of his magic buzzing against my skin.

For a moment, I wondered if I had actually reached the other side of the portal. Complete darkness encased me, so black that I could barely see where I was stepping. Carefully, I placed my bag on the floor and slid my backpack off my shoulder. The hairs on the back of my neck were standing on end, and my hand ran across my belt.

56

Kasra crashed into my back, and from the sound of it, Ryker crashed into hers.

"What's wrong, Zulli?" Kasra whispered into my ear and gently placed a hand on my shoulder.

"Someone's here." I pointed straight ahead to a closed door in front of us. A faint glow of light escaped through its cracks, the only light visible in the dark room.

"*Lumen*," Ryker's voice softly called out. A dull sphere of light illuminated in his hand from a glass marble, bringing a leather couch and a wooden end table into view.

I surveyed my surroundings, seeking any vibrations or sounds that might give away who the intruder was and what they were doing here. "It's a woman," I concluded from the feminine voice cussing on the other side of the door. The three of us crept closer, the light in Ryker's palm guiding the way.

"What's she doing?" Kasra asked, leaning in over my shoulder.

"Maybe I could hear something if you stopped breathing down my neck." She backed away a few inches, and I placed my ear to the cold wood. The sound of water sloshing around followed some violent movements as something was dragged, possibly kicked, across the floor. The woman's abrasive voice called out, "I wish I could destroy you with a sledgehammer and toss your filthy remains in the trash."

My eyes widened with alarm. That didn't sound good. "I'm going in."

"Be careful, Zulli," Ryker warned.

I twirled my finger, requesting both Ryker and Kasra to turn around. Letting my magic tingle through me, I transformed my human body into a creepy crawly with eight hairy legs. Just small enough to slip under the threshold, I crept my way inside the bathroom, where I was met with a blast of heat from a cloud of steam. It took a moment for my eyes to adjust to the brightness, but when they did, a female appeared off to my left. She was on her knees and hunched over. From where I was positioned on the floor, a large vanity blocked the view of whatever she was doing with her hands, but I could tell from the frustrated expression on her face that she was furious and struggling.

Determined to get a better look, I continued crawling across the damp tile floor, up the side of the vanity, and stared down at her from on top of the counter. The woman, perhaps in her early sixties, had thinning gray hair wrapped in pink curlers that stuck to her head. Her wrinkled skin drooped down her scraggly face, pigmented with dark age spots. Round, red glasses magnified the dark bags under her eyes.

She let go of the plunger and wiped her forehead with her wrist. Her hand reached for the side of the vanity to push herself up. That was when she glimpsed me.

"*Eek! Die!*" Her hand tightened into a fist and it came pounding down to squash the gross spider before her. With a flash of magic, my human form reshaped. As I was on top of the counter, there wasn't much room for my body. My fingers reached out to grab a towel rack on the wall but completely missed. Unable to steady myself, my torso twisted and I rolled right off the counter. My boot swept up as I fell, kicking the poor woman in the jaw. My other foot then landed in a plastic bucket, the contents spilling all over me as it tipped over. Panicking, I ripped whatever bullet I could find on my belt and attempted to jump to my feet.

"*Dormeo!*" As I slipped on the soapy water, the bullet loaded with sleep powder went soaring behind me instead of at the woman.

"Zulli!" The bathroom door whipped open and Ryker bounced in. The powder exploded in a colorful blue cloud of magic and hit Ryker square in the face. His eyes fluttered, his knees shook, and then he dropped to the ground.

Kasra stood in the doorway, watching the aftermath of the catastrophe that had unfolded. I pushed myself up and rested my back against the wall. The vile smell of the soapy water I was drenched in reminded me of a sewer. I did my best to suppress my gag reflex. When Kasra concluded that neither of her team-mates were seriously hurt or in danger, she stepped over Ryker and around me. Crouching down next to the woman, whose back was propped up against the side of the bathtub, she asked in a friendly voice, "Are you okay, ma'am? Looks like you took a nasty hit."

A pained and confused look crossed the woman's haggard face, and she rubbed her hands across her chin, groaning. She picked up the glasses that had fallen off her face and rested them on her nose.

"What's going on here? Who are you people? One minute I'm cleaning the bathroom and unclogging this damn toilet, the next I see this dreadful hairy spider on my vanity. And then ... and then it disappears and this young lady appears out of no-where!"

"Uh ..." I scratched the top of my head and bit my lip. Thank-fully, Kasra had things covered.

"You must be Mrs. Paxton, the owner of this building. We're so sorry to barge in on you like this. We're the three students you rented this apartment to for the next few weeks."

"But ... you weren't supposed to be here until this afternoon! It's three in the morning!" Mrs. Paxton adjusted her glasses and peered around me to Ryker. His face was covered in a shimmery powder and soft snores were coming from his mouth. "Is that ... a magic spell bomb? You tried to hit me with magic! You know that's illegal, right? Do you have a permit for that? I should re-port you to the police!"

"That's not necessary!" Kasra ran her arm across the woman's back to help her up. "I think you might have hit your head a little too hard, Mrs. Paxton. No magic is being used here. Ryker here is just ... really tired. Where we come from, there's a big time difference. We weren't expecting to arrive so early, and we got frightened when we heard someone in the bathroom. We didn't mean to startle you."

I quickly tossed a towel over Ryker's face before Mrs. Paxton shot any more questions at us about magic. "Next time, you might want to consider keeping the lights on when you're in an empty apartment," I added. Kasra glowered at me.

"And next time, Missy, you might consider knocking instead of barging in on an old lady! You nearly gave me a heart attack!" She wagged her finger at me.

"Why don't you head to bed and get some sleep? We'll clean this up. Don't worry, Mrs. Paxton." Kasra led the woman out of the bathroom, carefully avoiding Ryker's body, which was lying in a puddle of slippery water. I used the towel to wipe the powder off his face. It wasn't a strong sleep spell, and it wouldn't have much effect on someone who had been trained to endure such weak magic. I gave Ryker a sharp slap to the cheek. He startled awake, shaking his head as his gaze flitted around the room.

"What happened?" he grumbled, rubbing the back of his head with soapy fingers.

"Definitely nothing that had to do with me scaring an old lady and using magic. Come on, get up." He clasped his hand in mine and I hoisted him to his feet. He wiped off the rest of the powder and dried himself before we joined Kasra in the living room with Mrs. Paxton.

"Here's your key." Mrs. Paxton dropped the shiny piece of metal into Kasra's palm. "Make sure you take out your own trash and clean up after yourselves. There's a laundry room down the hall. I left a couple bottles of water in the fridge, but I don't keep food in the kitchen when nobody's here, so you'll have to go shopping."

"Thank you, Mrs. Paxton." Kasra beamed a friendly smile. "Again, we apologize for the abrupt arrival and thank you for allowing us to stay here. This place looks absolutely lovely."

"Oh, why, thank you ..." Mrs. Paxton's sentence trailed off and she tilted her head, lost for words.

"By the way, I'm Kasra. And my friends are Ryker and Zulli."

Mrs. Paxton gave a heartfelt giggle. "Such odd names you three have. Anyway, my number is on the refrigerator door if you need me, but I hope you don't. Enjoy your stay."

With that, Mrs. Paxton stepped out into the hallway and shut the door behind her. Now that the lights had been turned on, I could see the place we'd be calling home for the foreseeable future. Paintings of landscapes in drab pastel colors hung on the clean, whitewashed walls. Except for the fake marble title in the kitchen, the rest of the floor was covered in a thick cream-colored carpet, the area near the entryway dirty and worn from constant traffic.

Kasra let out a long, exhausted sigh and crashed on the large gray sectional in the center of the living room. "That was a close one. What were you thinking, Zulli? Magic is illegal here for most common people. We can't let anyone see our magic or the items we carry."

"How the hell was I supposed to know she wasn't some old lady sent here to kill us?" I snapped back at her.

"Did you bother reading the rest of the file Colonel Buckner gave us? Mrs. Paxton's name and picture were in it, along with all the rules and regulations we'd have to abide by while we stayed here." Kasra jumped to her feet and took a few steps toward me, her shoulders stiff and hands digging into her hips. "Zulli, magic on Earth is a relatively new discovery. They aren't as advanced as we are on Iradel, so it's regulated, since they don't completely understand how it works. Only certain businesses have permission to use magic objects. And they certainly don't know about harnessing individual magic powers. We can't be going around flaunting our magic if we want to stay off anyone's radar. We have to make sure we blend in."

I glanced over to Ryker, hoping he'd say something to defend me. "Kasra's right. Authorities on Iradel have no jurisdiction on Earth. We've kept our presence hidden to protect our society from crazy fools who might want to conquer us for our power and knowledge. If we get caught, we're on our own. We have to keep a low profile, not only to avoid raising any red flags from the people living here, but to keep out of sight of anyone who might also be tracking Colton."

I rolled my eyes, then walked over to grab my bags in the middle of the living room. "Fine. I'm going to go take a shower and try to wash this stink off me."

Kasra and Ryker also grabbed their bags and made their way down the hallway. Ryker grabbed the first bedroom, the small bed barely fitting in the tight space. Kasra snagged the master bedroom, which boasted a huge, fluffy mattress that looked like it might swallow her alive when she lay down on it. That left me with the remaining bedroom at the end of the hallway. Judging from the frilly pink comforter and pastel-colored walls, it must have previously belonged to a little girl.

After grabbing a new pair of jeans and another t-shirt, I made my way to the bathroom. Ignoring the mess, I stepped into the shower and scrubbed myself raw, trying to eliminate the rancid smell that had permeated my skin. After about twenty minutes, the water turned cold and I gave up. Steam escaped as I stepped out of the shower and goosebumps ran up my arms. I grabbed a white towel from the rack beside the tub.

"*Calor.*" I wrapped the thin towel around my chest, and the stiff cotton rubbed against my skin. The scratchy fabric remained rough and cold. "Damn it."

No magic for commoners meant no heated magic towels, one of the few magic luxuries I allowed myself to indulge in. This abrasive, cheap piece of crap sucked.

Hurrying up to cover my body, I dried off, threw on my clothes, and headed back down the hallway to my room. To my surprise, Kasra was waiting for me, staring out the window. It was an overcast day in the city of Lorith. Tall skyscrapers surrounded us, blocking what little morning sunlight might have escaped through a pocket of clouds.

Kasra didn't bother to turn around. I joined her, following her gaze, which was pinned to the busy street three stories below us.

The road was wet from a recent rain shower. Busy pedestrians scrambled in all directions on the sidewalk, avoiding puddles. A biker zig-zagged his way in between a crowd and right over a pothole that splashed dirty water onto the white blouse of a businesswoman.

"We take a lot of our magic for granted, huh? If that woman was wearing a spelled shirt to protect against stains, she wouldn't have even gotten wet," I commented, scratching my itchy arms.

"Yeah, I guess." Kasra tugged on the collar of her turtleneck and stretched out the ends of her long sleeves.

"Something wrong with your shirt?" I asked.

"It uses a magic fabric for extra protection. I figured I'd wear it since we can't use our tactical vests out in public. It's just a little tight."

"Oh!" I snapped my fingers and widened my eyes. "I think I have something that can help with that."

Excitedly, I jumped over to my duffle bag on the bed and dug through the pocket where I had stuffed Kasra's necklace.

"What's this?" she asked as I handed her the velvet box.

"It's a necklace spelled for protection like your shirt, except instead of just your torso, the magic wraps around your whole body. It should protect against sharp blades and most light magic spells, soften the blow of more intense ones. I had Catilda find it because I thought it might come in handy on missions when you go undercover."

Kasra removed the pendant from the box and smiled subtly as she ran her thumb over the shiny red jewel. She clasped it around her neck, the chain falling on her chest. "Well, tell Catilda I said thanks. I'm gonna go find something to eat and then we should start scouting the area to plan our rescue."

With that, she hummed a cheery tune as she left the bedroom.

6

―――――⟨⟨⟨⟩――――――

WHILE I WAS in the shower, Ryker had gone out exploring. He returned about an hour later with several bags of groceries and snacks. As he stocked up the cabinets, I handed him a plastic bag full of cookies.

"You brought snickerdoodle cookies with you? When did you have the time to bake those?" Ryker immediately opened the bag and grabbed two cookies. Kasra swooped in and snatched one herself.

"Last night. I couldn't sleep, so I figured I might as well make good use of my time instead." My fingernails furiously scratched at the back of my neck and then made their way to my scalp.

"What's wrong with you?" Kasra asked in a rather irritated tone. "Please tell me you don't have fleas. Do cat shifters get fleas?"

"Real funny." I slipped my hand under my shirt and started scratching my stomach. "I guess since you're not as sensitive to magic as I am, you don't feel it. But the raw magical energy in the atmosphere here … it's different from what I'm used to on Iradel. My body isn't liking it."

"Ha!" Kasra snorted. "Zulli's allergic to Earth magic!"

My nails started clawing at every pore on my body, and I scampered back into my bedroom to dig through my duffle bag for some lotion. Ryker followed, leaning in behind me and reaching toward my waist. "Let me help with that."

"It's fine. I can do it myself."

He was so close I could smell his sweet cinnamon scent and feel the warmth of his breath brush against the back of my neck. I tensed, twitching uncomfortably. Heat burned my cheeks and ran down my neck. He hesitated for a moment, then removed a white bullet from my belt.

"*Sana.*" Ignoring my previous statement, he lifted my shirt and started gently rubbing the healing ointment on my back. The warmth of the magic absorbed into my skin and the itching started to dull. "Sit," he commanded as he picked up my leather jacket on the bed and moved it to make space for me.

"Ryker, I said I can do this myself. Besides, I didn't bring a lot of refills with me. I have to save what I've got." Despite my resentment, I sat down on the mattress and let his hands continue to work up to my shoulders and then my neck. The gentle touch of his delicate fingers gliding across my skin was steeped in compassion that helped me relax. It brought me back to that magical but very confusing moment in the hot tub during our stay on Grestor Island.

A mixed cocktail of feelings coursed through me, and heaviness weighed down my heart. That evening, Ryker had been under the influence of magic that had heightened his emotions when he confessed how he felt about me. I had been trying to shrug off his affection, like maybe the magic encouraged him to say something he didn't truly mean. Ryker was my best friend, one of the few people I truly confided in, yet he had been straight up lying to me since the day I met him, working with my father behind my back. It was difficult for me to forgive him as a friend. I wasn't sure if I'd ever be able to move beyond that into something more.

As if reading my mind, Ryker brought it up.

"You know, I was thinking about that night at the hotel. Most of what I said was brought on by that, um, special magic, but the truth is ... I meant it. I wouldn't mind hanging out with you more, Zulli." Ryker stopped rubbing the ointment into my skin and goosebumps shivered down my arm. He let my shirt drop back into place.

"You ... remember that night? I thought maybe you had forgotten about it." I scratched the side of my head. My father had erased all the memories Ryker had of working with him. Although the incident at the hotel was only between us, we were there because of my dad and Ryker hadn't brought it up again until now.

"Of course. No memory drug could steal *that* away from me. I rather enjoyed our chat that night and eating dinner together."

"Seriously?" I laughed. "I thought the whole thing was pretty embarrassing."

"Your vulnerability is one of the things I like about you, Zulli. You never try to impress or suck up to people. You're never afraid to speak your mind and just be yourself. Even if sometimes it can be a little ... out of control." Ryker scooted closer to me and placed his hand on top of mine. "What do you say? Would you like to go out for a *real* dinner with me sometime?"

Two deep, childish dimples formed on his rosy cheeks as he smiled. Ryker wasn't what most women would call attractive, but there was something about his magnetic personality that drew me in. His modest innocence was soothing to the soul and warmed my heart.

"You mean, like a date?" I pulled my hand away and began fidgeting with my fingers. He had completely caught me off guard and I had no idea what to say.

Ryker shrugged. "Only if you want it to be. I wouldn't want to push you into something you aren't ready for."

"Oh, um ... I ... uh ..." My eyes didn't know where to look, so I stared out the window. Ryker removed his hand and leaned away from me, relaxing his posture.

66

"It's okay, Zulli. I understand now isn't a good time, but if you ever want to take me up on that offer, just let me know."

"No, I don't think you *do* understand, Ryker." The words rushed out of my mouth before my brain processed what I was saying. My pulse started racing and my heart thumped wildly inside my chest.

"I understand more than you realize, Zulli." Ryker's gaze became distant, reminiscing about something that seemed to trouble him. His shoulders sagged and his frown washed away the dimples on his cheeks.

"What's that supposed to mean?" I suddenly felt trapped inside my own body. My limbs wouldn't move, my lungs wouldn't breathe.

"Your father ... he's a very cruel man. I know this because the first thing that flashed into my mind when my memories returned was an image of you the moment I told you I was working for your father. Those striking green eyes slashed absolute hatred toward me. Your shaking voice spoke of agonizing disbelief. I could sense that all you wanted to do was run far away from me, so I've been giving you some space. I'm sorry, Zulli. I don't know why I did it, and I honestly don't remember any part of working with Zavyr, but I know I did. I know I hurt you and I know you're grieving."

"Why am I only hearing about this now?" I scolded. "I asked you if you remembered! Why would you lie to me again?"

"I didn't know what to do. I just thought that ... maybe you'd be more likely to forgive me and move on if you thought I didn't remember any of it. But every time you look at me, I still see the sorrow in your eyes—the disbelief swelling inside you, thinking that I could ever do such a cruel thing to you. I can't stand to keep seeing you like that. I know my apology isn't worth much, but I truly am sorry, Zulli. I promise you I will fix this."

"You can't fix everything, Ryker."

He looked at me with glassy eyes. "But I'd like to try if you'll let me."

I leaned back, surrendering to gravity as my back hit the mattress. "This team needs a group therapist. I kept secrets from Kasra. You lied to me. Kasra wants to murder me. We're all messed up. When will it end?"

"Now," Ryker confirmed with absolute assurance. His soft features hardened, and I knew he was sincere.

"So? What do you want to do, Zulli?" Ryker's hand went to brush a strand of hair away from my forehead but I sat up before he could. If we weren't holding back any more secrets, then there was something I needed to tell him about Colton. Consequences be damned.

"Ryker, I—" My throat constricted and I couldn't breathe. Tightness squeezed my chest.

"Zulli? Are you—" Concern flashed across Ryker's face.

"What's going on in here?" Kasra appeared in the doorway. She clapped her hands together to brush off the crumbs from another snickerdoodle cookie. "You two have been in here for quite a long time."

Once I stopped speaking, my airway opened back up and I could once again breathe.

"Nothing. We're done." Ryker stood up from the bed and strolled over to Kasra. "We should get going. It's late morning. Plenty of time for us to scout the area."

"Exactly what I was thinking." Kasra slipped out a piece of paper from her jeans and unfolded it. "Colton's apartment is located a few blocks from here. It's right across the street from a park. We can make a few sweeps around the building and camp out on a bench while we monitor the area."

I shrugged on my leather jacket over my baggy t-shirt, letting the oversized garment hide the bullets I kept on my belt. To the average person, they'd never know magic was inside the metal canisters, but it still wasn't something I wanted to advertise. Kasra continued wearing her magic-woven turtleneck and pendant while shoving all of our mission files into a zippered tote she carried on her shoulder. Ryker slung a single-shouldered bag across his back and traded in the leg holster where he usually kept his knife for one that concealed the blade horizontally across the back of his belt.

As we started wandering down the city streets of Lorith, my magic eventually adjusted to the new conditions. My stiff muscles unwound as I felt more comfortable and took in my surroundings.

Barely peeking out over the towering skyscrapers was a sliver of early afternoon sun, but it did little to warm the chilly wind that swept across my face and through my hair. The city of Lorith was similar to Chitol, but was also completely different. Cars and cyclists whirled by, pedestrians stormed the sidewalks on a mission to get somewhere fast. The charred smell of something being grilled mingled with the sweet aroma of freshly baked bread. But everything was void of magic. There were no magic-fueled vehicles on the road, no magical scents wafting out of the restaurants. While I was used to talented street performers using their magic to earn spare change, the people on the streets in Lorith wore rags that reeked of the trash they dug through.

We passed one beggar who had propped himself up against the side of a brick building. He held out his hand, and when he spoke, the powerful stench of tobacco rolled off his breath. "Can you spare a few coins for a poor man?"

The hood of his jacket shadowed most of his face, but as Liahm tilted his head upward, his dark brown eyes caught my gaze. He smirked, a cryptic reminder that I was being watched. He didn't bother us any further and let us continue.

Further down the street, I was met by a tall, slender woman in athletic attire running toward me. Her multiple braids swung from side to side with her motion. A ball cap and sunglasses concealed her identity, but it wasn't difficult to discern that screechy, nasally voice when she bumped into me.

"Oh, so sorry." She gave me a dirty look and kept running. I fought the urge to turn around and watch to see if she disappeared.

My breathing quickened and I stopped walking to hunch forward, rubbing my hands on my thighs as I tried to calm my racing heart.

"Are you okay, Zulli?" Ryker, who had a habit of following behind both Kasra and me, saw the whole thing unfold. He couldn't have possibly known who Liahm and Reeva were or what they were doing here, but I wanted so badly to tell him.

"You keep asking me that. I'm fine." I shook the panic from my thoughts. I'd find a way to tell Ryker and Kasra, but it wasn't now. When I lifted my gaze from the sidewalk, a vendor selling something on a stick caught my attention and I changed the subject. "What is *that?*"

Ryker's gaze followed mine to the man dunking a wooden skewer into batter and then straight into the fryer.

"I think that's called a corn dog," Ryker replied. "A hot dog coated in some kind of sweet cornmeal batter, then deep fried in hot oil."

"Dog?" I questioned warily. "As in … the animals often kept as pets?"

Kasra cut in to respond in a pointed tone. "It's actually some kind of processed meat shaped into a tube. I don't really get why it's called a hot dog, but I heard from others who've visited Earth that they're actually pretty good."

Despite the unappetizing name and questionable substance of the product, my mouth started watering and I licked my lips. Although Ryker had ventured out shopping, he had brought nothing back for lunch. My stomach was rumbling at the sight of this mysterious new possibility of a meal.

Reading my thoughts, Ryker grinned. "I'll pick up something for us to eat once we get to the park."

It didn't take much longer for us to reach the concrete building where Colton lived. The entire way there, the hairs on my neck stood on end and I couldn't help but constantly scan my surroundings. My unease didn't go unnoticed by Kasra or Ryker, but neither said anything about it.

"Here it is." Kasra looked down at the piece of paper and then at the rusty metal numbers drilled into the side of the building. It was nothing special—a square concrete block with rows of narrow windows stacked about twenty stories up. The steps were caked in dirt and the smell of exhaust fumes suffocated the air. The front door itself was in bad shape, painted with an ugly silver acrylic that was chipped and peeling. For extra security, there was another door with steel bars welded to a heavy duty frame, about fifteen different locks, and a keypad.

"Why am I getting the feeling this area isn't very nice?" My head swiveled from side to side as I did another check of the street. Neither Reeva nor Liahm were in sight, but it wasn't either of them I was worried about. Everyone we had passed within the last block had glowered at us like we were trespassing on their turf.

"Residents in neighborhoods like this make it a habit of knowing everyone's business. Whenever someone new or suspicious appears, they go on high alert. As long as we keep out of their way and don't draw attention to ourselves, we'll be fine." Kasra flicked her ponytail behind her shoulder and looked upward. "He's supposed to be on the second floor. Zulli, can you turn yourself into a spider and crawl up there to see what's going on?"

"If I can do it in less than five minutes, I can. My form won't hold much longer than that. Do you know exactly which apartment is his?"

"From outside? Not a clue." Kasra shook her head.

Ryker provided us with an alternative idea. "Let's start by making a pass around the building, noting all the escape routes and exits. Maybe we'll get lucky and catch someone entering or leaving the building and we can sneak inside."

While Kasra and I made a few rounds up and down the street, Ryker used his friendly charm to convince a young woman that he had left his keys inside and locked himself out of the building.

She was skeptical at first, but Ryker's puppy dog eyes and dimpled smile were impossible to resist. She eventually had no choice but to succumb to his plea.

With Ryker surveying the inside, Kasra and I circled the block a few more times. When our scouting was complete, the three of us found a spot in the park across the street. Like the rest of the neighborhood, it had a gloomy feel to it. A broken fountain tagged with graffiti stood in the middle, the benches that circled it suffering the same fate. We settled on a wooden bench with a clear vantage point to the main entrance of Colton's apartment building.

"Colton should be home from school any minute now." Kasra placed her tote bag on her lap, her foot impatiently tapping on the ground and her vibrating leg shaking the entire bench.

The sky was darkening, the promise of rain threatening to return. There weren't many people out and about, but there were a few who didn't slip my notice. Running in what seemed like an infinite circle was a woman in black athletic attire and a ball cap on her head. Over by the fountain was a homeless man in rags picking through the trash. Both Reeva and Liahm had followed us and stuck around to monitor me.

Ryker always had a keen eye for picking out things that didn't belong, but if he had noticed our audience, he didn't mention it. "I'm going to grab us something to eat. I saw a deli not too far away."

He got up and left without another word, strolling out of the park with his hands in his jean pockets. He could have created a portal to get there quicker, but we couldn't risk anyone catching a glimpse of our magic.

Kasra and I sat on the bench, an awkward silence settling between us. My hand slipped into the pocket of my leather jacket, where I had stashed the poison I was supposed to inject into Colton. There was also the crinkle of the plastic bag filled with white pills—Bliss—that I had been instructed to give to Kasra and Ryker to erase their memories. I opened my mouth, again trying to warn her about this impending disaster, when a tightness in my throat cut off my words. A deep croaking sound came out of my mouth instead, startling a cat sitting on the ledge of a nearby garbage can overflowing with trash.

Kasra, completely ignorant of my pain, continued to keep her eyes trained on the front door of the apartment building. "There he is," she confirmed.

Just like his photo, Colton's wavy blond hair shadowed his forehead. He appeared to be an ordinary teenager, perhaps a bit on the nerdy side, minding his own business and going about his day. I struggled to find anything threatening about him.

We watched as he jostled a stack of books in his arms and fumbled to reach the keypad that opened the front door. After steadying himself, he stepped aside and leaned against the door for an elderly woman taking her time to exit the building. My magic reached out to listen in on what they were saying. Their voices were low, but the conversation carried to my ears.

"Thank you, dear Colton!" The elderly woman beamed him a smile.

"No problem, Ms. Webber." I had no doubt he was returning the smile behind his tower of textbooks. "Will you be around this weekend? I found a new book about plant care I think you might like. I can read it to you."

"That sounds wonderful, Colton." She rubbed her eyes from under her glasses. "But you don't have to continue giving up your weekends to keep me company. Don't you have friends you'd rather be spending time with?"

"I don't mind, Ms. Webber." The stack of books in Colton's hands must have been getting heavy. The tower wobbled and he was starting to hunch forward. "I know you have trouble reading with your eyesight. Besides, I enjoy learning. Even if it's about plant care."

"Okay then." She chuckled. "I look forward to it." The woman hobbled out the door and carefully down the steps, disappearing down the street.

Heaviness swarmed my insides and my stomach twisted in knots. What was I going to do? No matter how many times I had tried, I couldn't tell Ryker or Kasra what was happening. After finally seeing Colton, I knew there was no way I could follow through with killing him. My dad had said he was a threat, and for all I knew, maybe he was, but I couldn't take his word for it. I needed to find out the truth before I did something I'd undoubtedly regret.

The bench creaked as Ryker sat down next to me. He pulled something out of a bag and handed it over. "One cheeseburger, no pickles. They didn't have milkshakes, but I found strawberry-flavored milk. Kinda the same thing, I guess."

I unwrapped my meal and stared down at the soggy bun. Most of the cheese had melted, sticking to the foil wrapper. The burger was a flat, unappealing, gray disc. My stomach rumbled, and I went in for a bite.

"What the hell is this crap?" I forced myself to swallow. "This isn't a cheeseburger."

Ryker shrugged. "I'm not surprised. On Iradel, we use magic to enhance the flavoring of our food. That's not done here on Earth, so it's going to taste different."

He handed a sandwich to Kasra then crumpled up the bag, getting up to throw it out. I noticed he had gotten anything for himself, and I had hoped that maybe he had eaten his meal on his way back.

I was about to offer Ryker half my burger when he spoke first. "We have to do this today."

"Agreed." Kasra wiped her hands off with a napkin.

"What?" I exclaimed. "We just got here and we haven't even been watching Colton for a full day. Don't you think we need to spend at least a week learning about his routines? We don't even know who's in the apartment with him."

"That would be ideal, but I don't think time is on our side." Ryker scratched the back of his neck, twisting it to the side toward Reeva. "That woman bumped into you on our way here, and she's been running around this park for hours. And that man over there …" Ryker yawned and stretched, his gaze flitting to the opposite side toward Liahm. "That man was the same guy who asked us for some spare change. He's been hanging around this park ever since we got here."

"So you saw them too," Kasra confirmed. "There's also a third person who looks suspicious."

"A third person?" I glanced around the park, searching for another mysterious body. I only knew of Reeva and Liahm watching me. Who was this third person?

"Stop being so obvious, Zulli!" Kasra mumbled through a fake smile that was followed by a slap on my knee. "There's a woman sitting over by the fountain. She's been reading a book for the past three hours. Every once in a while I see her glance up and look in our direction."

I stood up to throw out my trash, glancing in the woman's direction. Her eccentric floral trench coat and stiletto heels didn't quite fit in with this neighborhood. Although it was far from sunny, she hid her hair under a sun hat and sported a wide set of sunglasses that covered half her face. She peered up at me and smiled, a deep red lipstick painted on her lips. Whoever she was, she clearly wasn't trying to hide her presence. I flashed a sheepish smile back to her and returned to my teammates on the bench.

"Do you know her?" Ryker asked.

"She's too far away for me to get a good look, but I don't think so." I dragged my hands down my face and sighed, then narrowed my eyes on Ryker. "Do *you* know her?"

Before Ryker could answer, Kasra interrupted. "We have to tread carefully with this one. We've never had to extract a kid before, and we're working with limited information. We need to stay calm and stick to a plan." She widened her eyes at me.

"Why do you always blame me when something goes wrong?" I folded my arms across my chest.

"Because it usually does have something to do with you, Zulli. Chaos follows you everywhere."

Kasra had no idea how true her words were. My hand went to my chest and felt the pills in my pocket. If only she knew what was about to happen …

I gulped loudly. When I opened my mouth, a terrible burning sensation erupted inside my chest and I swallowed it back down.

"I can get us inside the building," Ryker explained. "But we have to hurry before the others watching us realize what we're up to and intervene. We don't know what this kid is capable of or if anyone is in the apartment with him. It's safe to assume that if anyone *is* inside, they won't hesitate to come after us."

"I don't like this." I flexed my fingers in a fist then uncurled them. My hands were shaking, my skin sweltering. For the first time, the reality of the situation kicked in. We were going in, and I'd have to come up with a plan of my own fast, because if my teammates found out what I had been sent here to do, it wouldn't be Colton fearing for his life. It would be me.

7

---⬦---

As THE LATE afternoon shifted into evening, angry clouds darkened the skies and a chilly wind intensified the shivers already running down my spine. I sniffed the air, the tang of rain warning of an impending storm. Most people were too focused on hurrying home and decided against any evening activities that involved being outdoors. Having few people roaming the streets worked in our favor, although that didn't mean we could let our guard down.

We followed Ryker into a dark alley shadowed on both sides by two tall buildings. After clipping a few magic objects to his belt he handed the bag to me. "The nosy neighbors inside the building were watching me earlier, so I didn't have time to explore as much as I wanted to. The file mentioned Colton's in apartment 202 on the second floor. I walked by it. Didn't notice anything suspicious."

I dug through the duffle bag, choosing to wear a few black rings spelled with useful magic. Paralysis daggers lined my belt next to my bullets. Once ready, both Kasra and I also ditched the bags through Ryker's portal.

Ryker winced, rubbing his forehead and sighing, then looked through his phone for a picture of our destination. As he stared at it, the spicy scent of cinnamon hit my nose, and a moment later, the three of us were crammed into a damp room that reeked strongly of mold and was surrounded by concrete walls.

"Where are we?" I blinked a few times before my eyes adjusted to the darkness.

"The basement," Ryker confirmed in a hushed voice. "I figured this would be the most discreet place for us to enter."

The three of us made our way up the stairs to the second floor, stopping at a wooden door marked 202 with plastic numbers.

"The coast is clear. Hurry up." Kasra's impatience was shining through. She bounced from foot to foot, unable to stand still.

Ryker removed a postage stamp from a pouch on his belt. He licked it and his shaking fingers positioned it just above the door handle.

"*Displodo,*" he whispered.

The explosion was more like a sizzle followed by a slight pop. It wasn't loud enough to alert the entire neighborhood of our presence but it was strong enough that it melted the lock, allowing us to push open the door and creep into the apartment.

Light spilled in from the hallway, but once Ryker had closed the door behind him, the room filled with silent shadows and darkness. We had seen Colton enter the building, but it was possible he'd left out of one of the other exits when we weren't looking. My heart rapidly raced inside my chest at the possibility of something I hadn't even thought about until now. What if this whole thing was a setup by my father? What if he wanted us to get caught, to trap us here on Earth so we'd no longer be in his way?

We cautiously crept into the living room. Kasra flipped on the light switch as a puddle of steaming acid flew directly toward her face.

"Move!" I dove at Kasra, both our bodies hitting the floor hard. The acid hissed and sizzled, chewing into the wall and eating away at the plaster. I rolled off her and rebounded to my feet as Kasra seethed at the blistering burn forming on the back of her hand. She pushed herself up and joined me.

Ryker flipped on a light and I scanned the apartment for the source of the attack. To one side was the kitchen, and the other was the main living area. A tile fireplace brought the single large room together, and standing right in front of it were two agitated predators that weren't going down without a fight.

"We're not here to harm you!" Ryker inched closer, holding up his hands in surrender. "We know someone is after Colton. We're with the Chitol military and we're here to help."

"The boy is no better in the hands of the military than the savages trying to kill him," a woman with a hissing voice spoke. Her skin shimmered with magic, transforming into a protective armor of iridescent scales. A long, thick tail sparkled with a rainbow sheen and curled around her leg. As she moved her head, her scales glistened and changed color in the overhead light. The beauty of her glamorous magic mesmerized me, at least until she peeled back her lips to show a row of deadly sharpened teeth. Steaming acid dripped down her chin.

"We won't give him up," the male next to her snarled, snapping my attention back to the situation. The man looked like a gym rat—strong, defined, and capable of crushing my head with a single squeeze of his hand. As he clenched his fists, they lit up a fiery red. "We have no reason to trust you. He doesn't leave our sight." He glanced over at the woman. "Let's do this, Lyra."

"I'm right with you, Alyx." The woman briefly flashed him a knowing smile then readied herself in a fighting stance.

"I guess we're doing this the hard way." Kasra swiped her hand down her sleeve to brush off some dust. She then narrowed her gaze on the lizard shifter who had tarnished her supple skin.

I stepped forward, claws out and ready to slice, but Kasra held out her hand to stop me.

"No, Zulli. She's mine."

Kasra charged into action. Her fruity-scented magic mingled with the stinky fish smell of her opponent. Kasra bounced on her rubber heels, launching herself at Lyra with an angry fist. The reptilian woman evaded her attack, whipping out her tail to lash at Kasra's legs. Kasra crashed to the floor, but immediately sprang back up.

The two of them started running, climbing, and clinging to tables and chairs that toppled over. They dodged each other's attacks, destroying the living room. Kasra had the advantage of her thick rubber skin, but Lyra's movements were swift, calculated, and serpentine. Her hands locked onto Kasra's shoulders and her lips parted. She spat out another mouthful of bile at Kasra, who couldn't jerk free. Ryker threw out his hand, redirecting the acid straight onto Alyx's chest as it narrowly missed Kasra's face.

The steaming substance melted Alyx's shirt, exposing toned muscles on his chest that glowed a reddish-orange, like embers of a flame. He growled, although more in rage than pain. As he burned away the corrosive liquid with his volcanic magic, his skin turned into molten rock and his entire body lit up like a wildfire. Tendrils of smoke rose into the air.

"Zulli!" Ryker called out. I didn't know what he had planned, but I knew exactly what he wanted me to do. I thrust my fist forward, straight into a portal.

"*Viribus!*" The black ring on my index finger warmed with magic. Strength vibrated through my muscles, the impact of my punch delivering a super powered knuckle sandwich directly to Alyx's jaw. The heat from his skin burned my own, but I refused to pull back. Most people would have been knocked out cold, but Alyx simply staggered backward. I slipped a paralysis dagger from my belt just as a glob of bubbling lava launched from his palm.

My cat-like reflexes took over and I leaped out of the way. I rolled across the dining room table, grabbing the edge with my hands to stop myself from sliding off. Plates and glasses crashed to the floor and shattered. Behind my opponent, Kasra's rubber body was bouncing off the furniture and repelling every fist or foot that came at her. She and Lyra flew back and forth in an expertly choreographed dance to the death, and I had no desire to get in the middle of it.

Ryker and I kept our focus trained on the volcanic man.

"What's so special about Colton?" I asked Alyx on a whim, using the distraction to get back on my feet.

He responded with two handfuls of hot molten magma, one heading toward Ryker and the other at me. Panic flashed across Ryker's face. He could only open one portal at a time, and I knew it wouldn't be to protect himself.

Snatching the tablecloth under me, I sprang off the table and flung it at Ryker. The boiling lava scorched holes into the thin fabric. Wisps of smoke rose into the air, only a few splatters having reached Ryker's arms and neck. I somersaulted across the floor, my momentum halted by a bookcase right beside Alyx's feet.

"*Torpens.*" I leaped up and sank a dagger into his bicep. He ripped it out and grunted, but the magic was already running its course. He struggled to keep control of his limb. Eventually, it dropped to his side, limp and useless.

I ducked to avoid his other swinging fist. As I did, my claws raked through the back of both his pant legs, tearing right through the denim. The monstrous man dropped to his knees, shaking the entire apartment as he did. I rolled backward, kicking him with the heel of my boot. He tripped over an overturned chair and the side of his face smashed into the corner of an end table.

Ryker had a knife in one hand, a dagger in the other. Both were spelled to paralyze their opponents. "Go find the Colton, Zulli. Kasra and I can handle the rest of this."

"But—" I refuted.

"Someone must have heard this racket by now. We have to finish this and get out before anyone arrives."

Glancing over my shoulder, I was confident that Kasra had things under control. The living room was completely demolished, but Lyra was running out of steam, her movements slowing. It wouldn't be long before Kasra completely overtook her. With Alyx only having one usable arm and wounded legs, Ryker would have no problem taking him down for good.

"Go!" Ryker demanded again, this time with a much deeper firmness to his voice.

With my heart pounding, I dashed across the room and headed for the only hallway in the apartment. Using the back of my hand, I wiped the sweat off my forehead. Nervousness bubbled inside me, the leather jacket trapping the heat that stuck to my skin like wet glue. I slowed down to a cautious walk, but my pulse kicked into high gear. All the rooms were dark except for one at the end of the hallway. The door was closed, but a sliver of light escaped past the threshold.

This was it. There was no turning back, and I still wasn't completely sure what I'd end up doing when I opened that door. I patted my jacket pocket, feeling the round cylinder filled with the poison, along with the capsules of Bliss. I didn't want to kill Colton, but the curious part of me wanted to know what was so special about him. What if he actually turned out to be a dangerous threat? What if he came after me and I had to defend myself? My mind knew what it wanted to do, but I wasn't sure my body would comply if I found out the truth.

Pressing an ear to the door, I listened for any movement inside the room but heard nothing. My fingertips felt the ground for vibrations, but all I sensed was the destruction going on down the hallway. My hand closed around the knob, its cool metal refreshing against my clammy palms. A haze clouded my mind as I drew in a deep breath and slowly exhaled to clear it. Thrusting the door open, I raised my claws in the air, ready to slash at whatever came at me.

"This ends now!" I cried out. But the boy didn't answer. In fact, he didn't even register my presence. He sat there on his bed, headphones covering his ears and nose buried in a book.

"Um, hello! Kid, a dangerous stranger just burst into your room!" I clapped my hands, but he didn't even twitch. Frustrated, I stomped my heavy feet over to his bed and slapped the book right out of his hands. That got his attention, but not much of a reaction.

He removed his headphones and looked up at me. Not a drop of fear registered in his mismatched eyes, one a striking icy blue and the other somewhat milky with a reddish hue. "Hello," he said calmly. "I'm Colton. Who are you?"

"I'm ... that doesn't matter. Stop trying to distract me." I squinted at him, looking for any slight movement in his body language that might give away an attack.

"Distract you from doing what?"

He did it again. I ignored his question and responded with my own. "Why are you so calm? How do you know I'm not here to kill you? Can't you hear what's going on out there?"

He tapped his headphones. "Noise canceling. The really good kind. And you're the one who interrupted me. If you wanted to kill me, you would have done it when I wasn't paying attention. Your body language gives off the impression that you're being more defensive than aggressive. You're not a threat to me."

Mildly impressed, but still flustered, I didn't quite know what to make of the boy. It was clear this wasn't the first time Colton had been approached by someone attempting to end his life. I peered over my shoulder at the door. Any moment, Kasra and Ryker would come barreling through it. I had to make this quick.

"Your life depends on your answer to my next question. Why are homicidal maniacs trying to kill you? Does the name Zavyr Taracula mean anything to you?"

My knees shook, and I tugged on the collar of my shirt as if it were strangling me. I then sucked in a deep breath and stiffened my spine, doing my best to hide the apprehension that Colton had so easily picked up on. My hand slowly descended to my pocket and reached in to grab both the syringe and Bliss.

"That's actually two questions, and I don't have the answer to either of them. I've been moving around my entire life, but no one will explain why. Is it because of this Zavyr Taracula person? Who is he?"

"He's my … " Damn it, he did it again. I held up the bag of pills in one hand, the syringe in the other. "That's not important. Look, kid. I'm sorry it has to be this way. I don't want to do this. It's nothing personal, but it's for your own good. It's best if you don't fight me. I'm going to—"

"Zulli! Stop! Don't do it!" My heart skipped a beat at Ryker's words and my whole body tensed. His voice traveled down the hallway before he'd even reached the bedroom door.

I stared dumbfounded at Ryker standing in the doorway, out of breath and holding on to the frame for support. "I won't let you do this."

"Wha—"

Ryker threw his hand forward. It disappeared through a small portal and clenched around my wrist holding the syringe. He squeezed tightly, compressing on the muscles and joints.

"Ryker stop! That hurts!"

He flinched briefly but didn't let go. I opened my mouth and hesitated, then bit down onto the back of his hand. My fangs began sucking out the very magic of the man who had saved me so many times. But at this moment, he had become a threat.

I had never extracted Ryker's magic before, and it tasted as sweet as it smelled. Almost like a warm snickerdoodle cookie right out of the oven.

"Zulli!"

My gaze shot up to see Kasra standing behind Ryker. She shoved him aside to enter the bedroom. I retracted my fangs and

Ryker let go of his grip, pulling back his hand through the portal. He stared in shock at the two puncture marks, small beads of blood bubbling from the shallow holes.

"I … I can explain!" I held up both hands in surrender, then remembered what I was holding in them.

"You have a bag of Bliss in one hand and what I can only assume is some toxic death serum in the other." Kasra cracked her knuckles and approached me. I took a step back and ended up bumping into the side of the bed where Colton curiously sat watching the conversation unfold. "There's nothing to explain, Zulli. I know what's going on here."

"I don't think you do. My—" A sharp pang hit the center of my stomach, the pain twisting and burning with fury. Bitterness and rage raced through me as I pushed to fight past the magical gag. I needed to tell them the truth. My lungs seized. Weakness dominated my limbs. Tears rolled down my cheeks.

Kasra charged at me, tackling me onto the bed. We tumbled across the mattress, miraculously avoiding Colton, and crashed onto the floor. She jabbed her elbow into my sternum, leaving me gasping for air. I dropped both the syringe and Bliss. Growling at Kasra, I flashed my claws and raked them across her stomach. She rolled out of the way, the turtleneck protecting her from my sharp weapons. I kicked out my boot and shoved it into her side. Her rubber body hit the wall and bounced off.

Quickly rebounding to my feet, I saw Ryker approach Colton and hand him an empty backpack. "Hurry up and pack."

"We don't have time for this, Zulli. Police will be here any minute." My attention was brought back to Kasra, stumbling to her feet.

I bent down to pick up the syringe and Bliss beside my boot. "I'm not going with you. I can't. Not until—"

A stream of air tickled the back of my neck, and Ryker stood behind me. Before I could react, his firm hands pinned my arms behind me. Ryker's strength wasn't overpowering, but his hold was tight. I wriggled, grunting and stomping my feet, trying to break free.

"I'm ready." Colton zipped up his backpack and stood next to Ryker. "What's going on?"

"I'll explain later, but you need to trust us and do as we say." Kasra kept her penetrating gaze on me. "Time to get this show on the road."

Kasra, Ryker, Catilda … they were all in danger if I didn't do something about Colton. I sucked in a deep breath and exhaled with zealous determination. I wouldn't let Reeva or Liahm get to them, and I sure as hell wouldn't let my father continue to destroy my relationships with my best friends. I had to do something about this right now.

"I said … I can't go! Not yet!" Heat collected at my core, so hot it felt like coals burning my lungs. The magical storm erupted inside my chest and I didn't hold it back. I screamed out in primal rage as my magic flourished, the intense energy saturating my veins. Adrenaline pumped through me. My eyes widened, then I squeezed them shut. The rush of magic consumed me. It had complete control, and it wanted to be set free.

"Zulli, what are you …" I pulled against Ryker's hold, seething and growling with all my stubbornness, until eventually I broke free. The momentum propelled my arms forward with a forceful swing, a sharp claw knocking Colton's shoulder and scraping his arm. Ryker lost his balance and fell backward, colliding with a dresser on his way down. I screamed with savage fury as magic exploded out of me in a concussive wave. The air crackled, the static buzzing across my skin with an electrifying, tingling sensation.

Kasra threw herself in front of Colton and spoke in a shaky voice. "Zulli, what have you done?"

Dread washed over me, the wave of magic subsiding. The world became a blur, but the empty syringe sticking out of Colton's arm was clear as day. I checked my hand to confirm my fear. It hadn't been one of my claws that had grazed Colton.

"Oh no …" A heavy numbness weighed down on my limbs. A moment ago I was coursing with power and now I was completely helpless. The poison was already inside him. There was no coming back from what I just did.

Ryker slowly rose to his feet and held out his hands toward me.

"Zulli, stop. Please. We can fix this." His hands touched my arms. This time, it had the gentle touch of a caring friend.

"We sure can." I turned just in time to be greeted with Kasra's open palm slapping my cheek. The thin glass marble between her fingertips shattered against my face and a plume of navy blue dust rose into the air. The light, fresh scent of jasmine and vanilla comforted my senses. My eyelids drooped, my body deciding it no longer wanted to stand up, and I went to sleep.

8

THE SOUND OF construction outside my window woke me up, the jackhammer pounding in time with my headache. I ran a hand through my hair, then flipped off the sheets and slumped out of bed.

Confusion filled my head with puzzling thoughts. I was back at the safe house in my bedroom. No one had bothered to tie me down or handcuff me to a bedpost. I was alone in the room. I still had on the same baggy t-shirt and jeans from our raid on Colton's apartment, but my leather jacket and belt had been draped over a desk chair in the corner. My finger ran down a rough, thin scab near the edge of my lip where Kasra had slapped me, the area tender and swollen.

"I probably deserved that," I said to myself as I rubbed some healing ointment over the cut.

I clenched my hand into a fist then splayed out my fingers. Straining, I tried to extract my claws but failed. Although I was currently magicless, for once I considered that a good thing. The oath spell would have dissolved and I could finally tell Kasra and Ryker what I had been trying to explain all along. Unfortunately, I might be too late.

After tossing on some clean clothes, I dragged my feet down the hallway. My brain was still trying to comprehend what had happened last night. There was an incessant throbbing in my heart and a suffocating, dense feeling in my chest as the vision resurfaced in my head. I had killed a young boy. That's what had happened.

Entering the main living area, I forced myself to look up. Although their backs were facing me, there was a blond, wavy-haired kid sitting at the breakfast bar next to Kasra. Ryker had taken command of the stove, spatula in hand as he placed a thick pancake on a plate. My eyes widened, my shoulders sagged, and I nearly collapsed onto the floor in a heap of tears. I ran over to Colton and hugged him.

"You're alive!" I pulled back and poked his arm where I had pierced him with the syringe. "But how?"

A stack of pancakes made its way in front of me, courtesy of Ryker. He took a can of whipped cream and made a smiley face on top. "Just how you like them."

I stared down at the plate and pouted. "Yeah, when I was five."

The last time I had smiley face pancakes was back when my mother was still around and the entire family spent every Sunday morning cooking breakfast together. Ryker wouldn't have known that. At least I don't remember telling him, but the gesture brought back some of the better memories of my family.

"Well, *almost* how you like them," he added. "They don't sell black flies here in the grocery stores so you'll have to settle for regular chocolate chips."

My gaze flitted between Kasra and Ryker. I anxiously rubbed the back of my hand and flexed my fingers. "I appreciate the fact I'm not being tortured in an interrogation room now, but what's going on? Why am I still … here?"

Kasra dropped her fork and held up her hand in front of my face. "First, I would like to apologize for slapping you in the face, although I did find it extremely satisfying in the moment. Given the circumstances, though, I suppose I can let this one go."

"Circumstances?" I questioned as I picked up my fork and shoveled a piece of pancake into my mouth. "I don't understand. Why isn't Colton dead? Why am *I* not in a cell awaiting a death sentence for betraying the military? And why are you being so casual about all this?"

Ryker leaned against the counter and clasped his hands in front of him. There was a dried smudge of batter on the side of his face and flour dusting parts of his dark brown hair. "I, uh, have a confession to make. I knew what was going on the entire time. About what Zavyr asked you to do."

"What! Why didn't you say something?" I clenched my fork a little tighter and speared the pancakes. "I thought I killed someone last night, Ryker!"

"When you brought me to your father's office and pleaded that he save me ... I, uh, wasn't quite *completely* out of it. I was still awake, and I heard the deal you made with him. I told Kasra, but I couldn't say anything to you because I knew you were being watched."

"Reeva and Liahm," I mused. "My father assigned them to make sure I finished the job."

"Reeva?" Kasra gasped. "You mean that woman I led right into your apartment was working with Zavyr Taracula this whole time?"

"Yup. I tried to tell both of you! I swear! But my father slipped some magic into my tea and made me promise not to say anything. Every time I tried, I'd choke on the words." I threw my head back and sighed. "I should have known he'd try something like that. I can't believe I fell for it. The spell only wore off this morning." I avoided eye contact and stared down at a massacred pancake, my fork stabbing and scraping the food around on the plate.

"You're lucky we knew what was going on." Kasra waved her fork at me, syrup dripping off it. "Ryker may be the forgiving type, but I wouldn't have hesitated to bring you right back to Iradel and have you locked up in a jail cell for murder."

"If you both knew, then the poison in the syringe ..."

"Wasn't really poison." Ryker grinned, a satisfying sparkle twinkling in his amber eyes. "I can be pretty discreet with my portals. When you weren't looking, I switched it out with something a little less deadly. Colton got a nice dose of multivitamins."

"I'm feeling better than ever!" Colton shouted, louder than necessary so early in the morning.

"So then you attacked me because ..." My voice trailed off and I kneaded the back of my neck.

"Because you were being an idiot." Kasra sniffed, brushing her ponytail behind her shoulder. "But mostly because if we gave off any sign that we knew what you were planning, we wouldn't have even made it up to Colton's apartment before Reeva and Liahm attacked us. We had to make it look like you'd completed the job. But it won't fool anyone for long. They'll both figure it out soon enough and come back for him."

Colton raised his hand and scanned the three of us. "Um, question. I'm sort of following what's going on. But is someone still going to kill me?"

Kasra and Ryker both glared at me. "Hey, I was never planning to kill him. I just thought maybe I could scare him into telling me why my dad is so intent on making sure he's dead. Then I was going to give him Bliss, hoping I could make him forget whatever it was my dad considered a threat."

Ryker flipped another pancake onto Colton's plate. "As long as you're with us, Colton, you'll be safe. The people who were taking care of you—Lyra and Alyx—did you know them well? Do you trust them? We weren't expecting them to have magic abilities."

Colton shrugged. "I have no idea what you're talking about with this ... magic ability stuff. But every time I move, I have a new set of foster parents. I've only known Alyx and Lyra for a few months. I guess they were okay, but they were very secretive people. If I had to guess, they're probably in hiding. They don't want to be found, by the police or anyone else coming after me. I'd rather take my chances sticking with you, if that's okay? I don't know you, but you seem more capable than they were at protecting me."

"Maybe we should take him back to the military. We at least need to update Colonel Buckner about the situation." There was uncertainty in Kasra's voice, and I knew why.

"No, not yet at least. Lyra said he was in as much danger with the military as he was in the hands of the people chasing after him." I remembered Liahm casually strolling down the hallway of the military base. No one has given a second thought to the fact he wasn't supposed to be there. "And besides, I think my dad has eyes and ears within the military. We don't know who we can trust, and that includes Colonel Buckner. For all we know, my father may already control him. It would make sense. Why else would he send us here?"

"So … what now?" Kasra leaned back on her stool and crossed her arms. "We live the rest of our lives on the run with a kid? No offense, Colton, but I'd rather not give up my life for you."

"I understand. I know you didn't ask to get involved with this." He picked up a napkin and wiped his mouth.

I shook my head at him. "You're taking this news very well. Most kids your age would be throwing a temper tantrum right about now, kicking and screaming that some kidnappers snatched him from his home. What's wrong with you?"

"Nothing," he retorted. "What's wrong with *you*?"

"That's not what I meant …" I brushed my hands across my lap. "What I was trying to ask is how are you okay with all of this?"

"This is my life. I'm used to it." He took a sip of juice. "The truth is, I *am* scared. Terrified, actually. I have lived my whole life under strict surveillance, warned to always stay on high alert.

I've never been to the movies. Never could join any school clubs and make friends. I've practically lived my whole life in my bedroom. I found a love for books and spent my time learning instead."

A frown pulled at my mouth, but the look on Colton's face was indiscernible. He caught me staring at his mismatched eyes.

"Go ahead. Ask. Everyone always does."

I hesitated for a moment. It was rude to ask, but I was curious. "Um, what happened? Was that from an attack?"

"No. I was told it was a birth defect. I can still see out of it, although not as well as my other one. So, I hear your name is Zulli?" he asked, changing the subject.

"Zulli Taracula." I held out my hand. "Zavyr Taracula is my father and the guy who's sending people after you. I just don't know why, but I'd like to help you find out."

"Sounds good. I'm Colton. Most people call me Cole." He reached out to complete the handshake. "I like your hair."

"And I like your ... dinosaur t-shirt."

He started firing off a barrage of questions. "Your magic was pretty cool. How did you do it? Do I have magic? Will you teach me? Ryker told me you're from a different planet. Are you aliens? What's it like there? Can I visit?"

"Uh ..." I gave a bewildered look to both Kasra and Ryker.

Kasra shrugged, then rose from her seat. Her slouchy sweater fell just above her knees, a pair of black leggings underneath. I couldn't help but smile at the pendant she still wore around her neck. "If we're going to figure this out, we need to tell Cole everything we know about what's going on. Why don't you and Ryker fire up the laptop and search the military database for anyone named Lyra or Alyx? I'll start filling in Cole with what we know and see if I can connect the dots."

I helped Ryker clean the dishes off the kitchen counter, then he powered up his laptop and began his search while I headed into the bedroom to retrieve my backpack.

Kasra was sitting next to Cole at the dining room table when I returned. Behind her, Ryker was scrolling through a sizable database of pictures at the kitchen breakfast bar, his hand propped up against his chin. "Without a last name, there are too many criminals and military personnel named Alyx and Lyra in this database to search. This could take us days to go through, and there's no guarantee either of them is even in here. Odds are those weren't their real names to begin with."

I reached into my backpack and retrieved a folded piece of paper. Using my fingers, I smoothed out the crumpled list of names. "Their names aren't on the list I found the night of the attack on NightFly Technologies, either."

I scanned the list thoroughly a second time. There were only about ten names written on it, most of them barely readable thanks to the water that had soaked into the paper, making the ink bleed. The last name, the only one handwritten in pen, was completely indiscernible except for both "T" initials.

"You still think it's a list of names of people working with your father?" Ryker didn't look away from his laptop screen as he addressed me.

"I'm not sure what to think. Cole's name isn't on here, and neither is anyone named Lyra or Alyx. But I've seen the Chitol city mayor, Ethin Henderson, being injected with a heavy dose of Bliss in my father's lab. Then at the coffee shop yesterday, I had an altercation with Cullin Maddox, also on the list."

Ryker stopped typing and raised his eyebrows at me.

"It wasn't anything serious. Don't worry about it. Although Cullin did say something a little concerning to me. I'm not sure if he was threatening me or warning me, but he said that my father has eyes everywhere."

"Well, Cullin wasn't wrong. If Zavyr has compromised the military and has people watching over you all the time, then he really does have eyes all over the place." Ryker propped his elbow on the counter and massaged his scalp, letting out a heavy sigh.

"You should really get those headaches checked out." As if a natural reflex, the back of my hand pressed against Ryker's forehead and I felt for a fever. But it wasn't him that was burning up. Embarrassment flushed my cheeks and I immediately retracted my hand, resting it on my lap.

"Checked out by who? Your father? Probably not a good idea." He gave a dark laugh.

"Maybe Lana can help? She's come through for me more times than I can count."

Ryker shook his head. "Going to a military doctor is probably worse. I did tell her about the headaches. She gave me some meds to help, but if I tell her the truth, that I was dosed with Bliss, she'll have no choice but to report it. That won't end well for any of us." His eyes widened. "Besides, I'm more worried about you."

"Me?" The pad of my thumb dug into my palm, making circular motions below my fingers.

"You've been fidgeting with your hands all morning. And when you just touched me, I felt how cold they were. Is everything okay?" Ryker leaned in closer to me, and I sat back on my stool.

"Uh, not really. My magic is … gone." My mouth went dry and an icy lump settled in my stomach.

"Well, you *did* explode in a nuclear bomb of magic last night." Kasra joined us in the kitchen, opening the refrigerator to grab a couple bottles of water. "How did you even do that? That's not normal."

"It's not the first time it's happened," I admitted. I went into the details about what had happened at the bar on Grestor Island and how I had sucked out the magic of some stranger that now seemed to be screwing up my own. "He said his name was Adrian. Short, kinda scrawny twerp with brown curly hair. He knew Captain Myra Llama and some other soldiers. But that's all I got out of him."

"Adrian?" Cole, sitting at the dining room table behind me, perked up at the sound of the name. "I keep hearing whispers about this man named Adrian Cotter. I've seen him on TV a few times and I think he matches your description. Could it be him?"

"Doubt it." I turned back around in my seat and slumped against the counter. "There are probably a million people named Adrian. What are the odds—"

"Is it this guy?" Ryker turned his laptop screen toward me. It displayed a news article from the Lorith city newspaper about the newly appointed assistant to the CEO of Arcane Enterprises, Daphne Canmore. The picture that went along with it showed a familiar head shot of a man who looked like he had just rolled out of bed.

"No way." I scrolled through the article. "This says Adrian Cotter was accused of murdering Sarah Canmore, Daphne's aunt and the former CEO of Arcane Enterprises, the leading magiceutical company here on Earth. The charges were dropped, and now he's Daphne's assistant." I scrolled past a few pictures of the both of them together, standing side by side and trying to wave off the cameras snapping photos. "There are rumors that the two of them are lovers and planned the whole thing so that Daphne could take control of the company. He sounds like a real winner."

"If he's from Earth, what is he doing getting mixed up with military soldiers from Iradel?" Ryker thoughtfully scratched his chin, staring distantly across the room. "How much do you think he knows about our culture and the magic we wield?"

Cole perked up curiously, but didn't fire off any questions.

"I don't know." I rubbed the back of my neck. "But we're already here on Earth and in the same city, too. It can't be a co-incidence, can it? We have to go find him. Maybe he knows something, and maybe he can fix my magic? If anyone has answers, it would be him."

I waited for either Kasra or Ryker to respond. It was Kasra who broke the silence first. "Fine. We'll go check out Arcane Enterprises. But *after* Cole and I go out shopping."

Cole looked down at his faded jeans. "How long ... do you think ...?"

"It's hard to tell how long it will take to sort this all out and make sure you're safe. But until then, we need to grab you a hat and a hoodie ... something that will help conceal your face."

He gave her a nod and went to grab a jacket on the coat rack by the door.

"I'll grab my things and come with you." I hopped off the stool and started making my way toward my bedroom to grab my jacket before Kasra stopped me.

"You and Ryker should probably stay here and figure out how we're going to reach Adrian. If it's just me and Cole, the two of us can blend in more easily in a crowd."

"You sure? How long will you be?" I looked at the clock on the fireplace mantel. It was just after noon.

Kasra shrugged, slipping on a coat and grabbing her tote bag. "I don't know. Just be ready when we get back."

I removed a cream-colored bullet from my belt and handed it over to Cole. "If you get into trouble, use this. There's a word etched into the metal. Say it out loud only when you want to activate the spell. It will deploy a smoke screen."

"I can actually use this?" Cole rolled the bullet around in his hand, his mismatched eyes assessing the magic object with extreme curiosity.

"Yup. Anyone can use magic. Don't worry, it won't harm you or anyone around you, but it'll give you a chance to escape if someone comes after you. Just keep it hidden and only use it as a last resort. Technically, you're not supposed to be walking around with it."

"Okay. Thanks, Zulli." Cole turned and followed Kasra into the hallway, the door softly clicking shut behind him.

9

---◈---

"It's been four hours. How much longer do you think she'll be?" I glanced out the window in the living room. As the evening drew near, the orange glow of the setting sun glared off the nearby buildings and reflected harsh shadows onto the street below. "She needs to get back here soon before it gets dark out."

"I'm sure she's fine, Zulli. She can handle herself." Ryker had moved to the couch, kicking up his feet on the coffee table. His laptop was resting on his thighs, the keyboard clicking as he typed. "Hey, check this out. This news article from a couple days ago says. It says this guy named Nolan Benson has discovered a way to give people their own magic. Like ours."

"Isn't that a good thing? He's advancing Earth's knowledge of magic."

Ryker scratched his head. "Maybe. But that's a huge jump, going from simple objects to drawing out the magic power hidden inside people. Up until a few days ago, the people on Earth didn't even know they *had* magic abilities. This article says he's working with the CEO of Arcane Enterprises, Daphne Canmore, to help him with the process. That's gotta be connected to Adrian somehow, right? Daphne hasn't commented on the matter yet.

Maybe we could pretend to be reporters and reach out to Adrian? Try to schedule a meeting so we can talk with him?"

Ignoring Ryker, I pressed send on my phone, hoping to reach Kasra. When she didn't answer, I grunted my frustration then plopped down on a stiff armchair. "You know what's been bothering me?"

Ryker peered over his screen at me.

"There were three people watching us, right? As far as I know, my dad only sent Reeva and Liahm to follow me. Who was that third woman?"

"Good question." Ryker sighed and rested his head on the back of the couch. "Whoever she is, she didn't seem threatened by us. She spoke to me on my way back from the deli."

"Really?" I focused my attention on Ryker. "What did she say?"

"She said, 'Looks like a storm is brewing. You should hurry home or you'll get caught in the downpour.' I thought she was with the other two and she was threatening us to hurry up and get the job done."

"Or she was warning us not to engage. She said to go home." My phone buzzed in my lap. "Kasra? Where are—"

"Hello, Zulli." A nasally voice interrupted me. "Guess who? I'm with your friend Kasra and a certain boy that's supposed to be dead. I suggest you hurry to the rooftop immediately before I toss them both off the ledge."

Kasra's scream was cut off as Reeva ended the phone call. My heart leaped into my throat. I bolted out of my chair and raced out the front door. I was still without my magic, but I'd never moved so quickly in my life.

"Zulli, what's wrong?" Ryker chased me down the hallway and toward the stairs, panic threading his voice.

"Reeva." I huffed out, climbing the second set of steps. At least fifteen more to go. "She has Kasra and Cole. And I think she's going to kill them. They're on the roof."

Even though Ryker hurried us along by opening a portal at the top of each flight of stairs, I was completely out of breath by the time I shoved open the rooftop access door.

"Kasra!" I cried out. My voice cracked and my thoughts were scrambled. Panting heavily, I sprinted across the rooftop, past some ventilation units and electrical boxes. I came to a halt near a small patio area furnished with a cheap picnic table set and a rusty metal fire pit. The intense flames roared an impressive five feet high and were a beacon of light in the rapidly approaching cloak of night.

To my left was Kasra, her hands and feet bound to a flimsy plastic chair. She was gagged, but that didn't stop her from trying to scream. Her frustrated cries for help were subdued by the din of city noises. Liahm stood behind her and kept her still, reminding her about the knife to her throat whenever she tried to wriggle free.

Ryker slowed to a jog as he caught up behind me. He reached for the knife on his belt and held it out in front of him. Reeva stepped to the side and appeared next to the wall of flames. Several flickering branches lashed out as a gust of wind swept through. Her obnoxious sneer would have made my ears bleed if I still had my acute sense of hearing. "You had one job to do, Zulli. And I remember Zavyr saying that we could intervene if you failed. But I'm feeling generous today. I'm going to give you a chance to redeem yourself."

"Let them go," I growled. "This is between us, not them."

The smokey flames roared with a toasty heat that brushed my cheeks. Reeva had Cole in a headlock, and from the looks of it, a tight one. The young, fragile boy could do nothing but accept Reeva's control over him. Although he must have been scared out of his mind, he didn't show it. He was blinking rapidly. One hand uselessly dug into Reeva's forearm, but his other dangled at his side. He clenched his fingers tightly, awkwardly flicking his wrist. It wasn't until I caught the brief glint of a metal bullet in his hand that I realized what he was trying to tell me.

"Well, now that this entire operation is out in the open, this very much concerns *all* of you." Reeva let go of Cole and shoved him forward toward the fire. A faint yelp escaped Cole's lips. I jumped with my hands outstretched, not that I could have reached him in time. Reeva grabbed the back of his t-shirt right before the flames reached the tip of his nose.

She kept him there for a minute, toying with me as she pretended to let him go. She then yanked him back into her chest. Her forearm crushed Cole's neck, her skin shining with a luminescent luster of her magic. "So, what's it going to be? Save this boy you hardly know or your beloved teammate?"

My hand ran along the length of my belt. Everything I had was useless to me without my magic. I couldn't even use my claws, and my reflexes were severely dampened.

"Zulli ..." Worry lanced through Ryker's words.

"Distract her," I whispered to him. "Then take Cole and get out of here."

"I'm not going to—"

"Just do it. I'll be fine, Ryker."

He gave me an uncertain nod but didn't question me any further. Ryker's attention turned to Reeva. He slashed his hand forward and it disappeared in front of him. The blade came swinging down right above her shoulder. Liahm snapped his arm out to his side, and like a stretchy piece of taffy, it expanded into a long, thin strip of flesh as it speared toward Reeva. His elongated arm reached Ryker's and his rope-like fingers lengthened. They coiled around Ryker's wrist, bending it backward. Ryker writhed in pain, hissing through his teeth as he struggled to free himself and bring his hand back through the portal.

"Ryker!" I slapped a bullet into his other palm, and he chucked it toward Liahm.

"*Fodio!*" Golden magic exploded out of the canister, the energy spell stunning Liahm and sending him into convulsions. He let go of his hold on Ryker, his deformed arm slithering back into its normal shape. Liahm twitched uncontrollably and pitched forward, dropping his knife right into Kasra's lap. She used her momentum to rock back and forth, the plastic chair bending but refusing to snap. With her rubber body, the ropes binding her wouldn't dig into her skin, but they were expertly secured.

Ryker dropped to the ground and kicked out his leg through a portal. He swept it past Reeva, taking out her feet. Her arms flailed above her as she attempted to balance herself. When she tripped, her grip on Cole was freed.

"Now!" I cried out to Cole.

He dropped the bullet to the ground at his feet and said the magic word in a very unimpressive voice. "*Fumus.*"

A thick cloud of smoke whistled out of the bullet and quickly devoured the patio. I heard a womanly *oomph*, followed by a burst of light magic that lit up like lightning through the haze.

"I'm coming back!" Ryker's voice reached me through the fog. I watched a scorching beam of light shot toward where I assumed Ryker was fleeing with Cole. When no one responded to Reeva's attack, my tense muscles relaxed.

The smoke was already dissipating. I stumbled my way over to Kasra and felt for the knife on her lap. Behind her, Liahm was bent down on one knee, clutching his chest. I gave him a swift kick in the stomach to push him out of my way. With clumsy movements, I sawed away at the ropes binding Kasra's hands behind the chair. I was about to start on her ankles when a bright light flashed before my eyes and everything suddenly went black. It took a moment for me to refocus, but I was still seeing dots in my vision.

"Why do you always have to make things so difficult, Zulli?" Reeva pushed me aside and stepped over to Liahm, helping him to his feet. He leaned his back against the railing that surrounded the perimeter of the roof, shaking out the stiffness in his arms and legs.

"Because," I snarled. "I'll do whatever it takes to protect the people I care about."

While Reeva was distracted by Liahm, Kasra finished cutting the ropes around her ankles. She bounced up from the chair, grabbed it, and swung the flimsy plastic at Reeva's head. Kasra's target held up her hands. A sheet of light shaped in front of her, but Reeva wasn't quick enough to melt the synthetic material, and the scorching hot chair leg scraped against her jaw. She backpedaled, almost tripping into the fire. If it wasn't for Liahm's stretchy magic hand reaching out to grab her, she probably would have fallen into the flames.

Fuming, Reeva channeled her magic into a single hand, her skin translucent and glowing a fiery red. She swung out her arm toward Kasra and me. Light exploded into the atmosphere like fireworks. I kicked over the picnic table with my boot and dove behind it. Kasra was right behind me.

"What do we do?" Kasra asked, flexing her fingers and bending her wrists.

An acrid smell burned my eyes and made them water. The plastic table was melting as Reeva's light magic chewed through it. Wisps of black, toxic smoke rose into the air.

"We run." I had no magic to protect myself or my teammate. Kasra hadn't worn her turtleneck this morning, and she had no other magic items on her. Fleeing was the only chance we had to escape alive. "Follow me."

She nodded, coughing on the fumes. I counted to three and leaped out from behind the rapidly disintegrating table. Reeva cried out in infuriated rage as a spear of light zapped my boot. Discomfort tingled my foot through the leather, but it wasn't enough to stop me. Another arc of golden light swept past me, reaching Kasra. She took the hit head on, wincing briefly as her rubber body absorbed most of the current.

Reeva increased the speed of her attacks, using each finger to blast multiple magical laser beams at once. Eventually, my luck ran out.

A stretchy hand snatched the back of my shirt and stopped me in my tracks. There was no punch that knocked me off my feet—there was nothing but the intense heat of Reeva's light burning my flesh. The feeling of my skin being peeled away from my body was enough to incapacitate me. I dropped to one knee and used every ounce of my strength to keep advancing. The door was a mere ten feet away. We could make it.

"Zulli!" Kasra crouched down beside me, wrapped her arm around my waist, and lifted me up. The friction of her arm rubbing against my scorched back ruptured every nerve ending in my body. Dizziness washed over me. She abruptly let go of me when she was yanked backward.

Kasra let out an ear-splitting shriek filled with both rage and surprise. Liahm stood about ten feet behind her, his arm outstretched and squeezing tightly around Kasra's torso as he reeled her in. She jumped up and down on her heels, launching her rubber body at anything nearby. Her shoulder collided into an electrical box, then ricocheted off an air conditioning unit. She took one more leap into the air, but this time she didn't come back down.

Both of Liahm's arms had coiled around her, wrapping her in a cocoon of stretchy limbs that lifted her into the air. His arms thrashed around wildly, and Kasra went along for the ride. For a seemingly gaunt man, Liahm's overpowering strength was surprising. He smashed her against the ground right at my feet and a scream burst from my throat.

"Kasra!" I shouted. "Hold on!"

Thankfully, her rubber body had softened Liahm's blows, but the agonizing pain etched into her dirt-smudged face was growing increasingly more severe. There were limits to how much her magic could take, and she was nearing them.

Liahm had spoken little since I'd met him, but when he did, he croaked like a poisoned frog. "What should we do with her, Reeva?" He kept hold of Kasra about three feet up in their air. Reeva joined to stand next to him.

"Both she and that Ryker boy know too much. It sounds like we're moving on to plan B. We need to eliminate all threats and

104

finish the mission ourselves." Reeva looked at me and feigned her despair with an over-exaggerated pout. "Your father will be very disappointed in you, Zulli, although probably not surprised."

My hand clutched my chest, the heat from Reeva's magic saturating my veins and burning me from the inside out. But then something happened. I could feel it, the icy cold numbness traveling through my bloodstream, turning into a molten hot lava. The magic coursing through me seemed to gather, transforming into a living ball of energy that threatened to detonate like a bomb. But, unlike the incident at Cole's apartment, this time I knew what was going to happen.

I closed my eyes and inhaled a deep breath, channeling all the energy into my core. The pressure in my stomach strained against my rib cage. Blood rushed from my brain in a dizzying surge.

My father had tried to kill Catilda. He had wiped Ryker's memories. And now he was going after Kasra. I wouldn't let my father toy with me any longer. I had to put an end to his devastating crusade to protect not only my friends but all the innocent victims who suffered at the hands of his drugs.

My insides were suspended in that combustible moment when the spark snapped into flame. My sharp senses surmounted Reeva's magic. Even at light speed, I could feel the patterned vibrations of each molecule of magic, taste the smell of burnt toast that it left in its wake. A flash of her sizzling hot light grazed the hem of my shirt sleeve as I twisted to avoid it. I gave Liahm a tight, determined grin with pointed fangs. I catapulted myself at him and was about to sink my teeth into his neck when the unbelievable power collecting in my belly let loose. A burst of light so bright torpedoed out of me. Reeva cowered and shielded her eyes. Liahm tumbled across the concrete.

Unfortunately, on his way down, Liahm hurled Kasra right over the ledge of the building and let go. Without a second thought, I leaped off the roof right after her.

10

PANIC SCREECHED ALONG my nerves. Seconds. That's how long it would have taken us to plummet twenty stories to our deaths if Kasra's shoulder hadn't bounced off the fire escape and her hand hadn't snagged hold of the ladder.

Suspended in midair, I went soaring past her, my boot tangling with the crook of her arm. Her grip slipped. Just before she let go, she snatched my ankle. I spun in an arc as she attempted to swing me onto the fire escape platform below us. She missed, my cheek smashing hard into the metal railing. My vision blurred and blood flooded my mouth. I threw up my hands, hoping to catch anything nearby to hold on to but grasped at air instead. The world spun around me and I couldn't make sense of any of it.

Kasra kept hold of my ankle, but with nothing anchored to grab onto and break our fall, we continued plunging toward the asphalt below.

"Zulli! Kasra!" Ryker's disorienting voice came from somewhere above. He had come back just as he promised, but not in time. He wouldn't be fast enough to construct a portal to transport us somewhere else.

The alley below us drew closer and I closed my eyes. The air whistled past my ears. My muscles tensed, as if it would somehow help save me from becoming the splattered remains of a human pancake. I fought back tears as I squeezed my eyelids tight. Painful disappointment rushed in and filled my chest. All I could think about was how I had failed my friends and teammates. And now Kasra was going to die—because of me.

The surge of magical power had weakened but still flowed heavily through me. Now wasn't the time to give up. With every ounce of determined strength I had left, I held out my hand above me. Magic gathered in my fingers, burning with a fierce need to escape my body. Thread-like spears shot out of my fingertips in strands of silky spider webbing, latching onto the fire escape ladder. Our descent came to an abrupt halt, but Kasra and I were now swinging full force toward the concrete side of the building.

Kasra kicked out her legs in panic, and her hip collided into the wall. Her rubber body softened the blow of the impact, but a sharp crunching noise was followed by her shrill, piercing scream. My webbing snapped and together, we fell the remaining ten feet into a dumpster that smelled like rotting food. A pointed edge protruding from a trash bag dug into my back, several other sharp objects digging into me from every angle.

"Kasra?" I choked out. The metallic taste of blood slipped down my throat as I coughed. My lips were the only thing I could move. Pain radiated from every muscle in my body, like I had just been hit head-on by a speeding train, beaten over the head with a baseball bat, and run then over by a tractor trailer. Even the thought of twitching made me cringe.

"Kasra?" I tried again. There was no answer, and I assumed the worst. I shifted my blurry gaze to see Kasra's motionless body across from me, her leg contorted unnaturally. I winced while pushing myself up and screamed an agonizing howl. Raw life flowed out of my bones, running riot through my limbs.

A cat leaped up onto the edge of the dumpster and pounced right on top of Kasra.

"Shoo!" My voice croaked, and I spat out a wad of bloody saliva. "Get off her!"

The cat gave a glaring look at me, its gaze hard and unyielding. The tabby cat meowed then turned its fierce emerald eyes away from me and started licking Kasra's chin. I froze. I remembered that cat and its judgmental look very well.

"Zulli! Kasra!" Ryker's head popped up over the dumpster and stared down at me splayed out over the heap of trash. Cole, a few inches shorter, jumped up slightly to see what was going on.

"Crap. She looks bad." Ryker hoisted himself up and swung a leg over the edge of the dumpster. He reached toward Kasra and placed two fingers on her neck. "She's still alive, but she needs help. So do you, Zulli."

The cat meowed again, a sound that came across a bit contemptuous.

"The cat …" I mumbled.

"Don't worry about the stupid cat."

Garbage crunched under Ryker's feet as he made his way over toward me and delicately slipped his arms under my legs and neck. I cried out in pain, tears spilling down my cheeks.

"It's okay, Zulli. Cole and I have to get you out of here first before we can lift Kasra." My face rubbed against Ryker's t-shirt, the scent of cinnamon filling my nostrils. Being held by Ryker gave off a calming effect that eased the pain rippling through me. Ryker would fix this. I knew he would, and I'd gladly accept whatever help I could get.

A fuzzy female voice reached me. "I can help … friends …" The rest of her words were drowned out by my pulse throbbing in my ears. It wasn't Kasra. It wasn't Reeva. Who did that voice belong to?

I barely noticed the pinprick in my upper arm.

Ryker jostled me in his arms, his voice just as muddled as the woman's. "What … that?"

The stranger's words were garbled, my brain only picking up bits and pieces of the conversation. "Sedative … relax … go now …"

I trusted Ryker was doing the right thing and let my mind slip into a haze.

"Don't pass out … Zulli."

I tried to smile at Ryker. My pulse pounded to the beat of my throbbing pain and my limbs felt heavy. Cinnamon filled the space around me, the warmth of Ryker's magic brushing against my ragged skin. The darkness we left behind was replaced with a sharp light that blinded me as I squinted to open my eyes. More voices sounded like they were garbling under water. They were shouting and talking over each other. I couldn't make out any of it.

"Kasra …" I nuzzled my nose into Ryker's hoodie before he placed me down on something soft and padded.

"Kasra's right here," Ryker assured me, although I couldn't see her. "She's gonna be fine. You're gonna be fine. Just rest and let them help you." He swept his hand across my forehead.

The sedative started doing its work. Blurry faces filled my vision, a bright light above shining down, right into my eyes. Someone slipped a plastic mask over my mouth and said, "Count to ten."

I only made it to one before I succumbed to the drugs. After that, I had no recollection of anything that my mysterious saviors did. But when I woke up, I was lying on a thin mattress, alone in a cold, dark jail cell.

The concrete box had one small, rectangular window high above on the wall. Judging from the bright sunlight filtering through it, I assumed it was mid-afternoon, although what day I wasn't sure.

The hallway beyond the metal bars was quiet and dimly lit. A damp chill brushed across my skin from a draft somewhere nearby. Both my duffle bag stuffed with clothes and backpack stashed with weapons were placed on a metal chair in the corner of the room. I pushed myself up from the cot against the wall and draped a fleece blanket over my shoulders.

A quick assessment of my body led me to believe whoever had treated me knew what they were doing. They must have had access to some high tech magic technology and medicine to heal such severe injuries. The superficial wounds were practically gone, just a few blotches of red and purple left from the remnants of cuts and bruises. My jaw was stiff, but the disorientation and skull throbbing had mostly subsided. Not everything was back to normal, though. Every time I inhaled, a sharp pain like a knife stabbed me in the gut.

I flexed my fingertips. In a desperate attempt to save Kasra's life, webbing had shot out of them. The silky stands were weak compared to my father's or brothers', but it wasn't a skill I had been able to use before. I wondered what made it suddenly manifest and what other abilities I might have that I had yet to discover.

When I rose to my feet, my angry muscles screamed at me. I nearly collapsed under my weight but shuffled my way toward the barred wall.

"Hello? Is anyone there? Let me out of here!" I wrapped my hands around the thick metal bars and shook them. The door was locked. If I hadn't been so exhausted, I could easily slip through them in my spider form.

I closed my eyes and listened for threats nearby. The clicking of high heels on the concrete floor echoed down the hallway and grew louder the closer they came. A shadow came into view first, followed by a woman wearing bright red pants and a loose-fitting top with a flower pattern. The lines etched on her face showed her age. Her light brown hair faded into a soft lilac at the end of her thick ponytail resting over her shoulder.

I sucked in a breath but, despite the pain that came with it, I couldn't let it out. My jaw dropped open, and I had to brace myself against the bars to keep from collapsing. The woman's glowing green eyes were fierce, yet sensitive and honest.

"Hey, kiddo." She folded her arms across her chest and leaned on one leg. "It's been a while. We have a lot to catch up on."

A million thoughts started running rampant through my brain, but only one came out in response. "Mom. You're alive."

11

---◈---

MY MOTHER STOOD before me, alive and well. It had been over ten years since I had last seen her. Thin strands of gray now streaked through her wild hair. Her skin was a little paler and thinner than what I remembered, but those vibrant emerald eyes full of compassion and sass, the same eyes I had inherited from her, hadn't changed one bit.

For a moment, relief loosened the tension in my shoulders. Then I remembered I was locked in a jail cell and she was making no attempt to let me out.

"Where are my teammates? What did you do with Cole?" I snarled at her, but she smiled politely back.

"Is that how you talk to your mother? I will excuse that attitude of yours since you've been through a lot recently. Your teammates are fine. Kasra is recovering, and both Ryker and Cole are with her."

"Why am I here? Let me out!" I gave the bars another shake. Not surprisingly, they didn't budge.

"You're in an abandoned prison back on Iradel, Zulli. Granted, that cell is no five-star hotel, but it's as close to a bedroom as you'll get around here. I asked one of my guards to lock the door because I didn't want you waking up and rampaging through my home, terrorizing my residents along the way. We're beat up and run down as it is."

"Home?" I let go of the bars and took a step back. "Guards? Residents? Mom, what's going on?"

"Ah, it feels so good to hear you call me that! I missed you, kiddo." She hugged herself and stared distantly at the ceiling for a moment then brought her gaze back to me. "Like I said, we have a lot to catch up on. So, are you going to poke some holes in my head with those claws of yours or will you agree to listen to me?"

While most modern jail cells on Iradel were reinforced with magic, this one no longer was. My mother held a silver key in her hand, waiting for my answer.

"Fine. I won't attack you."

"Or anyone else in this building?" She raised an eyebrow, seeing right through my cleverly crafted words.

"Yes! Fine. I won't attack you or anyone in this building. Just let me out of this damn jail cell and bring me to my teammates. I need to see them."

The door opened on squeaky hinges. I gave my mother a hard stare for about three whole seconds before launching my arms around her neck in a tight embrace. She seemed a little startled by the reaction but didn't hesitate to return the hug.

She patted my back, a slight tenderness from Reeva's burns surfacing with my mother's touch. When I let go, so did she. "Kasra is still sleeping, but she's safe with Ryker, and I have a doctor watching over her. Before I take you to them, we need to have a chat. Take a seat and I'll explain everything."

She left the cell door open. I hobbled back to the mattress and sat down. The springs were so worn that it didn't even bounce. My mother took a seat beside me, crossing her legs and placing her hands on her lap.

A million thoughts were buzzing through my brain, but I started the conversation with one particular set of questions that

I urgently needed the answers to. "What happened all those years ago? Why did you abandon your family, and why did you wait so long to let me know you're still alive?"

My mother let out a long sigh filled with sadness. She kept her gaze fixated on the cinderblock wall across from her. "Believe me, Zulli. I never wanted things to happen the way they did. Leaving you and your brothers was the hardest thing I've ever had to do, but I still believe it was the right choice."

She gave a sideways glance at me, and something unsettling reflected in her eyes.

Fury built up inside my chest. "It couldn't have been that hard if you just disappeared and kept your distance this whole time! You left us with a monster! I don't know if you've been following the news, but Dad's gone insane. He created this drug called Bliss and—"

"And he's going after you and your friends. I know, Zulli. I may not have been present in your lives physically, but I've been watching you and your brothers from afar. You've only recently been dragged into this mess, but your father has been planning something since long before you were even born."

My mouth opened then snapped shut.

"No one ever told you this, but my father—your grandfather—was Larris Gatlin, the founder of NightFly Technologies. He was a fairly private person and never enjoyed being in the spotlight. So while he technically owned the company, he always had someone he trusted be the face of the business and run day-to-day operations."

"Dad ..." It wasn't difficult to piece the information together.

"Correct. I also had a role to play. I was the ... product innovator, I guess you could say. It was my job to travel to medical labs and technology companies to evaluate their research and make an offer on behalf of NightFly Technologies to purchase the rights to manufacture their drugs and equipment."

114

"So, is that how you met Dad? And Catilda's mom?" I shifted uncomfortably on the flat mattress and pulled the blanket tight around my shoulders.

"Yup. I met Havanna Harper while she was helping to decipher some ancient medical book of magic spells thought to have long been forgotten. And your father and I met while he was working in another lab. A few months after I started dating Zavyr, Larris knew your father would be the perfect person to operate NightFly Technologies in his place. Zavyr had this powerful, confident aura about him that seemed to resonate with everyone. People trusted him, believed everything he had to say. But it didn't take long before I noticed something changing about your father. That once composed appearance became manipulative, sneaky, obsessed. The power he wielded at NightFly Technologies was eating away his soul. He stopped spending time with his family and buried himself in his work. Zavyr started arguing with your grandfather on how to run the business. When Larris unexpectedly passed away, the entire company was officially transferred over to Zavyr, and I started to think the worst."

"You don't think ... He wouldn't." Goosebumps ran down my arms.

"I don't know, Zulli. Your grandfather's death was ruled by natural causes, but we both know there's magic out there that can hide foul play." Her shoulders dropped, but she kept her expression confident and unyielding.

"So ... you just decided you no longer wanted to be a part of this family? You took off because you were *suspicious* about something? Did you ever think about your children? Me? Brodin? Maeck? About what would happen to us if you left?"

"That's not fair, Zulli." She pressed her lips together and frowned. "I wasn't exactly offered a choice. Your father wanted to be the biggest, the best, the most powerful in the business, and he'd stop at nothing to get there. Things were becoming more dangerous by the day. He started working with gangs and criminal organizations to gain access to illegal products, saying it was the only way to advance his research and 'help' those who needed it."

"He loved the attention fame brought him," I added.

My mother nodded. "He persuaded hundreds of patients to test his experiments with the promise of curing whatever disease or ailment they had. Unfortunately, many of them ended up dying. When things started spiraling out of control, the gangs no longer wanted to be tangled up in his mess. Of course, your father wouldn't just let them walk away. He decided he would force them to comply with his demands, and, well, their leaders weren't going to accept that. The gangs retaliated. Death threats started rolling in, on your life and your brothers. I finally confronted Zavyr about it and demanded this stop before something unthinkable happened. But he couldn't. The power had devoured him, and he was confident that eventually he'd be able to control the entire network of people as he saw fit. To get whatever he wanted without consequence. And he's found a way with Bliss."

My mother's eyes watered but she didn't shed her tears. She sniffed, wiped her eyes with the back of her hand, and continued. "The day I disappeared, I told your father I was going on a business trip scouting a promising new piece of medical technology. But the real reason was that I had set up a meeting with a young, eager reporter named Cullin Maddox to expose the truth about everything your father was doing."

My heart skipped a beat at the mention of his name.

"Before I had a chance to meet up with Cullin, Zavyr had someone come after me. Your father found out what I was up to, but the man he sent knew that your father was unstable and that killing me wasn't an answer to anything. He let me go and warned me never to show my face to anyone who would recognize me ever again. I didn't have the option to go back and take you with me. I couldn't call or say goodbye. All these years, your father believed that man finished the job he was sent to do."

"I … I had no idea." I squeezed the blanket tighter. My gaze dropped to linger on my dusty boots. My mother's delicate fingers found my chin and twisted my head so she could look directly into my eyes.

"Zulli, listen to me. Your father loves you, but if he tried to kill me, I have no doubt he'll eventually go after you too if you continue to impede his plans. He's not himself anymore. He's not the man I married all those years ago."

I thought back to the conversation I had with my dad before I'd left on my mission to find Cole. He had given me a cryptic warning about what would happen if I messed up. I didn't want to believe that he'd send someone to kill his own daughter, but deep down I knew I couldn't dismiss the possibility.

My mother continued speaking. "Until recently, your father believed I was dead. Bliss changed everything. After all these years, he finally found out how to control those who defied him. He's been dosing members of the Black Mark with Bliss and now commands about half their organization. He erases their memories and implants his own orders. Then he started going after everyone who had a connection to me, trying to use Bliss to turn them, too. And just like you, Zulli, I wasn't about to sit back and watch him so casually destroy lives, so I intervened."

"So what have you been doing all these years, then? Planning your revenge on Dad from this grimy prison?"

My mother gently tapped her hand on my thigh and beamed me a bright smile. "It'll be easier if I show you. Come on, let's go. I'll bring you to your friends and then I'll have the kitchen make you something to eat."

Paranoid as I was, I grabbed my backpack containing most of my weapons but left the duffle bag behind. As I followed my mother down the hallway, I noticed that many other jail cells were occupied. I hadn't felt their presence before because they were barely moving. Some didn't even look like they were actually alive.

117

A woman wearing scrubs rolled a gurney out of a cell and placed a white sheet over a pale, lifeless body.

"We can't save everyone from the effects of Bliss," my mother told me. "Your father may have acquired NightFly Technologies, but Larris left me everything else. Since I was dead, it defaulted to being donated to charity, conveniently one I had set up myself. It all went to this place—Sunshine Sanctuary!"

She raised her hands to gesture at the drab, gloomy dungeon. The walls seemed to soak in all the misery that had happened within this compound. Bloody fingerprint smears and disturbing carvings decorated the paint chipped walls. Dim yellow lights buzzed sporadically above us like dying flies that could no longer take flight. It was anything but bright and sunny.

"Over the years, I've built up my own team of people who have been wronged by Zavyr. Those he attacks with Bliss—we find them and bring them here to rehabilitate. The old prison isn't exactly state-of-the-art, but it does come with some security measures. Plus, it wasn't hard to convince some of my contacts to help me out. They want to see Zavyr pay for his crimes just as much as I do."

I stopped in front of a jail cell, where a middle-aged man was huddled up against the wall, rocking back and forth with a blanket wrapped around him. His bare feet peeked out from the bottom of his long sweats, and his dark blond hair was slightly mussed.

"Isn't that ... Cullin Maddox? I bumped into him the other day at a coffee shop. He went after me and told me that Dad has eyes everywhere."

"Your father got to him with Bliss not too long ago. He probably had just enough of his sanity left to warn you to watch out for threats. After I disappeared, the both of us continued investigating together, trying to find physical evidence proving Zavyr's illegal activities, but your father is a clever man. He uses others to do his dirty work and covers his tracks."

We rounded a corner and another familiar face stared back at me. The last time I had seen him, he was in my father's lab at NightFly Technologies. Tubes were snaking around his body and a technician had injected him with what I now knew was a more concentrated form of Bliss.

"And that's the mayor, Ethin Henderson. Dad told me he was treating him for psychosis. That Bliss could help stabilize his condition to keep his illusions separate from reality."

My mother let out an abrasive laugh. "You've got to be kidding. The man may be in his early sixties, but he's in better health than most people half his age. The mayor controls most of the city budget, including several research grants. He also has influence over a lot of important people. Your father was trying to manipulate him into giving all the funding to NightFly Technologies and gaining support from other politicians."

A thought suddenly occurred to me. I stopped walking and placed my backpack on the ground. I dug into a pocket and pulled out a crumpled piece of paper, handing it over to my mom. "The guy I went after when NightFly Technologies was attacked dropped this list of names. Does it mean anything to you?"

She hadn't stared at it for more than a second before she responded, "Sure does."

"What is it?" I leaned over to look at the paper as if something had magically decoded the meaning when my mom touched it.

"Well, you already know some of these names. Cullin Maddox and Ethin Henderson were working with me. So is Abril Penton—Zavyr's company lawyer before she got fired a couple of years ago. Brax Lichter is a private investigator I hired to dig into Zavyr's finances. These two names ..." she pointed at two lines crossed out in black ink. " ... these two names are Cole's parents. Herah and Cohlin Winchell."

She closed her eyes and exhaled a long breath. If their names had been crossed out, then it was safe to assume they had been eliminated as threats. While I was eager to learn more, I didn't press my mother for more information.

"This is a hit list, Zulli. In addition to the Black Mark, your father is coming after all these people connected to me."

"Who's the handwritten name on the bottom? It's too smudged to make out, but the initials are T. T."

My mother made a harsh, raucous sound when she laughed. It echoed down the long hallway. "That's the easiest one to figure out, Zulli. Tabatha Taracula. Me."

12

I OFFERED MY mother the list to keep. She folded it up and placed it in her back pocket, and we continued on down the corridor until we reached a set of double doors. When I flattened each hand to one of the thick slabs of heavy iron, I sensed the remnants of a now defunct magic spell. It smelled like glue and sent a mild shock to my fingertips when I pushed the doors open.

At one point, the chipped paint had been imbued with magic to identify employees allowed to pass through. Now the security measure was so weak, it functioned like any other door. We stepped right through and found ourselves in an infirmary.

I had to blink twice before my brain processed the vision in front of me. About twenty high-tech medical beds filled the large infirmary, half with occupants in them. At least a dozen doctors and nurses were treating patients with machines that far surpassed what most hospitals had access to. Unlike the depressing cell block we had just left behind, this section of the prison was bustling with activity and had recently been updated. Bright lights shone down from the ceiling, a fresh coat of yellow paint brightened the walls, and there even appeared to be an operating room through another set of doors off to the side.

"Zulli!" I heard Cole call out to me from the very last bed in the row. I hurried over and while Kasra wasn't awake, I was relieved to see her resting peacefully, a cast on her right leg and bandages everywhere else.

Ryker was sitting next to her, holding her hand and talking about nothing in particular. He had probably been speaking to her all night and ran out of things to say. " ... and I got all the way home before I realized I had forgotten cheese. How do you make grilled cheese sandwiches without cheese? I ended up having to order pizza."

"Hey, Ryker." He looked up at me from his chair and gave me a weak smile that immediately turned into a frown. He smelled like the dumpster he had dug me out of and a five o'clock shadow was starting to show on his chin.

"Hey, Zulli. Kasra hasn't woken up yet. I've been here all night hoping she would." He peered around my shoulder at the fashionably dressed woman standing behind me.

"Um, I guess you already must have figured it out, but Ryker ... this is my mom."

My mother took a step forward to address Ryker. "We had a brief encounter earlier, but with everything going on, I didn't have the opportunity to introduce myself properly. I apologize for being so cryptic at the park. I wasn't sure if you were aware of Zulli's situation. I had been following her in my cat form and was trying to warn you about the people following her."

"It's all right, Ms. Taracula. Thank you for your help. I'm not sure what would have happened if you weren't there." Ryker stood from his chair and held out his hand, but my mom greeted him with a hug instead.

"Just call me Tabatha. No need for formalities here."

A disheveled woman trotted over to us with a tablet in hand. Unlike the other doctors, she wasn't wearing a lab coat but had on a pair of flannel pajama bottoms, fleece slippers, and a thin yellow t-shirt. Her auburn hair was tied back into a stubby pony-tail, several loose strands framing her face. She pushed her metal-rimmed glasses up her button nose, then waved at us as she approached.

"Lana?" I shook my head to make sure I wasn't imagining things.

"Actually, I'd prefer if you addressed me as Dr. Lana Fischer, Chief of Medicine! It has a nice ring to it, doesn't it?" Lana put her tablet down on the side table and began examining the beeping machines hooked up to Kasra. "I see you're still getting yourself into trouble, Zulli."

"What are you doing here? And what are you wearing?"

She raised her eyebrows at me, ignoring the last question. "Your mother has the persuasion skills of the devil. She came knocking on my apartment door last night just as I was about to go to bed. I had no idea who this woman was, but her uncanny attitude and those vivid green eyes—it wasn't hard to pick up on the resemblance." My mom softly chuckled at Lana's statement. "So, I thought I'd hear her out. She flattered me for a few minutes, mentioned that she immediately needed assistance from someone with my expert skills. Not really understanding what her goal was, I refused. But then she started talking about all this top-of-the-line machinery I'd have access to and how I'd be helping to treat people who were affected by Bliss. I was still on the fence until she doubled my salary. I didn't even get to pack a bag before she demanded I come with her, so I'm still wearing my pajamas."

A weak moan drew my attention to Kasra. Ryker's eyes lit up with excitement and even Cole's bland expression seemed to hint at amusement.

"Good afternoon, Kasra!" Lana picked up her tablet and tapped the screen a few times. "How are you feeling?"

Kasra tried to speak but ended up coughing instead. Ryker poured her a glass of water from the pitcher on the end table and handed it to her. She struggled to swallow, dribbling down her chin, but got most of it down.

"I feel like some stretchy lunatic launched me over the edge of a building and I fell twenty stories into a dumpster. What's going on? Where am I?" She reached up to run her fingers through her tangled hair and plucked something out of it. "Is this … is this a chicken bone?"

"You're lucky, Kasra." Lana clutched the tablet to her chest. "If you hadn't activated that spelled pendant to cushion your fall, you'd probably be dead. Your leg is broken in several places, but Zulli's mother brought you here for treatment. With the innovative magic technology available in this place, I bet you'll be up and walking around in no more than two or three weeks. Just take it easy until then. Ryker went back for your duffle bag after you arrived, so all your clothes and other supplies are here if you need them."

Kasra gently squeezed the necklace around her neck. She looked at me, a face something halfway between both gratitude and annoyance.

"I thought your mom was … um …"

"Dead," my mother supplied. "It's a long story that I'll gladly tell you once you fully recover."

Kasra gave my mom a once over and snorted. "Well, I'm glad to see that Zulli didn't get her awful fashion sense from her mother. Thanks for your help, and it's nice to officially meet you."

"Likewise," my mother didn't embrace her like she did to Ryker but gently squeezed her hand to avoid aggravating injuries. "No need for thanks. I'm just glad you're okay."

"Are you comfortable? Hungry?" I asked my teammate. "There's a kitchen here … somewhere. Do you want me to bring you something?"

Kasra placed the back of her hand across her forehead and teased me in a dramatic voice. "Oh, Zulli, look at me! I can't even walk. How am I ever going to get dressed in the morning? Who is going to help me put on my makeup and do my hair?"

"Oh, I can help with that." I sneered at her. "I'll go get the buzzer and shave off your hair. That way, you won't need to take care of it! And our hairstyles will match!"

A scowl stretched across her face but her expression softened. "Actually, I am kinda hungry. The food here better be decent. I'm not sure I can stomach hospital food."

"We're actually in a converted prison," I reminded her.

She threw her head back into the pillow. "Ugh, that's even worse."

A nurse grabbed the attention of my mother, who left to join what appeared to be a serious conversation with some of the other staff in the infirmary. Not wanting to bother her, I left Ryker and Cole behind with Kasra while I ventured off to find out where the kitchen was located. I passed through another set of doors into a small recreation area. Although metal bars lined the thick glass windows, strong rays of afternoon sun shone through them. A deck of cards was scattered across one table, a board game on another. Plants and other cheery objects gave the cozy space a comforting warmth.

People kept coming and going around me. Some of them nodded as if they might have recognized me from somewhere. I nodded back, but an uneasy feeling settled in my stomach. I had no reason to doubt my mother's story, but if Cullin Maddox was right, my father had eyes everywhere. He had informants in the military and people monitoring me. How could I be sure I was truly safe here or that I could trust anyone I met?

Staying on high alert, I followed the sound of chatter and forks scraping plates at the end of the corridor. It was accompanied by the smell of something aromatic, like garlic and herbs.

Two doors opened into a large eating area. Round steel tables bolted to the floor were positioned throughout the cafeteria. The variety of people making up the afternoon lunch rush was astounding. Most seemed to be my age—somewhere in between their mid-twenties and thirties—but there were also a number of families. Young children, perhaps no older than ten, ran around the tables giggling as they played tag. An older couple, one with a cane and another in a wheelchair, made their way through the aisles, looking for a place to sit. Most were dressed pretty casually, with faded jeans and worn t-shirts. Clearly, they weren't living a luxurious lifestyle here at the prison, but I imagined most were just happy to be alive and safe from whatever my father had done to them.

At the far end of the room was a cafeteria-style buffet, and I started making my way over to see what was on today's menu. I made it about halfway before a middle-aged man in line turned around with a tray in his hands. My heart stopped beating and my blood boiled.

The man's skin was dull and droopy, except for one side of his face, which was mottled and tinged red from where the fire I set off had burned him. Despite his appearance, he strutted like a man with confidence, with long strides and stern shoulders. Stubble formed on the bottom of his chin and his cropped hair was peppered with gray. I'd recognize that khaki trench coat anywhere.

"Davian Grymes!" I snarled loud enough to garner the attention of those around me.

His gaze caught mine and a smirk bent his lips.

My feet moved on their own. "Out of my way!" I charged at a young woman in my path, swatting at her tray. It flipped over, drenching her in spaghetti and chunky red sauce.

Gasps erupted nearby. A brute of a man shot up from his seat and stepped in front of me. "*Sto—*"

I elbowed him in the sternum as hard as I could before he could finish the word. He wheezed as I swiftly darted past him but more people closed in around me. A shift in magic came from my left. Sheets of paper sliced through the air like spinning blades. A feisty punk with a red mohawk stood off to my side.

He held a single piece of paper between his fingers and fired off the deadly bladed sheet.

I twisted to the side, the tip of my boot scuffing against the tile. The sharp edge of the paper sliced across my cheek as I crashed into a table. My face was met with a bowl of scorching hot mashed potatoes. Grabbing the bowl, I tossed it at someone else running toward me and used the tray as a shield to deflect the lethal paper projectiles being shot at me.

"Listen to me!" I cried out. "I'm not your enemy. Davian is a spy!"

Panic and confusion consumed the cafeteria. Most backed away, not wanting to interject themselves in the fight, but others ran toward the action to protect their home.

A ceramic vase went soaring past me and shattered against the floor. "The only person we don't know here is *you!*" A dark-skinned man to my right held a magazine in his hand. His fingertips hovered above it as his magic started pulling another object out of the book.

Not waiting to see what it was, I chucked the tray at him and made a run for it. He threw up his hands to shield himself but not in time. As the tray hit him, his thick black glasses pressed against his face and he dropped the book he was holding.

"Davian Grymes!" There was nothing pleasant about the venom in my voice. As I approached Davian, I took a swing at him with my claws. He shifted out of the way. The fabric of his trench coat ripped, but I missed his skin.

"Nice to see you, too, Zulli." Davian placed his tray down on a nearby table. My hand reached for a bullet on my belt. He held up his hand and a blast of water shot out of his palm right into my chest. The impact ignited a deep pain from my injuries, still not completely healed. I gasped for air, breathing heavily to fill my lungs.

"What the hell are you doing here, Davian?" I wheezed. "Did my father send you?" The smell of summer sunshine and rainbows drifted in from behind me. Sensing the vibration of footsteps approaching, I hurried to rip a yellow bullet from my belt. I was about to throw it at Davian when a gray tail wrapped around my wrist to stop me.

"Zulli Adorabelle Taracula!" I clenched my teeth at the sound of my mother using my middle name. I had gotten it because she thought I was absolutely "adorable" when I was born. Embarrassment heated my cheeks. "I thought we agreed you wouldn't attack anyone here?"

My mother didn't let go of my wrist, squeezing tighter the more I struggled against her. Her claws extended. One hand was pushed against Davian's chest and the other held up to her side, warning onlookers not to intervene. Pointed cat ears twitched on her head and a threatening scowl was plastered to her face.

"Mom, this man is a spy for Dad. Davian has been working for him this whole time! He was helping Dad distribute the Bliss through the Black Mark—"

My mom's hand left Davian's chest and she held it up in front of me to cut me off. "Zulli, stand down."

My hand hovered above my belt and my eyes never left Davian.

"Zulli!" she challenged. "I said *stand down*. Davian isn't the man you think he is. You remember the man I told you about who spared my life?"

I blinked at her, then at Davian. "No ..."

"Yes. Your father sent this man to kill me. But he didn't. I owe him my life. It's true, Davian did work for Zavyr until recently, but he was doing so as our informant on the inside. He was feeding us information on everything your father was doing."

"I don't believe you. I was there when Davian met with someone at the bar to make an illegal deal. Then, at the dock, he attacked Kasra, and Ryker was shot in the leg. He was transporting the contents of a shipping container loaded with the bonding agent used for Bliss. Probably to the warehouse where it's manufactured."

Davian snorted. "First of all, *you* got Ryker shot. You attacked the poor fool helping me. Second, I knew Kasra's rubber body would have prevented any injuries from a mere fifteen-foot drop. You were supposed to have backed down when you realized you were outnumbered. And third, I was meeting with an informant at that bar who told me about the shipping container. I wasn't transporting drugs for your father. The Black Mark was helping me steal them to bring the shipment here to examine. So that Zavyr *couldn't* make more drugs."

"And the attack on NightFly Technologies? My dad made it sound like it was staged so no one would suspect him. Did you orchestrate that?" I leaned in, but my mom pulled me back.

"No one was supposed to be there that night." Davian shifted his weight to one side and his stance became more casual than aggressive. "I was working with the Black Mark to retrieve some valuable information from the secured records room on that floor. Unfortunately, your father had put in some extra security measures I didn't know about. The idiot helping me wasn't paying attention and triggered an alarm that set off a minor explosion."

"You tried to drown me! Explain that!" I dug my hands into my hips.

He bit his bottom lip before speaking. "Ah, yes. I may have gotten a little out of hand with that one. I wasn't trying to drown you. I just wanted to fill your lungs with enough water so you'd pass out and I could take you here."

"And what about Ryker and his memories?" Annoyance grew stronger with every word. "He almost died!"

"That wasn't part of the plan, and I swear to you, Zulli, I tried to stop Zavyr from giving Ryker the Bliss. I had to break my cover, and when Zavyr figured out what I was doing, he left me there to take the blame after you doused me with that sleep spell.

Thanks to your mom, she pulled some strings and I was later released."

"I'm not buying your excuses." I pressed my lips together and growled at him. His story made perfect sense—a little too perfect. He really had thought this through.

"Ryker was employed by your father to watch you, to keep you out of Zavyr's business, but his loyalty and dedication to keeping you safe went far beyond what your father ever expected. Ryker turned against him. When you went to your father asking for help to save Ryker, he no longer needed me. He saw the opportunity to use *you* instead."

"Zulli," my mom cut in. "I know this is difficult to accept, but it's the truth. I've known Davian half my life and I'm well aware of the questionable things he did while working for your father, but now he's in the same predicament as us. Your father knows what Davian did, and now his life is in danger too."

I studied Davian for a moment. His shoulders drooped and his hands were tucked into the large pockets of his khaki trench coat. He had dropped his defenses, all hostility toward me vanishing. The clever, sly man I had known as the criminal who had gone rogue against my father, the suspect that the military had thought was behind the whole creation and distribution of Bliss, was actually one of the good guys. And it was my father we should have been focusing on this entire time. Things were getting more messed up by the hour.

Davian's expression softened. His eyes, dark brown with flecks of amber, still had a sharpness to them, but his gaze was neither judging nor accusing. The thick, leathery side of his face where the burn marks were healing would probably scar, but thanks to the power of magic it would only end up as a slight discoloration.

"Fine," I relented. "But if I even suspect you're up to something, Davian, all bets are off."

He nodded, offering me a slight smile as he did.

130

"Great!" My mother's voice reverberated in the silent cafeteria. I hadn't noticed the noise had completely died down and everyone had been watching my temper tantrum. She glanced over at a terrified young boy standing behind a chair. "Alvyn, can you get everyone here to the cafeteria? I'm calling a meeting."

Alvyn, a chubby kid who couldn't have been over fifteen, closed his eyes and pressed a finger to his temple. His message echoed inside my head.

Attention all visitors and personnel: Boss Lady, Tabby Taracula, requires your presence in the cafeteria immediately for an emergency meeting.

Dialogue picked up and the noise grew louder as more people filed into the cafeteria, including Ryker, who was helping Kasra on a set of crutches. There was another familiar face following them I hadn't expected to see.

"Zulli!" Catilda came sprinting over toward me with outstretched arms, her short ginger curls bouncing as she did. She wrapped her hands around my neck and squeezed. I shoved aside the aches and pains and hugged her back.

"Catilda? What are you doing here?"

A woman who I could only describe as an older version of Catilda was by her side. Her red hair was a tad lighter, with a few strands of gray, and fell just below her shoulders in loose curls. A cascade of freckles filled the wrinkles around her eyes and down to her lips. "Mrs. Harper? Is everyone okay? Did something happen to your family?"

Catilda's father and two brothers appeared next to her.

"We're all fine, Zulli," her mother replied. "Tabby, I mean your mother, called us here last night. It seems like the gig is up. Zavyr has caught onto us and is probably planning his revenge as we speak. No one is safe."

"Us?" I looked over to Catilda. She held up her hands in surrender and took a step back.

"Catilda had no idea your mother was still alive and that I was still in touch with her. We kept it a secret because, well ..." Havannah Harper's gaze dropped to the floor.

"You couldn't trust me." I frowned and looked off to the side. "It's okay. I get it."

"More like we couldn't trust Catilda to keep a secret. She would have called you up immediately." Mr. Harper offered me a friendly smile that I eagerly returned.

"Oh, come on, Marx." Catilda's mom gave a gentle punch to her husband's chest. The man was a little rough around the edges with unkempt hair and scruff on his face, but he took pride in keeping his body in top physical shape. "Catilda is just ... very social with others. She makes conversation with others wherever she goes."

My mother approached and gave each of the Harpers a hug. "We had to make certain you were on our side. That's why I begged Colonel Buckner to have you take on the mission to rescue Cole."

"Wait, so Colonel Buckner is in on this too?" I rubbed my temples and pressed my lips together in a firm line. How many others had known about what was going on?

"Bucky and I go way back from my NightFly Technologies days, but he wasn't originally a part of this. I got wind that the team assigned to rescue Cole had been corrupted by Zavyr. I couldn't let them move forward, so I risked my secrecy and met up with Colonel Buckner to plead that he reassign the mission to you, Zulli, and your team."

"But ... how did you know I wasn't also corrupted?"

"I've been watching you, remember?" She placed a firm hand on each of my shoulders. "Of course I couldn't be certain, but I've seen enough to know what you've been up to. And besides, even if I had been wrong, you're a lot easier to take down than three expertly trained military operatives."

"So, it was all a test," I concluded. The thought that my own mother believed I might be some corrupt psychopath hurt more

132

than my twenty story fall off a building, but I couldn't fault her for it. Trust was earned, not freely given. I had to prove myself to her first, and before I truly trusted her, she'd need to do the same for me.

My mother scrubbed a hand through my hair. "Cheer up, kiddo! You passed the test! Come on, you're with me." She then clapped loudly and raised her voice to announce, "Everyone, take a seat and quiet down! The meeting is about to begin."

One by one, the seats were occupied with bodies and the noise dropped to a gentle murmur. My mother didn't have that same dominating voice my father possessed, but people obeyed her regardless. There was a matronly quality to her words—not a possessive command that forced you to listen out of fear, but a stern nudge that made you want to listen because it was simply the right thing to do.

My teammates, along with Cole, Catilda, and her family, occupied the nearest table facing me. My mother then climbed onto the table she was standing next to and pulled me up with her.

"Hello, everyone!" A mumble of greetings responded. "I know you're all busy, and I thank you for meeting me here on such short notice. I wanted to introduce you all to my daughter, Zulli Taracula." She gripped my shoulders firmly. "She's an accomplished military soldier for the Chitol army, risked her life to save one of our own, Colton Meyers, and now …" she paused and inhaled a deep breath. The tension in the room escalated. "… she will lead all of you in our fight against Bliss and bringing down Zavyr Taracula."

13

---◈---

FEAR PARALYZED MY joints. My heart beat wildly in my chest and my knees nearly buckled under my weight. I waited for someone to throw a slab of meat in my face, or even a round of disapproving boos. While the cafeteria spectators raised their voices in conversation, no one openly rejected my mother. In fact, they seemed more in shock, perhaps a bit confused, rather than aggravated by her decision.

"Breathe, Zulli," my mom encouraged with a smile on her face and a twinkle in her eyes. "Say something to them."

I drew a deep breath and exhaled my frustration.

"Are you nuts, Mom?" I threw up my hands and vented, although I kept my voice low enough so the rest of the cafeteria wouldn't hear. "You couldn't have warned me about this? I-I work for the military. I can't just leave my job behind! These people don't even know me, and they sure as hell don't trust me." I glimpsed at the man who I had jabbed with my elbow, the woman who was wearing her lunch, and the nerdy guy who I had chucked a tray at. "I'm not a leader, Mom. If you've really been watching me all these years, you'd know that."

"Oh, kiddo." Although we were still standing on the table, my mom turned her back to the crowd to give us some privacy. "Colonel Buckner and I have already discussed this. He thinks you'd be a great fit to help us, and he agreed that you and your teammates can stay here as long as you need to without any repercussions."

"He ... he said that? About me?"

My mom nodded with a smile. "He did. The military has many rules and regulations. Here ... not so much. You'll fit right in."

Well, she had a point there.

"Zulli, I understand your concerns. This has to be your choice. But I want you to know that, despite what you think of yourself, you *are* a leader. Rebelling against your father is dangerous. You know that and so do your friends. Yet here they are with you right now, following and supporting you. The people here don't know you like your friends do, but in time they will learn to trust and follow you. Now, go on ... give them a speech!" My mom turned around and raised her hand to quiet the crowd.

"Uh ..." A sea of faces full of different expressions ranging from disinterest to curiosity to excitement stared back at me. "Thank you for welcoming me here. My mother says a lot of good things about everyone."

It was obviously a lie and everyone knew it. I had known for less than a day that my mother was still alive and I hadn't even known what my father was up to until about a week ago. I watched as one woman turned around and continued eating her sandwich. A few others eyed the door, probably wondering if anyone would notice if they left.

I inhaled another deep breath, ready to speak whatever came out of my mouth. "Look, the truth is I don't know who most of you are, but I do know my father has targeted you, your family, and your friends. I'm truly sorry for what he has put you through." My voice softened and sincerity rang through my words. "No one is safe. He hurt me too—his own daughter. He forced me to grow up without a mother, making me believe she was dead. My father tried to erase the memories of my teammate and I nearly lost one of my best friends because of it. He attempted to kill someone close to me by forcing her to overdose on Bliss."

Catilda frowned at the reminder. My throat tightened as I brought up more painful memories. "My teammate, Kasra, fell off a building fighting alongside me, and I almost ended up poisoning Cole. Those are only my experiences, and I know between all of us here there are probably hundreds more stories to share. I won't lie. I will always love my father and my entire family, but what Zavyr is doing is wrong and he needs to be stopped. I can't take back the horrible things he's done or give back the people he's taken from us, but I can make sure I'll do my damned best to ensure our futures don't have to be lived hiding in the shadows. So, if you'll let me, I'd be honored to fight alongside each and every one of you until you no longer have to live in fear for your lives. You are all my family now, and I will do whatever it takes to protect you."

"Brilliant, kiddo!" My mom rubbed my back and smiled proudly.

At first, the silence was so profound that I could hear my heartbeat pounding in my ears. Then Kasra stood up from her seat. She adjusted her crutches and hobbled her way over to stand beside me.

"For the past six months, Zulli has been my teammate, and a damn good one at that. Yesterday, she didn't hesitate to jump off a building when I was thrown off it. She didn't have a plan but knew that if she did nothing, I'd certainly be dead. She put her own life at risk to save mine, and I know she would do the same thing for any of you, too."

Tears welled in my eyes. I swallowed the gratifying euphoria that bloomed inside my chest and constricted my lungs. Kasra turned around to address me. "I'm not angry at you, Zulli, for putting Ryker in danger or keeping your father's secrets from me. I was upset that you didn't trust that you could talk to me about it. That you wouldn't let me help. But I know that, deep down, you're a good person. I'm willing to put the past behind us and move forward. Together, as a team."

Ryker was the next to stand up and join Kasra. "I betrayed Zulli in the most horrible way imaginable. I was working for Zavyr Taracula." Gasps erupted from nearly everyone in the cafeteria. "I don't know why I did what I did. Zavyr permanently erased those memories from me, so I may never find out. But I do know that, despite how broken Zulli must have felt when she found out, she still believed in me. She saved my life by going to Zavyr himself and making a deal to kill Cole, knowing she'd never be able to follow through with something so treacherous. We all have our flaws, but Zulli sees the best in everyone and gives them a chance when others might cast them aside. I ask that you give her the same respect she'll give to all of you."

I really tried to keep my emotions in check, but a tear escaped down my cheek.

"Hi, I'm Cole." The blond-haired kid waved awkwardly to the crowd. "I haven't known Zulli for much more than a day, but in that brief span of time she saved my life too. Despite being ordered to kill me, she took me in and protected me."

Catilda and her family stood up next. One by one, the rest of the audience followed. Even Davian Grymes stood up. His slippery smile was replaced with something more agreeable.

I had joined the military to travel the world and aid those who couldn't help themselves, but the people who really needed me were right in my own backyard. I had failed to save Briyan, my friend and an innocent victim struggling with his own internal demons. If I could do anything to protect these people from the same fate, then I had to try.

Something inside me awakened, swelling as the spark fed the fire and ignited into a ferocious inferno of passion. I had always loved being a military soldier, but I had never felt like it was where I truly belonged. Something had been missing—my purpose. Now, standing in front of all these people, I had finally found what I was meant to do. Raising my fist into the air, I yelled out, "Who's with me?"

Elated cheers burst throughout the cafeteria as they all raised their fists.

"I told you." My mom nudged me with her elbow. "You're a natural leader."

Nearly knocking my mom off the table we were still standing on, I pressed myself into her chest and squeezed my arms around her in a suffocating hug. She wrapped an arm around my neck and kissed me on the top of the head. "I'm happy to have you back, kiddo."

"Me too," I whispered back.

We both hopped down from the table and I accepted a round of hugs from my friends. I found my way over to the group of people I had assaulted when I first entered the cafeteria.

"I'm, uh, sorry about earlier," I told them. "I didn't mean to take my anger out on any of you."

"Save it for Zavyr." The punk with a spunky red mohawk chuckled and held out his hand. "I'm Fynn."

White paper chains dangled from the belt loops on his baggy pants and he had a notepad sticking out of his wrinkled shirt pocket. His sharp jaw was smoothly shaved, and despite his hawkish features, his voice was quite friendly.

"Those sheets of paper you launched at me looked deadly enough to slice my head off," I joked, although I wasn't completely convinced it wasn't true.

"Yeah, death by a thousand paper cuts isn't the best way to go. I can turn simple sheets into blades as sharp as knives. I can also use paper to construct an object and animate it."

"I'm Zaydee. Nice to meet you." The petite female stepped forward to greet me. Despite the crusty tomato sauce that clung to her skin, her complexion glowed with a radiance that complimented a set of pigtails with blonde highlights. Her honey eyes

138

sparkled with delight when she smiled, and the multitude of fabric bracelets on her wrist dangled as she held out her hand. "My specialty is strength. I can rip a metal door off its hinges with a single yank."

I raised my brows and clasped her hand. She squeezed mine tighter than necessary. "Huh. Wouldn't have expected that."

The dark-skinned man who had thrown the vase at me introduced himself next. "You can call me Falk. I can pull certain objects out of books. Not people or tanks or anything, but stuff like clothes, weapons, and other survival gear. Helps cut down on the cost of supplies around here." He spoke swiftly in an excited, animated voice.

"That's pretty handy," I complimented.

"Sure is!" He rocked on his feet and hooked a thumb under his suspenders. I wasn't sure why he even needed them because his pants looked at least two sizes too small, the bottoms riding up his ankles, exposing his rainbow socks underneath.

The man I had elbowed in the sternum stood before me like a stone statue, an uncertain gleam in his eyes. His biceps were bulging, way out of proportion to the rest of his underdeveloped body.

"Oh, this is Evyn," Zaydee informed. "Although he *can* speak if he wants to, he chooses not to unless it's absolutely needed. His words have magic power, so this softie is just afraid that he might say something he'll regret."

Evyn started elaborately moving his hands in a series of gestures, pounding his fist into his palm and scowling as the expressions on his face changed along with his movements.

"He says he's glad you're here," Zaydee translated.

Evyn frowned and tucked his long, light brown hair behind his ears, then grunted his disapproval.

"Are you sure about that?" I questioned.

"Fine, fine." Zaydee rolled her eyes. "He wants you to know that your actions earlier were immature and uncalled for. Many of us have been living here for years. You barged into our home with no respect for any of us or what we've been through. If you want to be accepted into our home and as part of our family, you're going to have to work for it." She paused for a moment before adding, "And he's glad you're here to help."

A whisper of a smile danced across my lips and I scratched the back of my head. "You're right, Evyn. I promise I'll work on that, as well as making you and everyone else here proud."

His soured expression softened slightly. He grunted again—I imagined his way of agreeing with me.

"All right! All right!" My mom eventually called out. "While I'd love everyone to stick around and celebrate this momentous occasion, we all have work to do, so let's get back to it."

"We'll see you around!" Zaydee smiled at me before she skipped off toward the exit.

"The fun is only just starting, Zulli." Falk waved before following behind her.

The rest of them filed out of the cafeteria and silence rippled through the room. My mom had left, along with my friends. My stomach growled and I sighed to myself, realizing I hadn't grabbed anything to eat for Kasra or myself. I made my way over to the kitchen area, hoping to snag some leftovers, when I noticed a young woman sitting by herself at a table. She was paying no mind to the world around her. Her back was facing me, and all I could make out was her long, glossy black hair that cascaded down the entire length of her back.

"Hey!" I called out to her. Either she was ignoring me or she couldn't hear me. I switched directions and walked over to her. Placing a hand on her shoulder, I tried again. "Hey, is everything—"

"Don't touch me!" she wailed. She threw up her hands, slipped off the chair, and flattened right onto the floor. Her pointed elbow broke her fall, and she rolled over onto her side while rubbing it.

"I'm sorry, I didn't mean to—" I held out my hand to help her up but she scuttled out of the way until she was well out of my reach.

"I said, don't touch me!" She removed a set of earbuds from her ears.

"Okay, okay!" I held up my hands. "I was only trying to help. Everyone left the cafeteria. I just wanted to make sure you were all right."

"I'm fine. It's just, you can't touch me. It's dangerous." She stumbled to her feet and used a gloved hand to brush off the crumbs that stuck to her shapeless hoodie. She coughed hoarsely, and as she swept her glossy hair out of her face, I realized that was the only healthy-looking thing about her. Underneath her dry, flaking skin was a complexion so red that it almost looked like she had been burned. Her thick glasses were half the size of her face and magnified her dark, sunken eyes behind them. From the beanie on her head down to her black jeans that concealed her twig-like legs, almost every inch of skin had been covered.

"And *why* is it dangerous to touch you?" I asked curiously.

"My magic is poisonous. Literally. It creates a poison that radiates off my skin, and I can't control it. One touch can be enough to kill a person."

"That's absolutely absurd!" I took a step toward her and she took one back. I flinched at the sound of creaking metal that seemed to have come from under one of her pant legs.

"No, really. It's true. I … it's how my parents died." Her voice softened. She shoved her hands into her pockets and sat back down. I sat too, but at the next table over.

"Oh. I'm really sorry to hear that." I shifted in my chair, wanting to reach out a hand to comfort her but thought better of it.

"I killed my mom the day I was born," she continued. "My toxic magic ate away at her from the inside out the entire time she was pregnant with me. The doctors didn't realize how she died until a while later. Which meant that the whole time my dad was holding me after I was born, I was killing him too. Even the

141

doctors and nurses who handled me … some of them got extremely sick and one didn't make it. My aunt sent me to NightFly Technologies, hoping they could figure out a way to control my magic. They put me in some fancy medical program. The techs there tried a few different experiments, and, well, they only made it worse. They sped up the production of my magic, making my poison even stronger and more toxic." Anger burned in her eyes and fury was etched into every mark on her face. "Eventually, my own magic will kill me, too. So yeah, just don't touch me, okay?"

I flexed my fingers. I knew a thing or two about messed up magic. I wasn't sure if my unpredictable magic was actually killing me, but I knew if I didn't find Adrian and fix it soon it might end up *getting* me killed.

"Okay," I assured her. "So, if you don't mind me asking, you've been like this your whole life?"

"Yup." Her rage for my father's negligence softened into sorrow, and the despair behind her voice clenched my heart. If she had been avoiding touch since the day she was born, then she'd probably never experienced the uplifting experience of a hug or a kiss from someone she loved. I was willing to bet she had been cast aside by most people in her life and treated like a disease. "My magic took the bottom half of my leg about a year ago." She pulled up her right pant leg, revealing a sleek, metal prosthetic limb. "But on the bright side, I now have a way to kick guys in the balls if I need to."

We both awkwardly chuckled. Not knowing what to say next, I changed the subject.

"Your hair looks beautiful." The compliment drew a smile to her thin face.

"Tabby actually combs it for me. I told her not to. I don't want to be responsible for another death if she ever touches me, but she keeps insisting. The poison only comes from my skin, so while touching my scalp could be dangerous, my hair isn't."

"Well, maybe if my mom's busy, I can comb your hair some time?" I ran my hands across the buzzed sides of my head. "I don't have much of my own to work with." The confusion was easy to read on her face. "I'm Zulli. Tabatha Taracula is my mom. Did you miss that whole heartfelt speech I just gave like ten minutes ago?"

"I'm Salynn. Sorry, I guess I did. I had my earbuds in. They emit a magic pulse that helps me calm my magic. It's not a cure by any means, but it lessens the risk of something bad happening if someone accidentally brushes up against me."

A silence fell between us until she stood up from her seat. "Hey, it was nice to meet you, Zulli. I gotta get back to the control room."

"Oh. Can I come with you? I just got here. I don't really know my way around the place yet."

"Yeah, sure. Why not?" She started making her way toward the exit but I didn't immediately follow. "What's wrong?"

"Nothing." I stared at the untouched turkey sandwich Salynn had left on the table. "Are you, uh, gonna eat that?"

"All yours, Zulli. Have at it."

I shoved one half of the sandwich in my mouth and wrapped the other half in a napkin for Kasra, although the odds that I would end up eating that half too were pretty high.

"Okay. Now I'm ready," I said through a mouth full of bread. "Lead the way."

14

---⊛---

THE FORMER PRISON security room had been conveniently converted into the new control center that monitored the entire compound. Thick panels of glass overlooked the hallway and a single, continuous counter lined the perimeter of the room in a "U" shape. On top of it lay several computers and a dozen monitors the size of TVs. Some displayed a fuzzy video feed of the prison yard outside, while others monitored the magical alarms laid out in specific areas around the building. Like the equipment in the infirmary, everything looked high tech and was throwing off enough heat that my skin felt like it was melting off my face.

I fanned myself with my hand and watched Salynn occupy one of the empty chairs. She started typing something on the keyboard, then spoke, "*Aperta.*"

The empty desktop screen flickered, suddenly displaying something completely different. The heat leaking from the spell that she'd activated made the stuffy security room even hotter.

"What was that?" I leaned over her shoulder to get a better look at the monitor, careful not to get too close to make her uncomfortable.

"Magical voice-activated security protocol. We store a lot of sensitive information here and we don't want it getting into the wrong hands."

She started flipping through head shots, skimming the short biographies that went along with them. My mouth formed into a grim line. "That's the military database, isn't it?"

A cocky smile claimed Salynn's lips. "It is, but don't worry, Colonel Buckner gave Tabby access to it. He knows about it, and he's only giving us bare minimum information. We use it to cross-reference our intel."

Shivers of apprehension ran through me like a storm. My mom had met up with Colonel Buckner before the mission, but my team hadn't provided an update to him in over a day. I wondered if my mom had reached out when we arrived to let him know we were all safe.

I sat down on a rolling chair and spun myself in circles while Salynn worked.

"So, my mom never exactly explained where we are other than an abandoned prison."

Salynn's gaze never wavered as she kept her focus on the screen and answered, "Your mom isn't an idiot. She chose this place not only because of the good security but because it's on top of an icy mountain in the remote village of Clathe. Difficult for anyone to ambush it without us noticing."

"What? Clathe is like ... on the other side of the world from the city of Chitol!"

"There are enough people here with transportation magic. Not that I ever go anywhere." She shrugged like it was no big deal, but it clearly bothered her.

Continuing to occupy myself, I kept spinning in the chair. When I got so dizzy I felt like I was going to vomit, I stopped and unwrapped the other half of the sandwich. Before I could sink my teeth into it, a familiar picture briefly flashed across the monitor.

"Wait! Go back."

Salynn clicked on something and a file opened. "You know this twerp?" The picture showed the headshot of a brown haired male with frizzy curls, bushy brows, and distrusting eyes. Although his boyish features might let him pass for someone in his late teens, the information listed in his profile mentioned he was twenty-five years old.

"Adrian Cotter," I said, reading the name on the file in disbelief. "What's he doing in the military database?"

Salynn hummed thoughtfully as she scanned the data. "It looks like a lot of the information is classified, but this says he's a dangerous murderer wanted by the Chitol military. The Black Sheep unit of elite soldiers has been issued an order to terminate him. And according to this ... they're doing it tomorrow night."

"Oh, no." Captain Myra Llama's words resurfaced in my head. She had never said Adrian's name, but she had warned me to stay away from him. At the time, I didn't know why. Now it all made sense. Myra was a captain and member of the Black Sheep unit and she was likely the one tasked to kill Adrian. Staying away wasn't an option, though. I needed him to fix my magic.

"Oh no, *what*, Zulli? What is this guy to you?"

"Sorry, Salynn. I gotta go find my mom and my teammates. Thanks for this!"

I was already halfway down the hall when her raised voice reached me. "Uh, you're welcome!"

My heartbeat shot through the roof and my limbs shook. Adrian was a *murderer*? I found it difficult to believe that twerp had enough sense to kill a fly. Regardless, if the military killed him, I'd probably never get my answers.

Not knowing where I was going, I darted around the prison hallways looking for a familiar face.

"Mom!" I called out when I found her behind a desk in an office. Confusion froze my movements for a split second when I noticed my teammates, along with Cole and Catilda, were in the office as well. I refocused my thoughts and powered forward.

"Zulli, calm down. What's wrong?" Despite the terror grasping at my throat, my mother's voice was calm and her pale features remained as smooth and untroubled as a serene mountain lake.

"Adrian Cotter," I huffed out. "The military is going to kill him. I have to find him before they do."

Ryker gave up his chair so I could sit, and I recounted everything that had happened to me at the bar with Adrian.

"And you think this Adrian kid can help you, Zulli? We have a lot of talented physicians here. Why don't you have one of them check you out first before you skip off to ask a murderer for help?" Skepticism rang through my mother's words.

"Because if they can't, it might be too late. The only person who might know what's wrong with me will be dead."

My mother glanced over at Cole. Catilda was sitting next to him, gawking at his mismatched eyes. The seriousness of the situation hadn't really become tangible until now, seeing everyone in the same room, confined to this prison for their safety. My father had wanted Cole dead. My teammates and my friends' lives were at risk. I had just sworn to protect close to a hundred people, yet here I was thinking only about myself and my magic, asking to set off on my own adventure based on a simple hunch that Adrian would know what to do.

A sigh passed through my lips. "You know what, on second thought, you're right, Mom. I think I'll go get checked out by Lana."

My mom stood up from behind her desk. Her unruly ponytail dangled past her shoulder. The soft purple streaks that faded at the tips of her hair shimmered in the onset of early evening shining in through the window. "Zulli, I admire that you want to stay here and protect us, but part of being a strong leader is knowing when to take care of yourself as well. If you believe Adrian can help you, then I trust your instinct."

"Besides, hun," Catilda added, "Cole and I have a date in the library. He's going to tell me all about that odd-looking eye of his and then we're going to scour every book and see who can read the most. We'll be fine. Go on and do your thing."

Cole gave Catilda a blank stare before stating flatly, "It's not a date. I'm sixteen."

Kasra puffed out a heavy breath. "Well, you can count me out. I'll be of no use like this, Zulli." She tapped the cast on her leg.

"I'll go with you," Ryker offered, his voice eager and excited.

My mom raised her eyebrows at me and nodded.

"Okay, then," I agreed. "But what about Colonel Buckner? Does he know Cole is okay? Do you think he can push off the attack on Adrian until we find him?"

My mom scratched her chin. "I already updated him about the situation and let him know everyone's safe, but I doubt he can push off a military operation for us. It's not like we're an official government agency. We're just a bunch of rebels trying to do what's right, and the only reason he's not shutting us down is because all these people will have nowhere to go. They'd be exposed to Zavyr and targeted."

"Well, Ryker and I found out where he works. We can go back to Earth and pay a visit to Arcane Enterprises to see if he's there. But we need to go now before the military makes their move tomorrow."

"Zulli." My mom spoke in that stern, motherly voice. "You just fell twenty stories off a building. Not all of your injuries are completely healed yet. Are you sure about this?"

"I can handle it. Just a few aches and pains." Kasra let out a derisive snort at that. "Besides, it's not like we have much of a choice. Adrian could be attacked at any time tomorrow, and we don't want to end up in the middle of it."

"All right, then." My mom sat back down in her chair. She grabbed a pen and started tapping it against the desk. "Well, go on. We have a weapons supply room down the hall if you need to stock up on anything before you go."

I patted my trusty belt. "I'm good. I've got everything I need right here."

15

---◈---

"YOU ALREADY CARRY BULLETS on that belt of yours. You sure you don't want to bring a gun with you or something?" Kasra stood just beyond the metal bars of my cell, guarding the hallway while I changed. I could have made the long trek back to the locker room for some privacy, but I was eager to get out of there as quickly as possible. "Adrian's a murderer and we don't know what his magic power even is. If the military is conducting a mission to eliminate him, you know he must be packing some serious power."

I struggled to pull the plain purple t-shirt down over my head. The shirt, having come from Catilda, was a size too small and barely covered my midriff, but it was nicer than anything else I had in my bag. I selected a clean pair of fitted gray jeans from my duffle bag and tucked the pant legs into my biker boots as I responded to Kasra. "Any visible weapons are probably a bad idea. You said yourself that magic items are illegal on Earth without permits. Besides, if Adrian's already aware that the military is hunting him down, how do you think he'll react if we go in there with guns pointed at his head?"

The last piece of my outfit was a simple button up vest my mom had offered me. It didn't hug my figure like Catilda's clothes did, given that my mother was a little thicker around the waist than I was, but it helped make me look a little more polished. Ryker and I needed to fit in as employees of Arcane Enterprises so that we wouldn't raise any suspicions while searching for Adrian.

"I guess you're right. I have to admit, I'm a little jealous, Zulli. Sounds like a lot of fun infiltrating a magiceutical company that's *not* NightFly Technologies." Kasra nearly lost one of her crutches as her head whipped around to smile at me.

"Oh, believe me, I wish you could come too." I adjusted my bullet belt around my waist, then zipped up my bag and tossed it on the floor. "Okay, I'm ready. Let's go find Ryker."

Kasra and I made our way through the prison corridors and out into the main hallway, where we found Ryker with my mom in the weapons supply room. I knew my mother had made some friends in high places over the years, but whoever she had gained these weapons from wasn't someone I wanted to cross paths with any time soon. Just like everything else in this facility, the weapons were next-generation firepower. Some of them even the military didn't have access to.

"Woah!" Kasra exclaimed. "Is this a light launcher? I've never seen one this big before. I bet this bad boy releases a blinding magic that burns so hot it can melt the skin off someone's face."

Kasra marveled at the round canister about the size of a soda can. She picked it up, examined its smooth metal sides, then placed it back on the shelf.

"What's this thing do?" I asked, selecting a seemingly inconspicuous fountain pen and clicking the top to expose the tip.

"Poisonous ink pen," my mom answered. "Sometimes we have to be discreet about the magic items we carry. A small amount of ink on someone's skin will make them sick. A lot of it, though, depending on the person's tolerance, could kill them. You should take it. Might be useful."

I clicked it again, then delicately placed it back in its spot. "No thanks. I already stabbed myself once with a paralysis dagger. Don't want to try my luck with poison."

Next to the standard issued pistols that used simple metal bullets, there were other considerably powerful weapons—a magic-powered assault rifle that pulsed rapid fire magic to disorient and immobilize enemies, as well as a sniper rifle with special bullets that could lock onto a person's unique magic signature. The projectile would bend and warp, not stopping until it hit its target.

Ryker was eyeing the display of weapons that lined the shelves, but stuck to his trusty knife hidden in a sheath attached to the back of his belt. His baggy polo shirt mostly concealed it.

"Are you ready, Zulli?" Ryker asked. He always seemed to worry about me, but his apprehension was heavier than usual.

"Yes, I'm ready. Let's do this."

"Stay safe, kiddo." My mom pulled me in for a hug. She ruffled my hair and made it messier than it already was.

Ryker's cinnamon scent spilled past my nose as he focused on a photo that was on his phone. Although I had seen the black void of his portal before, the magic was currently invisible to me, but it still thrummed with strong, controlled vibrations and a steady stream of heat.

A warmth like the balmy days of late summer swept my skin as I passed through the portal with Ryker, who took us back to the safe house apartment on Earth. We couldn't risk anyone seeing two strangers appearing out of thin air and causing a panic.

Someone had turned over every inch of our temporary home. A box of cereal was spilled out over the kitchen counter and the dining room table was on its side. We checked the bedrooms, where each of the mattresses had been flipped over, the sheets torn off. Mrs. Paxton would have a heart attack when she saw what had happened here.

"You think this was Reeva and Liahm?" I asked Ryker, pocketing a stray green bullet that had been missed.

"Probably. But there was nothing here they could have used to find us. I mean, *I* wasn't even sure where we were going when Tabatha showed up." Ryker unlocked and opened the front door. "Come on, let's get out of here."

The spring day in Lorith was a damp one, and the moistness lingering in the air soaked into my clothes like a sponge. A thin layer of clouds masked the sun. Fog billowed across the city streets in a great gray mass, pedestrians emerging from its murky depths, appearing like ghostly figures. The Arcane Enterprises building in the distance was only a shadowy form, hidden almost entirely from view.

Because of the time difference between Earth and Iradel, it was early afternoon in the city of Lorith. We weren't positive Adrian would even be at work, but it was the only lead we had to follow up on.

After walking a few blocks, we approached Arcane Enterprises. Besides the gigantic sign out front and the building being slightly taller than the others nearby, it blended in with the rest of the cookie-cutter skyscrapers surrounding it. Rectangular windows were set in the gray metal frame that wrapped around the entire building, and an endless stream of people traveled in and out of the rotating front doors.

"So, what's the plan, Captain?" A slight smugness crossed Ryker's features.

"Captain, huh?" I laughed at the thought of one day rubbing that in Captain Myra Llama's face. Although my title wasn't officially issued by the military, it felt good to be recognized for something other than a screw up.

"Well, we could stick to the original plan and pretend we're reporters here to meet with the CEO's assistant, except Kasra isn't here to cause a distraction and persuade someone to let us in."

Ryker snorted. "You don't need Kasra for that, Zulli."

"Funny," I retorted dryly.

"No, I mean, your father runs the largest magiceutical company on Iradel. You know everything about how NightFly Technologies works. Aside from the outdated magic, I bet this place isn't much different."

I scratched my chin and hummed. "I guess. But it's not like my father was very forthcoming with me about how the company worked." I snapped my fingers and my eyes widened. "Oh! I got it! Back before my brothers were old enough to work in the labs, my dad would take advantage of their strength by having them unpack crates from the loading docks. It was a complete mess. No one could keep track of the orders, magic powders weren't stored properly, and there was no organization where anything was placed. What if we looped around toward where all the deliveries are dropped off? The workers there probably pay little attention to any of the Arcane Enterprises employees. We could sneak right in."

"Worth a shot. Let's try it." Ryker's dimples deepened with his smile.

"Let's just hope that, once we're inside, I can track down Adrian by his magical scent. I only got one good whiff of him at the bar and there's a lot of ground to cover inside."

Ryker followed my lead as we explored a quiet side street, searching for delivery trucks. We found the loading bays on the side of the building. A narrow side ramp led to a steel door that could only be opened with keycard access, so that option wouldn't work. My attention caught on the two overhead bay doors—one was occupied by a trailer currently being unloaded, while the other was left wide open with a clear view of the storage warehouse inside.

"Idiots," I muttered to myself.

Voices rose inside. I focused my hearing to listen in on two delivery men debating where the large crate they were handling should be stored. The vibration of their footsteps grew louder as they made their way back to the trailer to grab the next pallet of magical supplies.

"Ryker ..."

"On it." Ryker's magic thrummed with heat. Before anyone could spot us outside, we slipped into the warehouse through a portal and crouched down behind a stack of crates off to the side near the wall.

"Come on, Kenny. There's gotta be someone around here who can help us with this." I peeked around the crate to see a heavyset man with a bushy beard pointing at a large wooden pallet set in the middle of the floor. The cardboard boxes stacked on top were wrapped in clear plastic, reaching about as high as the tall man himself. "We can't just leave it here. What if it needs to be specially stored or something?"

"And I'm telling you, *Greg,* that the paperwork here says to just drop it off and leave. It's not our responsibility to figure out what happens after that. Let someone else figure out what to do with it." A much younger male with spiky bleached hair brushed past Greg and strutted back toward the truck.

Taking a moment to survey the area, I realized the warehouse wasn't all that large. On either side of the walls were stacks of boxes, crates, and barrels. The entire middle of the warehouse was wide open. The nearest exit I could spot was clear across the facility and right near where Kenny and Greg were unloading their haul. Even with Ryker's ability to transport, we wouldn't be able to reach the door to the lobby without being noticed.

"Follow my lead." I cracked my neck and tugged at the hem of my vest. I rose from my crouched position behind the crate and stomped toward the two delivery men. Ryker straightened up next to me and followed.

"Ahem. Gentlemen, what exactly do you think you're doing with this crate of ..." I glanced at the shipping slip laid out on top. "... of magic antiseptic? This magic powder is *very* delicate! You can't just leave it here. Its molecular structure will break down if it's not stored in the proper environment. This place is too damp!"

"Uh, right! We'll move it immediately, miss!" Greg narrowed his gaze on his co-worker and muttered, "I *told* you so, Kenny!"

Kenny gave me a once over. Unimpressed, he crossed his arms. "You don't look like you work here. Where's your badge and your fancy lab coat? What department do you work in?"

Damn. This guy was smarter than he looked. I cleared my throat, racking my brain to recall some of the information we had come across in our prior research of Arcane Enterprises. Ultimately, I winged it. "I don't need to have a badge to tell you that if this powder becomes tainted, Ms. Canmore will not be happy. This is thousands of dollars' worth of product just sitting here, waiting to deteriorate. You heard the news, right? Ms. Canmore is working on a super special project, and this magic powder is vital to its success. Do you know what happens when this powder breaks down? It emits a poisonous gas. That means, not only will this crate of magic here be rendered useless, but it'll destroy everything else stored in this warehouse as well. The toxic magic will get sucked into the vents and poison all the employees. You think the CEO of Arcane Enterprises will be happy about that? She'll go straight to your manager and have you fired from your jobs!"

Kenny licked his lips and ran over toward the boxes. "We're on it. Where should we put it?"

"Over there." I waved my hand off to the side. The thick steel door looked similar to the ones used for the temperature-controlled rooms at NightFly Technologies, and I had hoped I wasn't wrong. "That room should keep the magic stabilized until it needs to be used."

Both men disappeared into the walk-in refrigerator with the shipment of magic antiseptic, leaving Ryker and I alone on the loading dock platform.

"Impressive, Zulli. Was any of that actually true?" Ryker raised his brows at me.

"Doubt it. I just spewed out a bunch of crap my dad would always yell at employees. Let's get out of here before those two bimbos come back."

With both Kenny and Greg distracted, we hurried our way to the exit. Ryker cupped his hands above his eyes to get a good look through a tiny glass window set in the door. Without a key card, we couldn't open it but we were able to slip through to the other side using Ryker's magic.

The first floor looked to be administrative offices, but there were quite a few technicians, dressed in their flashy suits and skirts, walking around with their white lab coats, clipboards, and badges.

"We gotta get ourselves an access card," I told Ryker. A woman strolling down the hall passed by me, and I purposely bumped into her shoulder. She dropped her clipboard.

"Excuse me," she exclaimed, not in a very apologetic tone.

"Oh, I'm so sorry. I was just rushing to get to a meeting. I wasn't watching where I was going." I pressed a hand to my chest and feigned my apology.

As she bent down to pick up her clipboard, I did the same. "Let me get that for you." I leaned in to pick it up and lost my balance, knocking into the woman again. This time, my hand grazed the badge she had dangling from the pocket of her lab coat. Unfortunately, I dropped it right in front of her.

"Oh!" she gasped. "The boss would have my head if I lost that. Watch where you're going next time."

The woman clipped her badge back to her pocket and walked into an office, shutting the door behind her.

"Well, that didn't work out the way I planned. Kasra makes that look ridiculously easy." I scratched the top of my head and sighed.

"Oh really?" Ryker dangled the plastic keycard of Chief Director Megan Donnaley in front of him. "You forget I'm a master pickpocket with my portals. Although, I do feel bad that her boss is going to ream her out for losing it. You think we can return it before we leave?"

I frowned but also felt a tinge of guilt. I didn't know Daphne Canmore, but if she ran her company anything like how my dad ran NightFly Technologies, Megan would not only lose her job but her neglect for company security would mean she'd have a tough time getting another job elsewhere. "We'll drop it somewhere. Someone will probably find it and return it to her. Now we just need lab coats ..."

"I recommend the laundry room." Ryker pointed a thumb over his shoulder.

"Oh. Well that's convenient."

Ryker and I rifled through a few piles of clean laundry until we found two lab coats that mostly fit us. Ryker's was small, tight around his shoulders, and the sleeves an inch short, but it was good enough for what we needed. I shrugged mine on to cover my not-so-business casual attire and clipped the badge to my pocket. We left and I began putting my nose to work.

"Anything?" Ryker asked eagerly.

"Well, it's definitely almost lunchtime and I'm hungry. The cafeteria must be on the first floor because there are some delicious pizza vibes drifting my way. But no magic yet."

For supposedly being such a prestigious magiceutical company, the interior of Arcane Enterprises didn't live up to expectations. The lobby had the corporate taste of hideous plastic plants and a few cheap fabric chairs scattered around. Above the elevators were the words "Arcane Enterprises," the painted gold lettering peeling off the unattractive tan-colored wall. Stagnant air gave off the abrasive stench of musty carpets and dust, but no sign of Adrian's magic.

"How are we going to find him?" Ryker stared at the building map next to the elevators. "There are thirty floors in this building. He could be anywhere, if he's even here at all."

Near the front entrance of the lobby was a receptionist's desk. Lingering behind it was a woman checking in guests and smiling as employees scanned their badges and passed through the turnstiles on either side. A visitor strolled up and leaned across the counter.

"I need to speak with Ms. Canmore." The reporter slammed her fist against the desk. "I'm with the Lorith City newspaper. I just want to ask her a few questions. All I need is a few minutes."

"I'm sorry," the receptionist replied. "Her assistant gave me strict orders not to allow any reporters into the building. Ms. Canmore is not currently speaking to the press."

Well, there went that idea.

Pulling my phone out of my pocket, I dialed a number. The cheery woman at the front desk answered. "Hello, Arcane Enterprises. This is Bonnie speaking. How can I direct your call today?"

"Hello, Bonnie," I said in my best upbeat telephone voice. "This is Madison calling from the Journal of Magic Technology and Medicine. We're *so* excited to have selected Ms. Daphne Canmore for our Stellar Star award for her exceptional out-of-this-world contribution to the magic medical community! We'd like to schedule some time to interview her and present to her this prestigious award. May we speak to her?"

"Oh, I'm so sorry Madison. Unfortunately, Ms. Canmore is a very busy person. You will have to go through her assistant, Adrian Cotter, to schedule some time on her calendar." She started typing something on her computer. Trying my best not to look suspicious, I paced around to the side of the desk and squinted to see what was on the monitor. I was just far enough away that I couldn't make anything out, and if I got any closer, she'd be able to hear me.

"And how may I go about reaching him? Is he in the office today? I'm actually already in the area. I'd love to stop by and congratulate both of them personally."

A few seconds passed before Bonnie spoke. Ryker took the opportunity to exit through the turnstile, casually glancing over to view the monitor as he left the lobby.

"I'm sorry, Madison. Adrian is in a meeting with Ms. Canmore all afternoon. I'll patch you through to his voicemail and you can leave a message with your callback information."

"That's perfect! Thank you, Bonnie. I appreciate your help." The line clicked and started the transfer. I hung up after the first ring.

I sat down and waited in a chair for Ryker to return when someone walked up behind me and tapped me on the shoulder. My heart stuttered and I jumped to my feet.

"Sorry, I had to transport myself back into the laundry room to get back inside without anyone seeing me."

Breathing out a sign of relief, I followed Ryker over to the elevator and watched him press a button. "Did you get any-thing?"

"It looked like the calendar on the screen said room 1804, which I'm guessing is on the eighteenth floor. We should start there."

The elevator door rolled open. Ryker and I entered and made our way to the eighteenth floor. As soon as we exited, we were greeted with a closed door, a keypad blocking our advancement any further.

"Let's hope Chief Director Megan Donnaley has access." I swiped the card and the light lit up green. Ryker and I strolled up and down the aisles of the expansive lab space before us. Clunky, outdated machines hummed and groaned with purpose. Magical smells ranging from freshly baked apple pie to chlorine that burned my nose drifted past me as I surveyed the technicians conducting their experiments. With no sign of Adrian's vanilla bourbon-scented magic, we moved on to cover another five floors. Each one was just as unsuccessful as the last.

"This is ridiculous," I muttered to myself. I swiped some-one's clipboard from a desk and grabbed the first person who passed me. "Excuse me, I'm new here and I need to take this information to Ms. Canmore's assistant, Adrian Cotter. Do you know where his office is?"

"Office?" The woman snorted. "I don't think he has an office. He moves around, uses whatever random desk isn't currently being occupied. Last I saw him he was on the twentieth floor somewhere."

"Thank you! Much appreciated."

One glance at Ryker and we headed back toward the elevator, onto our next destination. I kept my nose sniffing every step of the way.

The twentieth floor was a grid of compact desks surrounded by cubicle walls. We strolled up and down every aisle to note which desks were occupied and whether the person sitting there might be Adrian.

"Nothing," I sighed to Ryker. "I guess this was a complete bust, after all. Let's take the stairs back to the lobby. I'll drop Megan's badge somewhere along the way where someone will see it. Then we can find a discreet place to return home."

"I'm sorry, Zulli," Ryker breathed out in defeat. "If he knows the military is after him, I wouldn't be surprised if he's hiding somewhere. At work is probably the last place—"

I abruptly stopped just as I reached the stairwell exit, and Ryker crashed into me. "Do you ... smell that?"

Ryker glanced over my shoulder. "Smell what? It's a closed door."

"No, there's like ... a very weak, faint smell of ... boozy cupcakes." I made sure no employees were looking before I ran my nose along the width of the door, stopping on the handle. Although it was barely noticeable, the tangy scent of lemon with a hint of vanilla bourbon was there. "He was here."

I stalked down the hallway, focusing my senses on figuring out where Adrian had gone next. Not having a great sense of how his magic felt, his smell was all I had to go on, and it wasn't very strong. He had certainly passed through here at some point, but there was a good chance he was already long gone.

We weaved through a few cubicles, passed a couple of executive offices off to the side, and strode down an empty hallway that very few people seemed to travel. The corridor was a dead end, but the last door on the right piqued my interest. A slight sniff of the handle confirmed my suspicion. "I think he's in here." Using Megan's card, I swiped the reader but it flashed red, denying me access. I stared down at the crack between the door and the floor.

Ryker shot me a concerned expression, the same one he always gave when he knew I was about to go something dangerous or stupid. "Zulli ..."

"Do you have any other ideas? We can't get in with the keycard." I dug my hands into my hips. "You don't know what's beyond that door, either. It's not like you can just portal inside."

"That's what I'm worried about, Zulli. If you go in there, I can't do anything out here. Just ... be quick. See if he's even in there and come right back. At least if we know where he is, we can keep an eye on him and approach him when it's safe." His amber eyes twinkled with his plea.

Of course, Ryker was right. Approaching Adrian on my own, not knowing much of anything about him, was an absolutely terrible idea. I promised Ryker I'd be in and out as quickly as possible, told him to turn around and watch the hallway, then let my magic take over. Its heat was a welcome warmth to my still aching muscles as my arms and legs vanished and transformed into the body of a hairy eight-legged arachnid.

I slipped under the door, scuttling across the linoleum floor. The room appeared to have once been used as a janitor's closet, now converted into some makeshift lab of sorts. The narrow space wasn't exceptionally large but had enough room for maybe five or six people to work comfortably. Unorganized shelves took up the far side of the wall. A few bulky machines were pushed up against the other side on a counter, and right in the middle was a mobile workstation lined with a few glass beakers and vials.

Directly in front of me stood the curly haired fugitive I had met not more than a week ago in the bar. His baggy jeans were faded, his red t-shirt wrinkled. Even though I knew he was short, in my spider form his shadow swallowed me whole. His puny arms stretched out from his sides, and I could feel the savage force of a powerful magic pulsing and vibrating around him. The murderous intent that washed across his childish face when he looked down at me was anything but amicable. He somehow had known I was coming and had been ready to take me down the second I crawled into the room.

He lifted a foot to squish me, and I let go of my magic. In a flash of heat, my body morphed back into human shape. Shielding my face, I rolled to my side just in time to avoid the incoming sneaker about to crush my head.

"Wait!" I cried out, but he didn't back down.

"*You* again. Did the military send you here?" Adrian pointed a finger at me and a bolt of lightning leapt out of it. I pivoted out of the way just in time for Adrian's attack to soar past me and burn a small hole into the wall. Smoke curled from it.

"Zulli? Let me in!" Ryker's voice was accompanied by his fist pounding on the door. If I let Ryker in now, he'd rampage and ruin my chances of reasoning with Adrian.

Ignoring him, I pushed myself up to my feet and held my palms out in front of me. "I swear I'm not here on military business. I need your help."

"Not here on military business?" He raised a bushy eyebrow at me but never dropped his guard. "Did your father send you, *Ms. Taracula*? You can let him know I'm not threatened by his daughter. I want nothing to do with him. He's already caused enough problems for me."

I stepped back as his magic continued building around him. The sizzling heat rippled off his skin in waves. The sound of his magic screeched like a sharp knife across rigid metal. "You know who I am?"

"Except for Zavyr's cold, heartless eyes, you look just like him. The spider-shifting ability confirmed it."

He extended his arm out in front of him. A thick black shadow shot out of his hand and snaked across the room. It coiled up my arms, around my waist, and squeezed my throat. Air was trapped in my lungs and tightness constricted my chest. My heart pounded louder, beating like a war drum in my ears.

My hand found a green bullet on my belt, and I tossed it at Adrian's feet.

"*Demitto,*" I choked out.

A sticky blob exploded from the bullet and locked Adrian's feet in place, but not his hands. He let go of the shadows holding me captive, and a fresh rain smell consumed the room. With a sweep of his arm, a fierce torrent of wind torpedoed right into my stomach. It sent me airborne, and I collided awkwardly with a heavy piece of machinery. My ribs rattled inside my torso, pain flaring from my side. Warm blood trickled down my lip.

I rubbed my forehead, willing my vision to return. The heat was suffocating, the vibrations of Adrian's power beating to the tune of his rage. Magic seemed to sprinkle out of his fingertips, a sound I could only describe as sand being poured over a grave.

The elastic sticking Adrian in place popped and sizzled. Smoke tendrils curled around him. His magic ate away at the spell, freeing his feet once more.

Fear spilled through my bones. Whatever magic Adrian possessed, there was an intense charge of energy radiating behind it. I could feel its steady vibration, building strong, growing reckless. It pulsed through me, my heart palpitating rapidly as the magic became a tangible, living thing inside me. Most people only had one type of magic, sometimes two. Adrian had just used three with perfect execution, and I had no doubt there would be more to come.

A trickle of sweat slid down my ribs beneath my shirt. *Murderer*, I thought to myself. How many people has he brutally killed? Would I become his next victim?

"Zulli! Come on!" Ryker's fist pounded on the door again. I wiped my sweaty palms on my pants then threw myself at the door and opened it.

Ryker came barreling in, his lab coat billowing behind him like a ghostly cloud. He had his knife in his hand and an infuriated expression on his reddened face. It transformed into something empty, his eyes inhumanely blank, when a dagger pierced him in the chest.

"Ryker!"

He dropped to one knee. Grunting and grinding his teeth, he leaned forward and clutched the dagger with his hands. In a wisp of magical smoke, it disappeared from his body. No blood. Not even a hole in his shirt. The illusion may have been fake, but the pain Ryker was experiencing certainly wasn't.

"This is your last chance to leave." Despite Adrian's warning, neither Ryker nor I made any attempt to exit. "Fine, then. I'm sorry, but this is going to hurt." Adrian thrust his arms forward. A dense cloud of magic energy surrounding him shot forward. An invisible wall slammed into my body, as well as Ryker's beside me. The intensity weighed down my limbs. It pushed me back and pinned me against the wall. The pressure kept building until I felt like my arms and legs would be ripped off my body. I struggled to free myself, as did Ryker, but there was no escaping Adrian's gravitational push.

"Do something, Ryker!" My words were strained by the magic, making it difficult to open my mouth. I coughed, a light splatter of blood spraying along with it.

A manic roar bellowed from Ryker. His hands clenched into fists at his side. Cinnamon wafted through the air, the only sign of the transparent blanket of magic opening before him. Adrian's magic vanished through Ryker's portal, the vicious attack thrown right back at him. Adrian stumbled and fell backward. A box of glass jars rattled on the shelf and came crashing down on his head.

Released from his hold, I picked myself up, sucked in a deep breath of air, and hobbled my way over to Adrian. Sharpened claws had formed on my fingertips and my fangs grazed my lips.

"I already learned my lesson by sucking out your magic once before. Now, as I was saying, I need your help to fix it."

16

---⟡---

ADRIAN PICKED HIMSELF up, crossing his arms and giving me a disapproving scowl. I studied the man for a moment, skeptically eyeing him up and down. He seemed more reserved than our last encounter, perhaps cautious. He was too formal, calling me by my last name. When he'd said it, it sounded like poison rolling off his tongue. The way he held himself, with a sense of purpose, was all wrong. Maybe I was being paranoid, since I didn't know the guy that well, but he seemed completely different. There was something off about him.

I sniffed the air and hummed thoughtfully. "The man I met at the bar on Grestor Island wasn't the brightest guy I'd ever met. In fact, he was somewhat of an immature brat."

"Says the woman who was slightly drunk, sucked out my magic, and now needs my help." Adrian huffed out a breath.

I brushed off the insult and continued. "Adrian spoke like a desperate teenager determined to save the world. He smelled like bourbon, vanilla, and lemons. But you ... you have many different smells. You stand here now all proud and mighty like the world owes you a favor. And your voice ... there's something off about your voice. It's a little deeper than I remember. Because … you aren't Adrian, are you?"

Ryker took a step forward and became my human shield. He had removed the lab coat, his unrelenting gaze locked onto Adrian.

"Well, congratulations to you," the impostor clapped. "Seems like you have it all figured out."

"But … that's Adrian's body isn't it?"

The man glanced to the side. "Yes." I followed his gaze. There was nothing there, but I sensed an obscure presence of magic somewhere in the room, like a ghost was watching over me. It sent tingles down my neck and arms.

"So … if you're not Adrian, then who are you?"

He hesitated for a moment, his dark brown eyes gleaming with harsh judgment. "You are truly not here for anything other than my help?"

I nodded. "I already told you. Something happened to me when I sucked out your magic. I'm just here because I want it fixed. I have nothing to do with my father or anything the military is doing."

He studied me for a few seconds before he seemed to loosen up a bit. "You know I can also sense when someone is telling me a lie …"

"I'm telling you the truth!" I shouted.

"I know." There was a tense moment that lingered, as he most likely debated on what information he'd willingly offer to both a military soldier and the daughter of Zavyr Taracula. I couldn't blame him for not trusting me, but I really needed him to. "Warmont Cove," he supplied. "Look it up."

Ryker scratched his chin thoughtfully as he pondered the name. "You mean the massacre at Warmont Cove? That happened over fifteen years ago. The entire military base there was attacked, and most of the residents died horrible, painful deaths."

Adrian, or whoever he was, bristled at the reminder.

168

"The man responsible was … Kellen Rezith," Ryker kept going, testing how far he could push this mysterious person. "They never found his body, but it was assumed he died. Could you be … But I don't understand how."

"I don't owe you an explanation of anything, nor do I have the time for idle conversation. Just call me Rezith." He gave Ryker a warning glower, and I didn't fail to notice his hand readying an attack. When Ryker made no attempt to counter, Rezith backed down. He turned toward the faucet, splashed some water on his face, then said, "You can come out now, Ms. Canmore."

A young woman removed the plastic tarp she was hiding under. She emerged from the corner of the room like a scared little kitten, confused and unsure of what was going on. Her straight black hair was cut into a sleek bob that fell just above her shoulders. Like most of the other employees we passed at Arcane Enterprises, she was dressed in a classy pantsuit that fit nicely on her slim frame. Her navy glasses shielded the vivid green of her eyes as she stared at both Ryker and me with extreme apprehension. She couldn't have been much older than twenty.

"Canmore?" I asked. "As in Daphne Canmore? The person who runs this place?"

"Y-yes, that's me." Daphne nodded, her hands trembling as they pushed her glasses up her nose. She sat down in an office chair and played with the hem of her shirt, listening but removing herself from the conversation.

"Nice to meet you." I gave her a nod, then turned my attention back to Rezith. "Look, I wouldn't be here if I had any other choice. But my magic is all over the place. Sometimes it's so overpowering I can't control it; other times it completely disappears. And I can … sometimes see magic. I don't know what happened, but it all started when I sucked out your magic. I need your help to fix it. Please."

"No." Power rang through Rezith's voice and his gaze slightly shifted. "I have too many problems to deal with as it is."

My knees trembled and my voice shook. "No? But … you have to help me. I *need* my magic back!"

Rezith raked a hair through his curls and I noticed his attention hadn't been on me, but was focused on that mysterious aura I sensed before. "Huh? Never mind that. Just sit down, Ms. Taracula. I hope I don't regret this."

I made myself comfortable on a stool beside his workstation and watched as the man plucked a vial from the test tube rack. Ryker stood beside me, eyes trained on the criminal like a hawk but not saying a word. My lips parted to say something, but nothing came out.

Rezith raised an eyebrow at me. "Just ask it, Ms. Taracula."

I gulped, my throat tightening. "You knew my father. What did he do to you? Did you really kill all those people?"

He continued stirring something in a vial as he answered. "I don't have time to explain my life story to you. I didn't know your father that well, but I knew him well enough to know he was up to something and that he decided to make me a part of it. It doesn't matter what really happened all those years ago. The only thing that matters is what people believe to be true, and I'll forever suffer the consequences because of it."

A few minutes passed as he worked, the awkward silence making my skin crawl. I adjusted myself on the stool. "Uh, can I ask you another question?"

"You have been asking me questions non-stop since you got here." Rezith glowered at me.

"If you're in Adrian's body, is Adrian … dead?"

Rezith glanced over to his right. He then returned his gaze to a small metal mixing bowl, poured the contents of a vial into it, and finished it with a pinch of another magical powder.

"He's alive. In a sense."

I closed my eyes, inhaled sharply, and relaxed my shoulders. My senses were so receptive I could hear Ryker's heart racing, Rezith's frustrated breathing, and Daphne trembling in the chair. But there was also something else that caught my attention. "I don't know if it's because I have your magic coursing through me or because of my heightened senses, but I can feel this … pocket of magic vibrating over by the desk. You keep looking over in that direction. Is that Adrian I'm sensing?"

Rezith snorted. "I'm not surprised that the daughter of Zavyr Taracula is so attuned to magic, despite not being able to see it. Here, drink this." He handed me the metal bowl. I was about to take a sip of the red liquid when Ryker stopped me.

"You never explained what's going on with her magic. What's in that bowl and what's it going to do to her?"

Rezith smirked at him. "She's experiencing the combined effects of both Adrian's and my magic—nullifying powers as well as the ability to copy magic abilities."

"What?" I gasped. "I've heard of objects that can dampen magic powers temporarily, but there are people who can completely neutralize it? Wouldn't the powers cancel each other out? I've never taken on the powers of magic I've sucked out. Why did it happen this time?"

"You ask too many questions. Do you want this fixed or not?" Rezith nudged the bowl closer to my lips. I took a sniff, trying to discern what his concoction might be, and wrinkled my nose at the awful stench. Holding the bowl in my hands, I waited for further explanation.

"Ugh. You seem to have inherited your father's stubbornness. Think about it, Ms. Taracula. The two powers that Adrian and I possess are both unique, powerful, and rare. The ability to nullify magic isn't even considered magic, and my ability to copy is probably one of the strongest types of magic you've ever encountered. Face it, you sucked the magic out of the wrong neck, and now you're paying for it. It's simultaneously trying to copy your existing magic and eliminate it at the same time. Tell me, can you fully shift into both of your forms? You crawled in here as a spider, but you slashed your cat claws at me."

"Don't tell him anything he doesn't need to know, Zulli. I don't trust this man." Ryker flashed his knife at Rezith.

"W-wait a minute!" Daphne jumped from her chair and scrambled over to Rezith's side. "I know it's hard to trust someone you don't even know. When I first met him, I didn't trust him either. But, this man, Kellen Rezith, isn't who you think he is. You can trust him."

Rezith actually blushed at Daphne's compliment.

My gaze dropped to the liquid. "Well, it's not like he couldn't find out more about me on his own if he really wanted to. I'm half cat and half spider shifter, although I don't have full control over either form. I never did, even before all this. I can only use limited magic from each animal, and not even at their fullest capacity."

Rezith beamed a mischievous smile at me. "Then today is your lucky day, Ms. Taracula. Extracting the magic to revert its effects is a delicate, painful process that I don't have time for. But this magic liquid will stabilize your magic. *All* of your magic."

"You mean …"

"It will unleash your full power. But let me warn you, Ms. Taracula, you'll have to learn all over again how to use your magic, how to control your new strength and abilities. If you're not ready—"

I chugged down the liquid in a few large gulps and wiped my lips with the back of my hand. It stung like gasoline all the way down my throat and lit my stomach on fire. "That was awful. It tastes like a mixture of rotten fish and moldy cheese."

"Well, then, you're not going to like the next part, either."

Rezith reached for something in his back pocket and pulled out a pink gardening glove, slipping it onto his right hand. *"Produco."*

He ran a finger across my forearm. My skin tingled, heat rising to the surface and my hairs standing on end. The tingling turned into a prickling sting, until eventually it felt like my flesh was being peeled off my body and melted by acid. My head snapped back and a scream ripped from my throat.

172

"It … it burns!" I tried to pull my arm away, but Rezith kept his fingers tightly locked around my wrist.

"Quiet down. People might hear you," he scolded.

"What are you doing to her? Let go!" Ryker gave Rezith a shove then pointed his knife at his throat. "I said, *let her go!*"

"If you value your friend's life, then you'll let me continue," Rezith spoke in an annoyed but steady voice. "The magic must be untangled before it can be stabilized. If I stop now, she'll never be able to use magic correctly ever again. Now *back off* and let me work."

The knife was shaking in Ryker's hand. He hesitated, eyeing me and the sweat dripping down my face like a melted popsicle. He withdrew his knife and spoke in a dark, menacing tone. "One wrong move and you're done for, *Kellen Rezith.*"

Rezith sniffed at the threat and focused solely on me. As the magic stabilizer did its work, the pain grew more severe. My muscles felt like they were disintegrating, my joints bending and snapping with my jerking movements. I could feel the vibration of magic rattling my bones, like it was trying to decide whether to shift into a cat, a spider, or a human. Pressure continued to build inside my chest, and all I could do to keep myself from passing out was grip the countertop. The laminate cracked under my fierce strength. I suppressed a harrowing scream from bursting out of my mouth.

Daphne walked over to me and held my hand. "You can do this, Zulli. Breathe."

Breathe. That was something my mother had always encouraged me to do when I needed to calm down. Such a simple act with such profound effects. Ryker grabbed my other hand and caught me in his arms before I collapsed off the stool. With both of their support, they helped me settle on the floor. I welcomed the cool touch against my smoldering skin.

I started panting, my hot breath fuming on its way out of my mouth. Claws flashed out of my fingertips, only to disappear seconds later. I bit down on my lip, my own pointed fangs drawing blood.

A haze crept in around the edges of my vision. With his gloved hand, Rezith seemed to analyze and carefully pick at something in the air. With precise movements, he used his fingers to separate strands as if untangling a ball of yarn. It was invisible to my eyes, but I knew he was working on unraveling my magic.

"Almost there," Rezith assured me.

"Hurry ... up." I took short, ragged breaths and glowered at him. Both Ryker and Daphne were holding me down, trying to keep me still.

In no rush, Rezith toiled away for a few more minutes, meticulously moving his fingers with precision and finesse. With every tug on my magic breaking apart, my insides twisted along with it. When I ran out of energy, I stopped thrashing. My head dropped to the side and my eyes fluttered closed.

"Zulli, stay with me." Ryker gently caressed my cheek and stroked it with his thumb.

"She's burning up. I'll go get some ice and water." Daphne's heels tapped loudly on the floor and I heard the door click shut behind her.

"It's done," Rezith confirmed.

Those were the last words I remembered hearing before I surrendered to exhaustion and let myself pass out.

When I stirred awake, I was still on the floor with my head resting in Ryker's lap. His lab coat was balled up underneath me as a pillow, and he was running his fingers through my hair in soothing strokes.

"Zulli, are you okay? How are you feeling?" Ryker removed the icy towel chilling my forehead. A vicious pounding inside my head threatened to crack my skull open, and that was only the beginning of my aches and pains. My limbs felt both tight and stretchy, heavy but light. Strength was coursing through me, but with each pulse of magic, there was a sensation of nails being hammered through my body. Some of it was from my previous injuries, but most of it felt new. I propped myself against a cabinet, rubbing my chest with my fingertips.

"I feel like I've got really bad heartburn, like there's corrosive acid burning away at my insides. Is that normal? Did it work? How long was I out?"

"Only about twenty minutes," Daphne answered.

Ryker helped me to a stool and Rezith did a quick examination of me. "I believe it worked just fine. But remember, you'll have to learn how to manage your new power. Your body isn't yet used to it, and until it is, you should probably wear this." He held out a thin piece of purple leather with a buckle on it.

"You've got to be kidding me. A cat collar? That's degrading, you know. I'm not wearing that." I swatted away his hand.

"I spelled the collar myself to contain your magic. It will only let you use what your body can handle. Over time, once you become better acquainted with your new abilities, you'll no longer need it. But until then, I suggest you wear it or you might end up snapping someone's spine when you go to hug them."

I gulped loudly, my throat parched and stomach queasy. Kellen Rezith was possibly the most talented person I had ever come across when it came to magic. With his ability to copy, his powers were limitless. How his consciousness had ended up in Adrian's body, I knew he'd never tell me, but I could understand why the military would think of Rezith as a dangerous threat. Whether he was or not wasn't my place to judge.

"Fine," I relented. "I'll wear the stupid thing. So, what happened to your magic inside me? Is it … gone?"

"It's gone, but the effects of what happened are irreversible. You might have some unexpected changes to your powers resulting from it. For instance, be careful next time you suck out someone's magic. Who knows what might happen with your amplified abilities?"

I fastened the stiff strip of leather around my neck. I tugged on it, my finger barely having enough room to slip through. "It's a little tight."

"Well, it was meant for a cat, not a human. If you don't want to wear it, be my guest and blow yourself up next time you try to use your magic."

My defensive expression softened and I caught his gaze. He may have acted like a tough guy, but I could tell that behind all the insults and frustrated gestures, he truly cared about helping people. "Thank you, Rezith."

"Don't mention it," he answered. "I mean, literally. Do *not* tell anyone about this."

I paused for a moment, staring at the remaining bottle of liquid in the test tube rack on the workstation counter. A thought occurred to me. "Say, um, could that stuff help stabilize someone whose magic is basically destroying her from the inside out with poison? And how would I go about getting my hands on some of it?"

A sigh escaped Rezith's lips. He picked up the tube and held it out to me. "Take it. Now get out of here. I have work to do."

I pocketed the vial and slipped a hand around Ryker's neck, leaning on him for support. Before we left, I turned around to Rezith. "I didn't know what to expect when I came here, but I appreciate your kindness and agreeing to help—the both of you." I nodded to Daphne. "And Adrian, I guess, even if he did nothing but cause this in the first place."

If he could hear me, I imagined the overly defensive brat was probably throwing a string of cuss words my way.

"I know my father has done some questionable things over the years. I want you to know that I'm trying to rectify that and help the people he's wronged. I believe there's more to your story. I don't know what it is, or whether my dad really had any involvement in what happened to you, but people deserve to hear the truth, whatever it is." I inhaled a deep breath, and slowly let it out. "That's why I'm going to warn you that the Chitol military

176

is planning to come after you tomorrow night. I don't know the specifics, but maybe run while you still can. One day, I hope I can find out the truth about what happened to you and set things right. You just have to survive long enough for me to do that."

A smile crept up Rezith's face, but it didn't reach his eyes. "I sure hope so, Ms. Taracula."

The door slowly swung shut behind us.

"Where should we drop off Megan's badge?" Ryker asked, searching up and down the hallway. Not a single person was in sight.

"Maybe we should give it to the front desk? That way we'll know she'll get it back."

Ryker agreed.

A weight had lifted from my shoulders and a sense of pride swept through me. My magic wasn't just fixed, it had gotten an upgrade. My smile stayed pinned to my face all the way back to the elevator. When the doors rolled open, the butterflies in my stomach turned to cold, hard lumps of coal.

Radiating a perfectly friendly smile at me was a petite female with skin the color of pale moonlight. Thick bangs covered her entire forehead, but the rest of her ashen blond hair was pulled back into a stylish bun.

"Zulli! What are you doing here?" Captain Myra Llama's voice sounded like she was greeting a close friend, but the firm grip she had on my arm as she yanked me into the elevator suggested otherwise. She pushed the button repeatedly to close the door, and Ryker slithered inside just in time to join me.

17

---◈---

"HEEEY, MYRA!" I backed into the corner of the elevator, although there was no escaping Captain Myra Llama's penetrating stare from her callous turquoise eyes. Ryker pressed up against me and unsheathed his knife.

"Get out of my way, Ryker." Myra never lifted a finger, but with a simple breath of air, Ryker suddenly dropped his knife and he stepped to the side. The clean cotton smell of Myra's magic permeated the small, confined space.

Without warning, she lunged at me and pressed her forearm up against my neck. The more she leaned into it, the more my esophagus crushed under her force.

"I warned you, Zulli. I warned you to stay away from him. That man is *mine*." She still refused to say his name, but now I knew for certain who she was talking about. It wasn't just Adrian she was after, but the man camping out in his body—Kellen Rezith.

The elevator jerked to a halt and the door chimed open. In one graceful move, Myra swiftly bent down to snatch Ryker's knife and twirled around so her back was facing me. She had her hands clasped behind her, the tip of the blade pinching my gut.

A janitor entered with his supply cart, then left two floors later. Myra immediately swung around to face me again, this time with the knife to my throat.

"What are you doing here?" she demanded, her uplifting spirit turning into something harsh and abrasive. I dared a quick glance at Ryker. His eyes were distant and his posture slumped. He stood there like an empty, emotionless husk, unaware of anything going on around him. What had she done to him?

"That's none of your concern," I spat back at her. "Why don't you stay out of *my* business!"

My fingers wrapped around her wrists and I pushed against her hold on me. To my surprise, it was easy. Too easy. With just a slight shove, she flew across the elevator. Her head made a crunching noise as it slammed hard against the wall. Her hands swayed in the air as she stumbled on her feet and a knee hit the floor. There was a visible dent in the metal siding.

Less than ten minutes with my new magic and I had nearly killed someone. "Myra, I'm sorry. I didn't mean to—"

"Don't you move another inch." Myra let out a sharp breath. The fresh linen scent of her magic was cold and numbing as I inhaled it. My mind froze, unable to think or command my limbs to move. I couldn't turn away from her hardened gaze. "You are interfering with a classified military operation. I don't know what you're planning with that piece of trash, but once I report you and your teammates ... let's just say the military doesn't tolerate traitors."

My thoughts snapped back to reality and Ryker shook the cobwebs out of his head.

"Traitors? No, we're not ... it's just ..." I couldn't tell her what had happened to me or, despite Rezith's kindness, what he had done. Whether or not he meant well, I'd be Rezith's accomplice just for seeking help from a deadly criminal. Even Colonel Buckner wouldn't be able to get me out of *that* mess. Plus, I had warned Rezith about the military's ambush.

"I promised not to meddle in your business if you didn't interject yourself into mine." Myra's nostrils flared, fury swirling in her eyes. "Yet you seem to keep testing how far I will go. I'm warning you now to stop before it gets out of hand. You won't win." The elevator door chimed open. Myra straightened her shoulders and smoothed a few wrinkles from her blouse then casually strolled out of the elevator.

"What the hell just happened?" Ryker took quick breaths in between his words. "Myra's magic ... it felt different from the last time. Like I was trapped inside my own mind."

I held out my hand to stop the door from closing, and we stepped out into the lobby. Myra was already gone.

"I don't know what dirt she thinks I have on her. She had told me that if I kept her secret, she'd keep mine about what happened in the vault when I tried to steal the spatula. She said nothing about the warehouse either. Whatever she's hiding, I think it has something to do with her magic."

"Let's just get out of here." Ryker started heading toward the front desk and I followed behind him. I handed over Megan's badge, explaining that she must have dropped it in the stairwell.

The nearest place we found where we could discreetly use Ryker's magic was the parking garage below Arcane Enterprises. The spicy scent of cinnamon mingled with the sticky dampness and the harsh smell of car fumes. We both passed through his portal, back to the gloomy prison on Iradel.

With the late afternoon of Earth left behind, night was upon Iradel. Moonlight filtered in through the window of my mother's office and lit up the vacant desk.

I turned to see Ryker smiling at me, even as his fingertips massaged his temples. "You okay?" I asked him.

"Yeah, I'm fine." Ryker's dimples deepened as his smile reached his amber eyes. "I'm just glad everything turned out all right. It's not often we come out of these missions without causing more problems."

We strolled out into the hallway, a cold draft sending shivers up my arms and down my neck. When Ryker wasn't looking, I stretched out my tongue, licking my busted lip. The surface tingled lightly, my saliva absorbing into the open cut. Tightness pulled at the skin as my magic healed the shallow wound much faster than I expected.

There were no other bodies roaming the halls. The overhead lights were turned off, the end of the hallway before me disappeared into a vast ocean of darkness. The striking absence of noise was so profound it seemed to have its own quality.

"Where is everyone?" I asked Ryker.

"Asleep?" Ryker grabbed my hand and started dragging me behind him. "Come on, let's go to the cafeteria and find something to eat. I'm hungry."

I followed, although with extreme wariness. Ryker never complained about being hungry, and most times when we sat down for a meal, he never actually ate.

"Something's wrong, Ryker. There's no way everyone's—"

Ryker pushed open the cafeteria doors and a blinding light brought dots dancing in my vision. The silence was replaced with an eardrum-shattering cheer from about a hundred people. *"Congratulations!"*

My heart leaped into my throat and I let out a squeal like a cat whose tail had just been stepped on. I wanted to run back out the door but Ryker was blocking it.

"What the hell is this?" With a hand to my chest, I did my best to steady my racing pulse.

Dimples formed in the center of Ryker's cheeks, the redness of his face growing a shade brighter. "Why did you think we were all in your mom's office earlier? We were planning a party to celebrate your ... promotion of sorts. And to make up for your mom missing all those birthdays over the years."

Adorned with party hats and streamers, everyone in the entire prison was crammed into the cafeteria and had their gazes pinned on me. As someone who had always tried her best to stick to the shadows and fly under the radar, I absolutely hated being the center of attention. My head sank into my shoulders as if I could make myself less noticeable.

"This is unnecessary. I don't deserve to be treated any differently than anyone else here." I tried to sidestep around Ryker to leave, but he shifted to match my movements.

"Come on, Zulli. Everyone worked hard to put this together. I know you don't like surprises, but Catilda insisted." Ryker gave me an opening to escape, but the promise of food outweighed the awkwardness of mingling with strangers. Besides, if I was going to be the one leading them from now on, protecting them, I should probably attempt to get to know them and gain their trust.

"And who told you I hated surprises? It's not like you've tried to throw me a surprise party before ... have you?" I could think of one surprise that got to me: his betrayal. I wouldn't dare say that to him though.

He scratched the top of his head and tilted it to the side. "I don't know. I guess I just always assumed, or maybe your mom said something."

"You look in good spirits. I take it everything worked out?" My mom excused herself from a group of chatty women and walked over to me. She had changed since earlier, now wearing her hair in a messy bun and choosing more casual lounge pants and t-shirt, the bright orange color making her easy to track from anywhere in the room. She had a can of beer in one hand, and although she wasn't drunk, her flushed cheeks told me it wasn't her first drink of the night.

"Yeah. Better than expected, actually." I offered a cheery smile, and she responded with one of her own.

Catilda skipped over to me and looped her arm through mine.

"Come on, Zulli! I want to introduce you to my new friends!" She whisked me away, Ryker heading off in his own direction, and she started introducing me to a few unfamiliar faces. I wasn't paying attention to any of it, though. My eyes were glued to the extravagant display of food and my nose was drawing me toward it.

A three-tier platter of mini cheeseburgers sat on a long table stockpiled with other various greasy finger foods. Chicken tenders, pizza, a sheet cake half the size of the table, and a five gallon tub of strawberry ice cream. Bowls of magically-enhanced flavored toppings, like sprinkles and syrups, sat next to it.

"So, what's everyone else eating?" I joked to Catilda, but she had already left me to socialize with the next group. It was actually Salynn who was standing behind me, and she looked even more like death than she had when I'd last seen her a few hours ago.

She opened her mouth to speak but kept choking and gasping for air in between each hoarse cough. She put a napkin over her mouth, and when she removed it, speckled blood had soaked into it. Noticing the horrified look on my face, she said, "It's fine. Happens all the time."

She sat down on a folding chair next to the far wall, out of the way of most traffic. I snatched a chair and pulled it up next to her. A little too close, she scooched her chair another few feet away from mine.

"Anything exciting happen while I was gone?" I asked in between her coughing fits. She uncapped a bottle of water and guzzled the entire thing down in a matter of seconds.

"Nope. We spent the entire time planning this. We don't usually get to have a lot of fun around here. Look at everyone. They're so … happy."

But Salynn wasn't. Her wishful words were filled with painful longing. She was barely strong enough to stand, let alone dance. She could join a conversation, but being so close to others would make her anxious. Her prosthetic limb clanked against the metal chair as she adjusted herself in her seat.

My heart broke for her. My hand twitched, wanting to grab hers and give it a squeeze. Even with gloves on to prevent contact with her skin, I knew she'd object if I tried.

"Do you ever think about what it would be like if you could get your magic under control? What would you do?" I asked her.

She pondered the thought, sighing as she looked out into the crowd. "I'd like to dance. At least as well as I can with one weak leg and a metal contraption attached to the other." She chuckled to herself and her gaze softened. "And hug someone. Maybe kiss a cute boy. Ryker's cute. You think he'd kiss me?"

My stomach flip-flopped at hearing that. He probably would just because he was such a nice guy, but a part of me felt a twinge of bitterness at the thought of him doing it. "Maybe," I answered. "But more importantly, what if I told you I might have found a way of allowing you to ... live? You could dance and kiss as many cute boys as you wanted."

She pouted and gave me a dissatisfied look. "Don't joke with me, Zulli. That's not funny."

"No, I mean it." I leaned forward in my chair and pulled out the vial of red liquid from my pants pocket. "When I went to Earth, someone gave this to me. It's a magic stabilizer, similar to the bonding agents they use in labs like NightFly Technologies. But unlike what they use in labs, this one is used to tame your *internal* magic, not mix and stabilize spelled liquids and powders."

Awe crossed her ghoulish features. Her mouth parted, and a spark of hope flashed in her dull eyes.

"Are you serious? That stuff could ... I could ..." Tears rolled down her red, flaking cheeks.

"I can't make any promises, but I have it on good authority that the guy who made this is good for his word."

She balled her hands into fists and bounced up and down in her seat, squealing with excitement. I handed over the vial and she caressed it between her fingers with extreme delicacy.

"Bring it to Lana over in the infirmary. I'm sure she'll know what to do with it."

Sticking alongside Salynn, I avoided speaking to anyone else for the next couple of hours. As the night grew late, tired party goers left to head to bed. I was about to call it a night as well when a rambunctious laugh full of energy rang through my ears.

Ryker was having a very engaging conversation with an unfamiliar female. She drew a hand up to her face to hide her giggle, shying away like she was embarrassed about something. She had a few extra pounds on her that stuck mostly to her hips, but the periwinkle sweater dress seemed to melt into her curves. I was too far away to get a good look at her, but I could tell she had that same magnetic attraction as Ryker—a sense of beauty that conveyed a personal sense of warmth. It poured over her skin, flickered over her clothing, and dazzled the very air around her.

She brushed her hands behind her dark brown hair and flipped her loose curls off her shoulder. She said something to Ryker, then reached out to give him a tight hug. The smile he returned was so pure it twisted my stomach in knots.

"Who is *that*?" The words came out more bitter than I expected.

"Oh, that's Maycee. She's like everyone's big sister around here. She spends a lot of time with the younger kids, teaching them about magic and other school subjects. She's always in high spirits and adds a much needed ray of sunshine around here. Her magic is pretty cool, too. She can turn herself into a shadow. I don't know how she ended up here, though."

I focused my hearing to listen in on their conversation when a piercing screech filled my ears instead. I clasped my hands to my ears and rubbed them.

"Damn magic," I grumbled to myself.

"Huh?" Confusion flavored Salynn's words.

"Nothing. I'm heading to bed. Come get me when you go see Lana? I'd like to be there when she starts the procedure. It's, uh, let's just say, less than pleasant, but the results are worth it."

"Sure thing, Zulli. I'm gonna head to bed too."

Salynn walked a good six feet behind me as I passed by Ryker and Maycee. Maycee didn't see me, but Ryker had a perfect vantage point as he glanced over her shoulder. He flashed me a quick lopsided smile. It was warm, authentic, but also had an undeniable level of uncertainty. He didn't follow as I wandered back to my cell.

18

———◈———

I LAY ON the uncomfortable cot in my dark, drafty jail cell with my hands behind my head, staring up at the ceiling. A sliver of moonlight passed through the tiny window high above me.

The vision of Ryker chatting with Maycee was at the fore-front of my mind. It wasn't jealousy that provoked me, at least not completely. After all, Ryker had brought up the idea of a date with me and I hadn't given him an answer. What I felt was … annoyance that I couldn't place what it was about Maycee that brought out a side of Ryker I had never seen before. The clear depths in his eyes had shone with raw passion, and the bright glow of his enchanting smile had radiated pure bliss. He wasn't smiling to be friendly; he had truly felt happiness in that moment. What was so different about Maycee that made Ryker genuinely content? Why didn't he act that same way around me?

I rolled over onto my side and tucked the blanket under my chin. Giggling echoed down the corridor, and I watched as Maycee and Ryker passed right by me.

"Let's have lunch tomorrow?" Maycee asked innocently.

"Sure. My treat."

She laughed again. "The food here is free, silly. Unless you had somewhere else in mind?"

"Maybe. I'll think about it." Ryker, who had been adamant about choosing to sleep in the jail cell directly across from mine, opened his squeaky barred door and strode inside. "Sleep well. I'll see you tomorrow."

Maycee left, and I stared off into the distance toward Ryker's bedroom cell. Not more than a half hour later, his soft snoring was amplified by the near silence that consumed the cell block.

I shoved the thoughts out of my head and exhaled a deep breath. Ryker was an outstanding guy and deserved all the happiness in the world. If Maycee could offer that to him, then I couldn't ask for anything more for my best friend.

Closing my heavy eyes, I wished for sleep but it never came. I eventually got up from my bed and found myself outside Ryker's cell, staring at him through the bars. The metal screeched as I put a hand on the door, waking him up.

"Zulli?" He used one hand to push himself up and the other to rub his eyes.

"Yeah. Sorry, I didn't mean to wake you."

"So you were just creeping outside my room, watching me sleep? Come here, sit down."

I sat down on his mattress, no different from the same shapeless pad made of flat springs that I had. I'd have to talk to my mom about giving this section a much needed upgrade. "There's just a bad draft in my cell. Thought maybe I could sit here for a bit and warm up."

He grabbed my arm and gently pulled me down to the pillow until I was lying beside him, then flung his blanket over me. He squirmed to make room, the tiny mattress not nearly big enough for two people. "Better?"

His warm breath tickled the back of my neck. My muscles tensed as he brought his arm around me and rested it on my shoulder. He was so close, the heat of his body drawing out the cold of my skin. His protective embrace stole the strength from my muscles as I released the stiffness of my spine. "Well, it's no honeymoon suite, but I guess it'll do."

My eyes fluttered. After a moment of silence, they shot open when Ryker spoke. "You know, I meant to tell you earlier that you were amazing today. The way you handled those delivery people, the technician, and even Rezith. Your mom was right to choose you as a leader. You're going to do great things and save a lot of people. I'm sure of it."

My cold cheeks heated under the compliment. "Thanks, Ryker."

I hadn't meant to stay there very long, but I felt so comfortable in his arms that I eventually fell asleep. When I woke up, there was sun spilling in through the small window in my cell across the way. Careful not to disturb Ryker, I slithered out of his bed and went back to my room. I hit the shower, ate some breakfast, then went off in search of my mom.

I flexed my fingers, wiggling them as I tried to recreate the silky threads I had shot out of them once before. There was a slight tingle, a numbness, but I couldn't figure out how to activate it. Rezith was right. I'd have to learn how to use my magic all over again, and it wouldn't be easy.

The sound of high heels clicking on the cement floor reached my ears before I saw the womanly figure responsible for them. "Zulli, there you are. Come with me."

This morning, my mom was wearing red pinstripe pants and a crimson rose in her hair to match. The ruffles on the sleeves of her white blouse swayed with her graceful movements as she waved at me to follow. Cole was walking alongside her, his nearly white-blond hair slightly mussed, dark circles under his mismatched eyes. He was tightly clutching a book to his chest.

My mother was lively this morning, as was I. My limbs felt stronger, my muscles more defined, and my movements more agile. I had an overabundance of energy, more than I had ever thought possible, and I was eager to do something with it. Even most of my pain from the lingering injuries seemed to have vanished. Light on my feet, I skipped after her.

To my disappointment, we ended up in the infirmary. It wasn't as hopping as the day I'd first arrived. Most of the patients were just waking up, and the nurses were making their rounds to check in.

"I'm fine, Mom. Better than fine, actually. I don't need to be checked out."

She shook her head at me, the red rose decorating her ponytail showering her with a light dusting of magic. It didn't seem to have any special power other than to provide a pleasant floral scent—a perfume—that constantly drifted around her.

"We're not here for you, Zulli. But I do have to ask. What's with the cat collar?" She gave me the same discerning look I gave to Rezith when he presented it to me.

I began recounting my visit with Adrian, leaving out the whole confusing part about the other man trapped inside him. "He set my magic free then stabilized it, so now I have access to both my shifter powers. But he told me to prepare for new abilities to develop, and the ones I already have are changing. He gave me the cat collar to prevent me from releasing too much magic before I'm ready to control it."

My mom stared at the ground while thoughtfully stroking her chin before glancing over at Cole. "We'll deal with that later. Right now, let's focus on Cole. I have a hunch, but I need to be sure about something. We need to test his magic."

"Magic?" Cole questioned as he sat down on the exam bed. "But I don't have any magic."

A smile slipped across my mom's face. "But I think you do. You've been using it all this time and haven't even known it. If you don't mind me asking, do you remember anything about your parents?"

Cole shook his head.

My mom pulled up a chair and sat next to Cole, resting a comforting hand on the boy's lap. I remained standing beside her. She softened her voice as she spoke. "Your birth parents, Herah and Cohlin Winchell, were lovely people, originally from Iradel. They owned a successful winery that both Zavyr and I frequented often. The magic they infused in their grape vines made the leaves impenetrable to many diseases and gave the fruit a perfect balance of both sweet and tart. Another magiceutical company was trying to acquire the leaves for medical purposes, but Zavyr worried it would make his own business suffer. When your parents refused to sell Zavyr the formula, he burned their entire vineyard to the ground so that no one else could ever use it. I'm sorry, Cole. They did everything they could to save you, but they died in that fire when you were five."

Anger swelled inside my stomach and I clenched my teeth, but Cole's reaction was less subtle. He blinked a few times, clutching the book in his arms just a little bit tighter. "But, if I was five, would I even remember something like that happening?"

"A normal child might remember bits and pieces of it." The lines around her eyes and mouth turned serious. "But your father had the gift of knowledge, while your mother's magic was the gift of memory. I believe you have both powers, Cole. Despite your young age, you would have remembered everything that happened that day and seared it permanently into your memory. Zavyr knew about your parents' abilities, and likely assumed you had inherited them. Just like he saw your parents as a threat to his business, he saw you as one as well."

"He was a five-year-old kid!" I blurted out rather loudly. My outburst received a few scowls from nurses, warning me to keep it down.

"Yes. He was," my mom responded with sincerity as she continued. "I had just gone into hiding, so Zavyr didn't know I was still alive. When I heard about the fire, I went to investigate what happened. Miraculously, Cole was still alive. I made the tough decision to have someone seal away his powers and the memory." Guilt flashed in her green eyes. "I sent you to Earth,

Cole, and I had hoped you'd grow up to live a normal life there. But when Zavyr found out I was still alive, he found out about you, too. I feared for your safety, so I asked my best people to look out for you, but even they struggled against Zavyr's forces and the Black Mark. I'm sorry your childhood was less than ideal, but it was for your own protection. Your body was never found in that fire, and I knew Zavyr wouldn't stop searching for you until he had confirmation that you were dead."

Cole's shoulders sagged and his chin hit his chest. "So, what happens now?"

"You will always have a home here, Cole. We'll do whatever it takes to make sure Zavyr never gets to you." My mother inhaled a deep breath and exhaled with a sigh. "But I would like to remove the seal on your magic, and it won't be pleasant. Years of suppressed knowledge, memories, and emotions will come flooding back to you in the blink of an eye—including the night your parents died. There's no guarantee anything useful will come of it, but you might have suppressed information that could help us get one step ahead of Zavyr. Of course, I would never force you to—"

"I'll do it," Cole stated boldly. "I'd like to honor my parents' sacrifice, and if there's any chance I can be of help, I'll do it."

"You're a brave boy for doing this, Cole. Thank you." My mom stood up from her chair, the metal legs screeching on the floor as she did. She waved over Dr. Fischer. "Can you run a full medical exam on Cole? We need to release his magic, and I want to be certain there won't be any complications with the process."

"Of course. I'll do that right now." Lana immediately got to work, running a handheld scanner across his forehead.

"So, what's next?" I asked my mother.

She cut me a stern look loaded with purpose. "We find a man by the name of Ozcar Thorne."

19

"OH, HELL NO! Ozcar Thorne *cannot* step foot in this building, Mom!" I leaned forward until I was an inch away from her face. "That man is a notorious drug dealer known for his sleazy trans-actions. And now he's trafficking ... I don't even want to know what kind of illegal contraband he's trafficking into the hands of other dangerous criminals. He sold me and Catilda out. If it hadn't been for Brodin ..." My mouth went dry and I swallowed, knowing that, despite saving me, my brother had still tried to erase my memories of what had happened. "If it hadn't been for him, I probably would have been kidnapped and tortured or worse. Maybe even killed. You *can't* bring Ozcar here."

My mother pressed her lips together and, despite her heavy breathing and flaring nostrils, held back her anger. "Zulli, I know who the man is. I know what he's capable of, and I know we'll have to make a deal with him in exchange for his help. But the woman who did this to Cole all those years ago ... we never kept in touch and I have no idea how to reach her. For all I know, she might not even still be alive. We need someone who can do this now and do it quickly. He's the only one who can safely break such a complicated spell."

I tugged on the ends of my hair, threw back my head, and grunted. I had to find Ryker and Catilda. Maybe between the three of us, we could convince my mother to reconsider. Just as I was about to storm off, a shrill cry for attention cut through the stillness of the infirmary. "Help! Someone help her!"

Maycee straggled into the infirmary, struggling to drag a lifeless body across the floor. Two nurses immediately rushed over to her but stood frozen.

"What are you waiting for?" I pushed a nurse out of the way to take in the pile of baggy fabric completely covering a decaying, frail body. My heart dropped to my toes. "Hurry! Get Salynn to a bed!"

A nurse shook her head. "We can't touch her without protecting ourselves first. We need to make sure none of our skin is exposed."

At the sound of the commotion, Lana rushed over to Salynn's side. "Zulli, grab the shirt by her shoulders. I'll grab her shoes. Be *very* careful."

Cautiously, we hoisted her up and brought her over to the nearest bed. Lana snapped on a pair of gloves and grabbed the face shield an assistant brought over. "Who found her? What happened?"

"Me! I did!" Maycee stood off to the side, catching her breath. "I heard a crash in the hallway, went to see what had happened, and found her lying there. She had this in her hand." Maycee placed a vial filled with red liquid on a metal rolling cart next to Lana.

Dr. Fischer began thoroughly examining Salynn. Through all the clothing concealing her body, it was impossible to tell how bad things really were, but I knew it wasn't good. Pieces of her hollow face were peeling off like a snake shedding its skin. It left behind a globby, viscous substance that coated her in a glossy sheen. Slowly, Lana slipped off one of Salynn's gloves to reveal

194

her skeletal hand covered in the same slick substance. She attempted to roll up a sleeve when she pulled back and hissed. "Damn it. The poison is eating through the gloves." She turned around to address whoever was listening. "Someone get me some thicker gloves! *Now!*"

A moment later, an aide returned with a new pair of gloves. Lana inserted a needle into Salynn's arm, injecting some kind of magical potion that snaked through a thin tube and into her body. Salynn was breathing ... but barely.

"It looks like her condition took a turn for the worse." Lana pinched the tip of a syringe into a vein and expelled another liquid. "The IV drip has a mix of magical nutrients and liquids that will help slow the poison, but not for long. At this rate, it will devour her entire body in a matter of hours unless we do something about it."

Salynn twitched, her eyes squeezing tight and teeth grinding. She groaned, gripping a fistful of bedsheet and squeezing through the pain. I could only see what was happening on the outside, but inside, her poison magic was likely eating away at her very muscles and organs. I couldn't even begin to imagine the horrific pain. "Da ... da ... ah ..."

"I can't understand what you're saying, Salynn." My mind raced with hundreds of possibilities of what she might be trying to say, but the panic that clouded my mind wasn't helping me think clearly. "Dead? Do you think you're dying? Because we're not gonna let that happen."

Two other nurses, now decked out in fully protective clothing, swarmed around Salynn's bed. They shoved me to the side and worked, extracting blood, taking swabs of the poison, and placing ice packs over her body to help keep her rising temperature down.

"There's gotta be something I can do. Lana, I ... I can suck out her magic! If I suck out enough, maybe it'll stop the decay!" Lana's mouth opened but she didn't get a chance to respond.

"I won't allow that, Zulli," my mother answered. She was standing a short distance away from Salynn, arms crossed and worry written all over her face. Cole hadn't moved from his spot on the exam bed but watched with an intense gaze as the medical staff worked. "If your magic is changing, you don't know what it'll do to Salynn, or to you. It could end up killing you both. Just let the doctors work."

Salynn's back arched, her arms and legs locking stiff. Her lips puckered and the corners of her mouth twitched. Suddenly, it was like a surge of electricity jolted through her. Her taut muscles became pliant, jerking violently with involuntary movements. The bed started rattling and shaking, the metal pieces clanking together. Salynn slapped a nurse with her ungloved hand, knocking the shield right off her face. Panic flashed across the woman's face. She took a step back, frantically feeling for any possibility of contact. With one fearful look at Salynn, she exclaimed, "I need to go wash myself." In the blink of an eye, she was gone.

"Another dose of Edeprofen," Lana cried out to the nurse next to her. "We need to sedate her before we continue working. We can't have her accidentally touching us in this state."

The male attendant assisting her held a syringe in his hand but couldn't get near Salynn's flailing body. "Dr. Fischer, I can't. She'll knock it right out of my hand before I even get close to her."

"Give me the damn needle, Lero." Lana inhaled a deep breath, and in one swift movement grabbed Salynn's wrist and plunged the needle into her arm. Sweat beaded down Salynn's face, soaking into the thick hoodie. Her eyes were glazed over, dazed and confused. There was a brief moment I glimpsed her awareness returning. She gazed at me, weakly smiling. Then the convulsions resumed.

"Here! Put these in her ears!" Maycee, who I hadn't even realized had left, returned to the infirmary with a pair of earbuds in her hands. "She uses them to calm her magic. Maybe it'll help."

Lana struggled to put the small pieces of plastic into each ear. Pain funneled into my heart as Salynn's miserable shriek sent trepidation screeching along my nerves. I hadn't known Salynn for very long, but I knew she didn't deserve this. There had to be something I could do to help.

Lero stepped back and hunched over, swiping a hand under his face shield to wipe the sweat pouring off his face. Lana lost her footing trying to evade a strike from Salynn, crashing into the rolling medical cart. She shook her head and blinked a few times. She, too, seemed to struggle to stay focused.

A vial filled with red liquid rolled around on the tray as Lana struck it. "Lana, the liquid! Salynn has to drink it."

Dr. Fischer glanced down at the vial before flashing me a disturbing look. "Why? What is it?"

"It's a special magic concoction that will help her get her magic under control … permanently."

Salynn's erratic behavior subsided as the sedative kicked in, but the pain she was experiencing was apparent by the whimpering sobs and tears rolling down her cheeks. The corrosive magic was leaking out of her and growing around her. I couldn't see it, but I could feel its magical heat suffocating the room—a toxic cloud of poisonous magic with a thrum so ominous even I wanted to back away and run. My limbs grew heavy, my strength slowly being sapped out of my body.

My mom stepped up beside me. "I don't like that idea, Zulli. We need time to analyze that magic liquid before we can officially call it a cure and give it to her. But I'm not a medical professional. Dr. Fischer, what do you think?"

Lana hummed to herself before speaking. "She's stabilizing. I think we should hold out as long as we can before trying something so drastic."

It might have looked like she was relaxing, but Salynn wasn't out of the clear yet. How much damage had her magic done to her internally? She had already lost the bottom half of a leg to her own magic. What would be next? Only after Lana had conducted tests would we know how badly it had damaged her vital organs. At that point, it might be too late. The magic potion could only stop more damage from happening, not revert what was already there. Something had to be done, and it had to be done now. Waiting wasn't an option.

Lana and the other nurses took a moment to breathe, sitting down to catch their strength. Even though they hadn't actually touched her skin, Salynn's magic was clearly affecting them. If they couldn't contain her magic soon, they might suffer the same poisonous fate as Salynn. My mom gave me a warning glance, like she knew exactly what I was about to do.

"Zulli ..." My mom reached out to grab my arm, but I was too quick. I swiped the vial on the tray, popped it open, and leaned over Salynn's deteriorating body. "Zulli, don't!"

"Drink it," I told her. She blinked her acceptance, lucid enough to know what I was offering. I tipped the vial to her lips and she swallowed down every last drop.

My mom's fierce green eyes gleamed with anger. She clenched her fist like she was holding back from slapping me across the face.

"Mom, you told me I'd make a great leader because I trust my gut and stray from the rules. My gut tells me this is going to work. Plus, it's Salynn's choice to make. Not yours."

Lana jumped from her chair as a monitor started angrily beeping. Salynn gasped, no air reaching her lungs. "She's crashing. Get more ice packs!" Dr. Fischer commanded Lero. "We need to get her temperature down."

The feeling was still fresh in my memory. When I had taken the medicine myself, the discomfort had been unbearable, like there was lava boiling through my veins. My mind had shut down, the world still spinning around me when I collapsed. But Salynn didn't have two types of magic battling for her body, nor did she have Rezith to help walk her through stabilizing it. But she had been training her whole life to keep the poison under control. She was tough, and I knew she'd pull through.

Lero dumped a bunch of ice packs around Salynn. Lana kept her eyes glued to the monitor, the beeping turning into a more mild warning until eventually all the red numbers turned green. She let out a sigh of relief. "I think Zulli lucked out with this one. Look, Salynn's vitals are stabilizing." She pointed a finger to a number slowly declining. Salynn's temperature was returning to normal, her racing heartbeat steadying. "I'll give her some pain medication to get through the next day or two while her body heals. The earbuds should also stay in her ears in case she has another episode."

Lana and her team conducted a few more tests on Salynn before they deemed her out of the danger zone.

"Is she going to be okay? Did it work?" Cole, having kept his distance and staying quiet throughout the entire ordeal, joined me by Salynn's side.

Lana pushed her glasses up her nose and tucked a loose strand of her auburn hair behind her ear. "Everything is looking good right now. I'll run a test on her current level of magic and compare it to her previous records over the years. It's too early to say for certain if it's a cure, but these magic readings on the monitor? It certainly looks like something changed."

A dark shadow loomed over me as my mom approached. "That was utterly irresponsible of you, kiddo. But ... I know why you did it. Had that been you on the table, I wouldn't have hesitated like I did with Salynn. Just remember that your actions can cause undesired consequences. If that antidote hadn't worked ..."

The alarming truth of her words twisted my stomach into knots. I knew what message she was trying to convey. She had tried to do the right thing by exposing my father and it had ended up costing her family and nearly her life. One day, my luck might run out too. It was important to take risks, but she was warning me to calculate which were worth taking before acting on them.

My mother left to go about her daily business, while Lana and her team turned their attention to other patients. The noxious cloud of magic that Salynn was giving off dissipated after a few hours and, while I didn't want to speak too soon, the color was coming back to her ghostly face. The healing ointment slathered all over her body would take some time to regenerate the blistering skin. Lana kept the IV stuck in her arm to dispense a magical cocktail of pain medications, nutrients, and antibiotics to help speed up her healing.

Cole stayed with me for a while until Catilda swooped in and they left for another visit to the library. She was teaching him all about the magic of our world, and the curious bookworm would take any opportunity to learn about everything he could.

Salynn was still sleeping when Ryker and Kasra came to visit. Ryker handed me a hamburger and a strawberry milkshake. "I was eating lunch with Maycee when she told me what had happened—she said you haven't left the infirmary since this morning. I figured you might want something to eat, so I asked the kitchen to whip up something special."

"Thanks." I wrapped my fingers around the cold cup and sucked down a long slurp of milkshake. I was starving, but it wasn't because of an empty stomach. A nervous energy buzzed through my chest. Each second sitting by Salynn's bed felt like hours, each minute like days. I anxiously waited for her to wake up and give me the final verdict of whether the potion had worked. After Kasra had received her daily check up, both she and Ryker stayed with me a little bit longer until they, too, headed out.

Without windows in the infirmary, it wasn't easy to tell how much time had passed. It wasn't until I heard one nurse say they were heading to bed that I realized how late it was.

Lana handed me a cup of water tinted a faint pink. "You look like crap, Zulli. Drink this. I added some vitamins and other nutrients to the water for you." She placed a delicate hand on my shoulder. "Salynn won't wake up for a while. She needs her rest, and so do you. Go to your own bed and get some sleep. A team is always on call and nearby, so if anything happens, we'll tend to her immediately. If she wakes up, you'll be the first person we call. I promise."

I sipped down the water, a light fruity flavor tickling my taste buds. It tingled my insides, the warmth inviting and refreshing. I watched as Salynn's chest gently rose and fell with each breath, her long black hair fanned out like a blanket underneath her. She had been that way for hours, with no change either good or bad. I had wanted to be there when she woke up so that the first thing she saw was a friendly face, but I knew I wouldn't be able to stay up the entire night. I had been sitting in this uncomfortable plastic chair for nearly twelve hours, and it was time to lie down.

"If *anything* happens, if she so much as sneezes, have someone wake me up immediately."

A small grin stole across Lana's tired face. I pushed out the chair from under me and headed to bed. My mother had stopped by earlier to bring me a snack and to inform me that Catilda's parents had reached Ozcar. They'd agreed to meet tomorrow.

Could Ozcar really help Cole? I believed he could, but what would it end up costing us? My mom had told me to trust my gut, and my instincts told me never to trust Ozcar. Tomorrow was another day, and I needed to save my strength in case he doubled-crossed me and my friends for a second time.

20

---◈---

THE WALK BACK to my jail cell was lonely and dismal. Since I had arrived at the prison, more of the cells had been filled with victims of Bliss. Some cells that had been previously occupied were now empty. I stopped to peer through the bars of Cullin Maddox's cell only to realize that no one was in it. Fresh sheets had been placed on the cot, a folded blanket and pillow placed at the foot of the bed. The only sign that anyone had once slept in the stuffy box was the lingering smell of his skunky cologne. My stomach churned and an agonizing sadness gripped my chest.

"Good night, Cullin," I whispered into the silence. His mind had lost the battle with Bliss. I hoped he could finally rest in peace.

The cold, damp draft in my own jail cell sent goosebumps racing up my arms and down my neck. I wrapped the blanket tightly around myself and felt my eyelids grow heavy. Whatever Lana had given me, I suspected there was something in it that would knock me out and put me to sleep. I yawned, letting out a long breath of air as I did. Worried thoughts about Salynn swirled around in my mind, along with a nervous fear of what might happen when Ozcar came to visit. I hadn't seen Reeva or

Liahm since I'd leaped off the building to save Kasra. Were they still looking for me? A shudder ran down my spine. I hadn't been back to my apartment or the military base since it had happened. It wouldn't have taken much for my father to figure out that it had been my mother who'd rescued me and taken me in.

Sleep claimed my anguished soul, and for the first time in a while, I woke up completely recharged and ready to tackle the day. Part of it must have been the sedative that Lana gave me, but the other part was because of my newfound magic. It coursed through me like a fiery river, devouring weakness and replacing it with an eager heat bursting with vitality.

The first thing I did was race to the infirmary to check on Salynn. As Dr. Fischer had suggested, my friend had slept clear through the night and hadn't yet woken up. One nurse informed me that her vitals were strong and the poison hadn't had enough time to do much internal damage. She would be just fine once she regained her strength.

I stayed with her for a while, but my magic was itching to let itself out of its cage. Changing into a pair of workout pants and a tank top, I decided it was time to test my new limits in the gym.

The musty odor of testosterone wafted through the atmosphere. As soon as I stepped through the door, five macho men glistening in sweat started showing off in front me. There was a floor fan pushed up against the wall, and when the breeze stirred in my direction I could pick up their scent of manliness and arrogance.

Their dramatic grunts mixed in with the loud clanking of metal failed to impress me. I rolled my eyes and found an unoccupied space as far away from them as I could get. The shabby workout bench just happened to be right next to my mother running on a squeaky treadmill. She may have had a lot of connections when it came to state-of-the-art medical technology, but she had clearly never made friends in the fitness space.

She slowed down and grabbed the towel off the railing. For a fifty-something year old woman, she was in fantastic shape. Cat shifters often lent themselves to lean bodies, but my mother was naturally athletic. The definition of her muscles was on clear display thanks to her crop top and tight pants.

"Good morning, kiddo! Glad you could join me." My mom hopped off the treadmill.

"You were expecting me?" I eyed the bench as a challenge, wondering how much I could press with my new level of strength.

"No, but I had a feeling you'd show up here. We need to do some training. Have you been able to fully shift into a cat yet?"

I shook my head. "I haven't exactly had enough free time to even try."

"How about forming ears and a tail?" She swiped her sweaty ponytail off her neck.

"Nope."

"So what *can* you do, kiddo?"

I sat down on the bench and flexed my fingers. "My senses have gone into overdrive to the point that sometimes normal smells make my stomach churn. My strength has also increased, but I'm having trouble controlling it. I was trying to shoot spider webs out of my fingertips. It happened accidentally once, but while I can sort of feel the magic, I can't get it to release on command."

"Because you aren't letting it. Follow me." I followed her to a practice mat at the far end of the gym. "I can't teach you much about being a spider shifter, but I can help you through everything I learned about shifting into a cat and the powers I possess. What were you able to do before?"

"Um, well, I have claws. I always relied heavily on my senses. I can smell magic, and if I really focus, I can hear it and feel its vibrations. I'm pretty quick on my feet, and I can heal minor wounds by licking them with my tongue."

My mom made a sour face. "Yeah, that's a gross one, but it *does* sometimes come in handy. For me, my skills lie in agility, and I bet yours do too. I have exceptional balance. I'm swift and, combined with my senses, I can usually predict my opponent's movements before they happen." She closed her eyes and inhaled a deep breath. "Try to hit me."

"What? Why—" She slapped me across the face, her eyes never opening. "*Ouch.* What was that for?"

"You think your father or anyone he sends after us will hold back? You shouldn't either. Don't try to kill me or anything, just try to land a hit."

I heard a whistle from one of the gym rats. "Hey guys, check it out. A real life cat fight! My vote's on Tabby."

Frustration coiled inside me, my magic seeping out of my pores. It was an all too familiar feeling reminding me of Captain Myra Llama making a fool of me back at the military base.

The sounds of multiple heartbeats pulsed in my ears. The air shifted around me, delicately brushing my skin from all directions. I staggered slightly, the disorientation blurring my vision.

Focus. One single heartbeat remained—my mother's. Her eyes were shut. Her breath was steady, but quick. The smell of her magic was like fresh lemonade and tulips, and it mingled in the air as she tightened her ponytail. She shifted slightly on one foot, the vibration dampened by the mat.

I pressed my lips together and lunged. Without opening her eyes, my mother snatched my swinging wrist and redirected it. The whooshing sound carried past my ears and made them pop. She twisted my arm behind me, the heel of her palm digging into my back. With a firm press into my spine, I lost my footing and dropped to my knees onto the padded mat.

She let go and backed away. "Don't just dive blindly into a fight. Work *with* your magic, not against it."

The heat of my magic rose to the surface and the cat collar around my neck seemed to burn against my skin. I rubbed my clogged ears, trying to clear the muffled hearing. My magic wanted to be set free, but the more I let out, the less control I had over it. Sounds became deafening, vibrations like earthquakes rippling through my bones. If I unleashed it before I was ready, I'd likely harm either myself or someone else.

I counted to three and exhaled deep breaths to calm my frustration. Rising to my feet, I assumed a crouched position with my hands raised in front of me. I didn't unleash my claws, but my fingers curled as if they might be there. My military training took over, my muscles acting on memory.

I threw a right hook at my mother's jaw. Eyes still shut, she stepped back and guided my hand past her shoulder. With her other hand, she chopped me in the side. A subtle pain erupted on impact, but nothing that injured me.

She pushed two palms into my chest, knocking me off balance. A flash of pain rippled up my forearm as I blocked her punch. It created an opening, and I slashed my hand like a knife toward her neck. Her head snapped to the side, but she rebounded quickly. Taking hold of my elbow, she thrust it upward, spun me around, and locked it behind me. The pressure of her weight sunk right into a tender joint. Anger, more than anything, seethed through my teeth. She wasn't trying to harm me, just subdue me. This might be a fun exercise for her, but all I felt was humiliation.

Strength swelled inside my core. I lurched forward, carrying her weight with me. She rolled across my back, landing perfectly on her feet. My foot immediately shot up. In an extreme show of her dexterity, she back-flipped to avoid a kick to the gut. Her own leg swung up as her body arched, my arms crossing in front of me to parry her attack.

My movements quickened, my limbs feather light. One punch after another, I evaded my mother's attacks—ducking, dodging, retaliating. Currents of air rushed by my face, the vibration of her magic laced within it. My hands smacked away hers, my legs firm and strong with each kick.

"That's it, kiddo! You're finally getting the hang of it."

A few cheers came from the sidelines, the small crowd driving us on.

206

Evading my jab, my mother ducked and dropped to the ground. With a sweep of her leg, she took out my ankles. Before I knew it, she was on top of me, pinning my arms to my chest. My lungs struggled to take in air, my ribs crushing under her weight. Unleashing my strength, I shoved her back but didn't let go. I tucked in my feet and pressed them firmly against her chest. Rolling on my back, I kept a firm grip on her wrists and launched her right over my head.

Her back slammed against the mat, the air wheezing out of her lungs. Scrambling to my knees, I laced my two hands together and raised them high. They plunged down toward her head like a hammer hitting a nail. Her eyes widened and her mouth dropped open. With a few centimeters to spare, she rolled sideways. My fist punched right through the padding and ripped it wide open. The floor shook upon impact. My hand went right through to reach the rubber flooring underneath.

The cheers from the crowd of onlookers abruptly stopped. Horror churned inside my gut. Had my mom not moved in time, I would have pulverized her skull.

With both hands on one knee, she kneeled and pushed herself up. "I said *don't* try to kill me, Zulli."

"I ... I ... I'm sorry." I took a step back from her. My whole body was trembling.

A bright smile crept across my mother's face, one of her cheeks red from where I had landed a nasty hit. "Don't be sorry for your power, Zulli. You have two very ferocious animals within you. Cats have stealth, and spiders, despite their small size, have strength. Learn to combine them and you'll be unstoppable. Come on, kiddo. Let's call it for today. Ozcar should be here around lunchtime."

On my way out, I glowered at the five show-offs and smirked. "Mess with me or my friends and you'll have to deal with *that*." I nodded toward the gaping hole in the mat. Without saying a word, they dropped their chins and resumed their workouts—

this time without all the grunting and desperate need for attention.

21

CATILDA'S PARENTS HAD left early in the morning to meet up with Ozcar. For the next few hours, until they arrived back at the prison, I anxiously paced around the hallways and found myself in the lab waiting for their return. My stomach boiled, twisting in a tangle of knots. Cole was with me, poking around and asking question after question about all the fancy magical equipment he had never seen before. Kasra was leaning against a stool, her crutches resting against a counter, and Ryker stood guard by the doorway. He switched between kneading his palms with his fingertips and rubbing the heel of his hand against his forehead.

My belt was replenished with magical bullets, several paralysis daggers strapped to my thigh. Although I didn't typically use guns, I opted for a pistol filled with stun bullets to immobilize anyone who got in my way. Under my purple flannel was a white t-shirt, the threads of fabric spelled with magic to soften both physical and magical attacks. The expensive piece of clothing wasn't something I could afford myself, but my mother seemed to have a stockpile of them lying around in a storage closet.

"I'm not sure you have enough weapons. You should strap the grenade launcher across your back. Just in case, you know, a stampede of elephants attacks us," Kasra teased. Her playful smile dropped off her pretty face as I glared at her.

"You weren't there the first time, Kasra. Ozcar was helpful, sure, but he plays his own game. When we raided that bakery for the magic spatula, he abandoned everyone there, even his girlfriend, to save himself. When Catilda and I met with him, he saw the opportunity to sell us out to the highest bidder. Gangs and other criminal organizations tried to kidnap me, hoping to bargain my life in exchange for my dad supplying confidential information from NightFly Technologies. Ozcar might be able to help Cole, but I worry about what it might cost us."

"That's understandable, Zulli." My mom wandered into the lab, her lilac-tipped hair pulled back into a messy bun. A single button closed the black blazer across her chest, and peeking out from under it was a silky floral top. "But Catilda and her parents have dealt with Ozcar for years. They know how to negotiate with him, and I trust they'll make this work out for everyone."

Magic roiled inside me. If I was to accidentally unleash too much during a fight, I hoped it would be directed right at Ozcar. My ears twitched and my spine straightened. I could hear heavy footsteps approaching, accompanied by several voices. "He's here."

Ryker peered up and down the hallway. "He is?"

I focused my enhanced hearing to pick up on their conversation. The sound waves came from the right side of the hallway, bouncing off the walls as they traveled in my direction. The voices generated a slight ringing in my ears, and although I was struggling to pinpoint their location, it sounded like they were somewhere close by. "I can hear his annoying rambling. He just told Catilda that he's surprised she made it out of the skating rink alive, but *so* happy to see she's okay." I rolled my eyes.

Ryker's head twisted to the right and his gaze traveled down the hallway. "There they are. They're coming."

I stood firmly, directly next to Cole. Ozcar didn't know about my recent magical upgrade, and if he so much as blinked at Cole the wrong way I'd be on him faster than a mouse trap snapping a rodent's neck.

"I'd just like to tell you, Mrs. Harper, that I am *honored* you have recognized my exceptional skills to help you with this project!" Ozcar's voice drifted in from the hallway, his pretentious tone full of candy-coated fluff.

Catilda's mom snorted. "Don't flatter yourself, Mr. Thorne. You were our only option on such short notice. I am trusting you will remain professional throughout this partnership?"

"Why of course—Zulli! What a surprise to see you again!" He pushed Ryker aside as he entered the lab. His ball cap and thin, wiry goatee shadowed the devious expression he slipped across his face. "I never properly thanked you for keeping your end of our bargain. That magical spatula has improved my business tenfold, and it's all thanks to you!"

"Quit the chit-chat, Ozcar. Get this over with and get out of here. I never want to see you again." I crossed my arms and leaned on one foot.

"Charming as always, I see. You know, you mentioned the last time we met that you never wanted to see me again, and I distinctly remember confirming that you would." He threw up his hands. "And now, here I am! It's always a pleasure doing business with you and your family, Zulli."

My mouth went dry and I swallowed a lump in my throat. Nervous prickles shot down my spine. What other business had he conducted with my family? Was he referring to my mom or my father?

Ozcar began strolling around the lab, taking in all the finery of his surroundings. Peeking out from under his zipped up jacket, he had the collar of his green polo upturned, hiding his neck and framing his round face. Suspicion rang through me, wondering if he was planning to steal something or if he'd come prepared, concealing something alongside that gut of his.

"What a lovely place, Ms. Taracula. Or is it still Mrs.?" Ozcar's sly voice and the way he was acting so casually made my skin crawl.

"Just call me Tabatha." She held out her hand for a greeting, smiling politely as Ozcar took it. I couldn't tell if it was genuine or if she was seething underneath like I was.

Ignoring both Kasra and Ryker, Ozcar went straight for Cole. "And this must be the boy in question. May I?" He held up his hands toward Cole's face. Cole glanced over to me and I gave him a wary nod of approval.

"My, what a strong spell we have here. The woman who did this was very talented. There are many types of skills and potions out there that can suppress magic. Zulli is very familiar with my own handiwork." The corner of his mouth twisted upward in a smirk, and I wanted to rip that goatee right off his face. "But I have never seen one last for such a long time. In most instances, they wear off in a few hours, a couple weeks if you're lucky. But years? Unbelievable."

"So, can you use your crazy voodoo magic to break the spell or not?" Impatience shivered through me. Ozcar tilted his head up at me, removing his hat to scrub a hand through his messy brown hair. A mischievous determination was set in his hazel eyes.

"My magic can only break down the composition of spells, but I can't actually *break* the spell. I can only offer you a solution to what might counteract it. However ..." He slipped his hand down the front of his jacket and I whipped out my gun.

"Relax, Zulli. I believe this should look familiar to you, no?" He revealed a baking utensil in his hand. The purple scraper was just how I remembered it.

No one spoke a word, but Catilda stifled a gasp. Kasra nearly fell off her stool, holding a crutch in her hand as a weapon, and Ryker tightened a fist. The smell of his cinnamon magic drifted across the lab.

"What do you plan on doing with that magic spatula?" I kept my gun aimed at his temple.

Ozcar waved the spatula in the air like a magic wand, its shiny silver handle glinting in the overhead light. "Once I know how the original spell works, I can use the magic spatula to mix the perfect antidote that will break it down completely, freeing Cole's magic. Simple as that."

"And what do you want in exchange for this?" My mother knew this was going to cost her. Without even knowing what Ozcar wanted in return, the anger etched in her voice made it very clear that she knew she wouldn't like it.

Ozcar slipped out a piece of paper from his jacket pocket and handed it to her. With each blink of her eyelids, the green of my mother's eyes grew more livid.

"Absolutely not," she scoffed, crumpling the paper in her hand. "What you're asking for is enough magical liquids and powders to build a deadly bomb full of toxic poison large enough to decimate an entire continent."

Ozcar shrugged. "That is my price. Agree to it and I can have this boy's magic restored by nightfall."

My mother and Catilda's parents stepped out into the hallway for a discussion. I kept my weapon pointed directed at Ozcar, watching as he examined Cole like he was a precious jewel. Fascination crept along his thin smile and skepticism raised his eyebrows. He attempted to grasp Cole's head in between his meaty fingers to continue assessing him, and I grinned proudly when Cole slapped him away.

My mother re-entered the room and spoke in a confident voice. "We agree to your price on one condition. Inform us who you plan on selling this to and what they intend to use it for. We know the nature of your business, and we're not about to hand over something so powerful that could start a war between nations, killing hundreds of thousands of innocent people."

A low chuckle came from Ozcar. "Well, under normal circumstances, I would tell you I can't because I value my clients' confidentiality. However, because this is for personal use, I will let you know I do not plan on selling these assets to anyone you consider a threat, nor will I go about using them to start a war between nations. Unfortunately, if I let you know what I am planning, you'll try to meddle with my affairs and stop me, so that's as much information as I am willing to provide."

My mom gave a hard glance to both Harpers standing beside her. They knew that was as much as they'd get out of Ozcar, and they'd have to trust that they wouldn't regret making this deal with him.

The three of them shook on it, and Ozcar got to work, continuing to examine Cole while scribbling something down on a piece of paper. "Here is a list of what's needed to release the spell."

Catilda's mom removed a clunky machine from a shelf. She struggled to carry the bulky object across the room, tripping over dangling wires as she did. With a loud clatter, she released it on the counter next to Ozcar and Cole, then plugged it into the wall.

"What does that do?" Cole asked. Ozcar reached for the applicator, a small plastic handle with a metal ball attached to the end. A thin coiled wire connected it to the machine which was about the size of a computer printer. A loud buzzing noise grated in my ears as he turned it on, pressing a few buttons to program the correct settings.

"Does it matter what it does?" Ozcar scoffed.

My mother interjected. "This is what we call a Mindray Imager. Ozcar will use the applicator in his hand to roll the little ball around your forehead. As he does, a magical pulse emanates from it. This pulse will relax the tense threads of magic that have created the spell so we can more easily break it down and get rid of it."

The second Ozcar touched Cole with the contraption, the teen flinched. "It shocked me!" he exclaimed.

214

I trained my gun on the back of Ozcar's head. My finger was itching to pull the trigger. He didn't seem threatened by my actions when he turned around and rolled his eyes. "I can't help what the machine does, Zulli. The magic gives off a static charge. The boy has to deal with it."

Cole squirmed on the stool while Ozcar continually yelled at him to sit still. Five minutes later, the process was complete.

"Now, what about the rest of the items on the list?" Ozcar stood up straight and proud, but his belly jiggled as he did. He was still wearing his jacket, his hands tucked into the front pockets.

"I have already sent for Karise. She's our best and strongest empath and will keep Cole relaxed, allowing him to open up to his new magic as we release the spell. She'll also be able to help him call upon his memories. But we don't have any of this other stuff," my mom informed him.

"What do you mean, you don't have any of it? You're running a high-class facility here. There's an endless supply of magical medications and other supplies in this very room, yet you conveniently don't have what I need?" Ozcar's eyes narrowed under the shadow of his hat, his tone threatening. "If this is some kind of trick ..."

My mom raised a firm hand. "I assure you it isn't. We have a lot of different medicines here, but the items you're asking for on this list are plants and herbs. Everything we have here was manufactured in a lab."

"Synthetic magic won't work," Ozcar scoffed. "It'll be too much of a strain on someone who's unfamiliar with their own magic. It needs to be something natural." Ozcar dipped his chin toward Catilda and she shot her gaze in the opposite direction. "Yes! Yes, I know what you're thinking, Catilda. That glitzy shop owner friend of yours on Grestor Island. The one with the sandals and tie-dyed shirts. He was a master with plants. I bet you he has what we need."

I ran my fingers through my hair. "Yeah, but after you destroyed the Bliss antidote Bailee was working on and obliterated his work area, I'm pretty sure he won't welcome you back with open arms."

"That *antidote* had enough Crowroot in it to kill someone. I was doing him a favor." Ozcar huffed, his lips pressed so tightly together they turned white.

Tension descended upon the room. Eventually, Ozcar raised his voice. "Well? Time is of the essence here. You have agreed to this deal, *Tabatha*. It wasn't very smart of you to bring me here to your hideout. The second I arrived, I broke down all of your security measures. I would hate for this information to fall into the wrong hands. I'm fairly certain I could retrieve a good fortune for selling it to a certain *someone* who would absolutely love to have it."

"Fine." My mother closed her eyes and exhaled a deep sigh. "We'll go see Bailee."

A darling old woman entered the lab, using a cane for balance and dragging her loafers on the floor as she shuffled in. Age had swallowed her youthful spirit. Her long white hair was thin and frizzy, tied back to reveal her dull eyes. She looked like the type of person who had experienced life and had come out stronger because of it. The crows feet around her eyes warned of constant worry, but the lines around her mouth spoke of happiness. Each wrinkle on her face was an emotional scar, now a sign of her overwhelming knowledge and wisdom.

Despite this, she gave off a glowing radiance with her soothing voice and sweet smile. "You called for me, Ms. Taracula? Can I assist with something?"

"Yes, Karise. We're going to break the spell that's suppressing Cole's magic and we need your empathic abilities to keep him relaxed during the process. He may also need your guidance to bring forth specific memories."

"It would be my pleasure, Ms. Taracula." She gave her a slight bow.

"Can this old hag handle what we're about to do?" Ozcar assessed the old woman from head to toe. "This is a pretty violent spell. We need someone powerful—"

Karise whipped out her cane and smacked Ozcar across the back of his knees. "Powerful enough for you?" She beamed him a delightful smile. I bit my lip, stifling a laugh.

Ozcar muttered a few choice words under his breath, rubbing the discomfort from his legs.

"All right. Catilda, can you give your friend a call and let him know we're stopping by? The Harpers and Kasra will stay here and hold down the fort. The rest of us will be back as soon as we can." My mother held out her hands as if to haul everyone in toward her. "Ryker, can you take us to Bailee's shop?"

"Of course." He flipped through some pictures on his phone and studied one for a moment. The smell of his cinnamon magic helped release some of the tension that had set me on edge. A nervous swarm of bees still buzzed around my stomach, but I focused on the potential positive outcome. If this succeeded, we Cole's memories would offer us valuable information that would put us one step ahead of my dad.

The spark of hope snuffed out when the electricity cut off and the lab went dark. All the cat shifters in the room trained their attention on the door. It was quite a distance from where I was standing, but the glass shattering and raging screams that rang through my head sounded as if it was happening directly in front of me.

22

---◈---

"WELL, THIS IS unfortunate," Ozcar huffed, more bored than alarmed at the fact someone had just infiltrated the prison. Almost as if ...

"You told him where we were!" I hollered at Ozcar.

"Told who? Your father? Now, why would I do that while I was still here in the building with you? *How* could I have done it? I didn't even know where we were going until we got here. Did anyone bother to check if we were being followed?"

Catilda's parents averted their gaze from Ozcar and looked at each other with shameful eyes.

The tortuous sounds grew louder, my senses amplifying every movement. My whole body shuddered as the panic flared inside me. Anguished screams filled my ears, their piercing cries making my eardrums throb. Intense vibrations rumbled at my feet as bodies slammed against the wall. I could hear it all, feel their very fear riding through my bones. I slapped my hands to my ears, wishing I could block it out.

A dangerous male voice called out to me—stern, commanding, and eager for control. Shivers of apprehension worked up my spine as my father spoke. "I'm coming for you."

The buzz of magical energy was heavy in the air, the strong, metallic stench of blood making me gag. Maycee. I could hear Maycee calming down a small child wailing for her parents. A lover's painful cry pleading for someone to aid her injured husband. Fear gripped at my throat and I clenched my eyes shut. This was all my father's doing.

"Zulli, it's okay." Ryker wrapped his arms around me and guided me to a stool.

"Make it stop! Make *him* stop!" The world was lost around me. My palms crushed into my skull. The voices were deafening, exploding inside my head. I begged for obedience from my magic, but I lacked the mastery to control it.

"Out of my way!" The command, much closer than before, was followed by the sickening crack of bone. Tears slipped down my cheeks.

Pressure built up behind my eyes, the pain gnawing away at my very sanity. My heartbeat raced uncontrollably, my fingertips pounding as the blood rushed through my body. Power continued to build, pulling up from my roots, bubbling and turbulent. Confusion, fear, and anger were warring for control over me. My senses throttled into overdrive.

"Zulli." I reluctantly opened my eyes. Karise hobbled over in front of me, using her cane for balance. She placed a hand on my arm. "*You* are in control, child. Not your magic. Focus only on what *you* want to focus on. Right now, I need that to be me. Push everything out and focus on me."

There was something enchanting about her aged voice. Her peaceful, harmonious tone was uplifting and soothing to my soul. Warmth emanated from her hand, a tingle of her serene magic caressing my insides and relaxing me. My shoulders relaxed and my breathing steadied. A feeling of calmness was instilled within me as Karise forced her own emotions to take over mine. "That's it, child. Take back control."

My pulse slowed, and as my lungs filled with air, I exhaled the hysteria with it. The sudden attack had caught me off guard.

So many people needed my help, and all I could do was cower. I tugged on the snug cat collar burning my neck. So much for holding back my power. Or if it was, how much was it still suppressing?

"Zulli, look at me." Sincerity was etched in my mother's eyes and urgency in her tone. "I know this is tough for you, but right now we have a problem to deal with. We need to get out of here with Cole."

"What? And just leave everyone here to fend for themselves? I promised I would help them!" I jumped to my feet a little too fast, the world momentarily spinning around me.

Ozcar butted into our conversation. "If I might add, the MindRay machine only temporarily relaxes magic. Once it wears off, it will be much more difficult to get the same effects a second time. We will have to amplify the magic power, and the more magic we pump into Cole's delicate brain ... Well, I'll let you figure that one out."

"Zulli," my mom placed a firm hand on each of my shoulders. "We have protocols in place for this. Everyone here knew an attack was a genuine possibility and they've all prepared for it. Trust in them to do their job and they'll trust you to do yours. You felt the vibrations, heard the warning in his voice, right?"

I nodded.

"Then you know your father is here for Cole. For us. The best course of action is to get out of here now, with Cole, and hope he'll come after us instead. So let's go."

"And where are you off to so soon? I just arrived here." A figure loomed in the doorway, a cunning smile on his face and darkness in his silver eyes. The entire room fell silent. My heart stopped beating, my stomach writhing with pure nervous energy.

Light blanketed the room as a soft glow overflowed from Reeva, wearing some kind of impractical skin tight catsuit and heels. Shadows danced across her glamorous face and she showered me with a conceited grin. Five leather-clad men filed into the lab, black crosshair tattoos visible on their exposed skin.

"I thought you said the Black Mark was rebelling *against* Dad," I muttered to my mom.

"Most are," she replied softly back to me, "but the ones under his control with Bliss are a different story."

I surveyed the room, trying to sniff out the scent of any hidden magic or feel for others concealing themselves in the shadows. I didn't sense Liahm, but that didn't mean he wasn't somewhere nearby.

My mother approached our unwanted visitor. "Zavyr. How did you find us?"

My father brushed a hand down his suit vest and smoothed an out-of-place lock gray of hair on top of his head. He scoffed when he noticed a crimson streak of liquid that had blemished his white dress shirt. The stain continued to blossom, the blood coming from a small but deep wound on his arm. He casually strolled over to a shelf on the far side of the lab and selected a tube of healing gel.

He spoke as if having a friendly conversation, although there was nothing kind about his words. "You have been sloppy, Tabatha. You may have deceived me all these years, but Davian was your undoing. You thought you were using him to spy on me? Well, I can play that game too. I drugged him with a low dose of Bliss and had him do my bidding. Don't blame him, though. The poor pawn didn't even realize what he was doing, couldn't remember a thing. He may have been feeding you information about me, but he was also spying on *you*."

Ozcar shot me a prideful "*I told you so*" look.

Ryker and I stepped in front of Cole. Longer, sharper claws than I had ever seen before shot out of my fingertips. Ryker winced, shaking his head to clear whatever had distracted him, then readied his knife in his hand.

"Zulli, my little spider, can't we all just have a civilized family conversation? I had wanted the boy dead, but it seems your reluctance to obey orders may have paid off for me. I heard enough of the conversation earlier to know that it sounds like

Colton might have some helpful information. So, what are we waiting for? Where are we going?"

"*We* are not going anywhere. Especially with Cole," I spat at my father.

"Like you have a choice, my little spider. Let's compromise. I will hold off on killing him. Let's find out what information he's hoarding in that genius brain of his. If it's nothing, I'll leave. No questions asked. But if it's something I could use, then the boy comes with me. I'll need to experiment on him. He might live or he might die. That all depends on how willing he is to cooperate with me."

"That's hardly a compromise." My gaze hardened, but my father's expression was unrelenting. I knew he'd never let us walk free, whether or not we agreed to his offer.

"Fine. Let's make this quick, Zavyr." My mother grabbed a few things and shoved them into a bag. "We've already started the process and time isn't on our side."

My jaw dropped open. I wanted to refute, but the unamused tone in her voice offered no room for negotiation. What was she thinking? Did she have a plan?

Ozcar, Cole, Karise, my parents, and I gathered together, but my father pushed out his hand when Ryker tried to join. "He will not be coming with us."

My mother frowned, exhaling loudly. "We can't do the procedure here. We need someone to transport us to Bailee's shop. Ryker can take us there."

Ryker squeezed his eyes shut and slid his hand through his hair, failing to hide the pain of his headache. A light sheen glistened from his forehead.

"Rusl will take us. I know how crafty this boy and my daughter can be. I don't want them trying anything. Besides ..." My father tilted his head to assess Ryker and the corners of his mouth pinched upward into a smirk. His eyes burned with something deep and cleverly amusing. "I can tell he's in no condition to be of any assistance to anyone. It's best if he stays out of our way."

Ryker wobbled slightly on his feet, choosing to lean against the counter for support. "You're not going without me. I promised to protect Zulli and I will do everything in my power to keep that promise."

My father snorted. "You're still rambling on about that? Maybe one day you'll remember why you spied on my daughter for me, but for your own sanity, I hope you don't."

"Ryker." I pulled him in for a hug and whispered in his ear. "We'll be fine. Protect Salynn and ... Maycee needs your help. Go find her."

Annoyance twitched in his muscles, but he knew what had to be done.

"Rusl. Please come in here," my father called out. My father's own personal transporter, an older man with wispy white hair combed to the side, flowed through the door like a silent ghost. He clasped his white-gloved hands in front of him and stood tall, waiting for orders.

"Do you remember that barn I sent you to a while back? When I asked you to bring Zulli and her dying friend to me?"

The transporter nodded.

"We need to go back there. All of us."

"Of course, sir. But I don't have a strong connection to that place, and with this many people—"

"I know," my father cut him off. "Deal with it." He glanced over to Reeva and commanded, "Stay here and monitor things. Find everyone in this building and lock them in the prison cells. Cut off their magic if you can, and make sure the fools don't follow. If anyone rebels, I give you permission to burn the place to the ground, along with everyone in it."

Light in Reeva's eyes covered the madness I knew lurked in the depths of her soul. "Of course, sir. With pleasure."

My father turned his attention to me and my mother. "I am taking everyone in this building as hostages. No harm will come to them unless you break our deal. Try to escape with the boy or feed me lies about what he knows and everyone will pay dearly for it."

Unease clenched my stomach, and I felt nauseous. I was hit full force by the cold reality of my father's words. *Burn the place to the ground, along with everyone in it.* When had he become so ruthless, so detached from the world that he would be so cruel? How far would he go to gain power and protect his business?

Rusl's earthy magic warmed a pocket of air around me but struggled to attach to all six of us traveling with him. I wasn't sure what his limits were, but he was certainly pushing them, trying to transport this many people at once. Slowly, the magical heat strengthened. With my new powers, I felt closer to the energy that surrounded me. It had a fractured thrum of detachment as it tried to rip my body away from the place I was currently anchored to and transport me to where Rusl was trying to go.

Sweat poured down Rusl's face, the discomfort visible through his hunched stance and heavy breathing. It was time. With one last glance over at the friends I was leaving behind, a soft smile pushed up my lips. Catilda, Ryker, and Kasra all smiled back weakly. What had started as a way to get one step ahead of my father had turned into handing him the very information we were trying to keep secret.

With a final grunt, Rusl pushed himself over the edge, and Reeva's light vanished as the world turned to solemn darkness around me.

23

⎯⎯⎯⎯◈⎯⎯⎯⎯

WARMTH ABSORBED INTO my skin, a cool breeze soothing the heat. Rusl's magic had been fractured and unstable. When we landed in front of Bailee's cottage shop, it vanished immediately. My knees shook, and while I threw out my hands for balance, I ended up falling backward onto the rocky ground. The others didn't manage a graceful landing either.

Bailee's shop was located on Grestor Island, and was a couple of hours outside the city of Estine. While it may have been early afternoon in Clathe, where we had come from, here it was the dead middle of night. The black to navy gradient stretched across the endless open sky. The moon, glowing a yellowy white, loomed large, surrounded by an ethereal glow. It was a rare sight for me, having spent most of my time in the city of Chitol, where the lights never went down and perpetually hid the beauty of the nighttime sky.

The plants surrounding us danced in the gentle wind and cast moonlit silhouettes upon Bailee's eclectic magic shop. During the day, the bright sun would soak into the terracotta roof and glisten across the mosaic pathway. Under the cloak of night, only a dim porch light illuminated the rustic wooden door, along with the colorful "Rainbow Unicorn" shop sign that hung above it.

The door slowly creaked open, and before us stood a bleary-eyed zombie still in his pajamas, which were decorated with cartoon sharks. Bailee dragged a hand down his face, then ran it through his tousled bleached blond curls.

He yawned loudly, then started rubbing his eyes. "You know, Fuzzy Fangs, you're lucky I like you so much, because when Catilda woke me up from a dead sleep like five minutes ago, she—" He blinked open his eyes and saw all seven of us lining the pathway. His penetrating stare stopped on Ozcar. "She did *not* mention there would be a dirty roach joining you. Zulli, what have you dragged me into this time?"

"Hello again, *Twiggy*," I jested, using Catilda's nickname for Bailee. "We had a slight change of plans. Sorry to intrude on you like this, but we need your expertise on plants to help release a spell holding back my friend's magic. Ozcar here so graciously offered us his skills in breaking down spells to assist with the process."

Bailee's gaze slowly roved over the group. He had met Rusl briefly, and Ozcar had stamped his mark by stopping by to claim the spatula and destroy Bailee's progress on making an antidote for Bliss. Everyone else was a new face, and he stared at each one of them with a tired but irritated glower.

"Ugh. I can't believe I'm letting you talk me into doing this. Give me a minute to change. I'll meet you in the back by the barn. *Touch nothing!*" His last statement was directed toward Ozcar, who innocently held up his hands.

The group followed me around the back and down the pathway to the barn. Even at night, the grounds were a tranquil sanctuary of pleasant floral scents and insects buzzing freely in the open air. NightFlies lit up the surrounding field with their colorful fluorescent glow, and Bailee's fountain of youth, as he called it, trickled with magic-infused water that sounded like a peaceful running stream. Rusl stayed behind and took a moment to rest beside it, cupping his hands to splash the nutrient-rich liquid on his face.

By day, Bailee ran a shop similar to Harper's Treasure Chest, offering unique and rare magic finds. During his time off, he dabbled in mixing herbal concoctions using his magical connection to the earth. The barn, overwhelmed with exotic plant life, was entwined with nature. The raw timber siding had a natural weathered look to it. Inside, oak beams curved across the loft like a wooden rib cage. The floor was mostly packed dirt, with some areas cultivated to create a natural garden for his plants to grow. A few tables, shelves, and chairs were placed around the open space. Potted plants were *everywhere.*

Ozcar stared at some liquid samples stored in glass mason jars, humming loudly and with a purpose. If he wanted someone to ask what he was thinking, no one did.

No more than ten minutes later, Bailee joined us in the barn wearing a pair of striped board shorts, a pink tie-dyed polo shirt, and purple flip-flops. He hid his mussed up hair under a red baseball cap, but his flawless bronze skin seemed to glow brighter than the sun itself.

"Okay. What is it exactly that you need from me?" Bailee tied a worn out work apron around his waist then rubbed his hands together.

To Bailee's dismay, Ozcar replied. "For ten years of his life, this boy has had his magic suppressed by a powerful spell. Synthetic magic processed in labs would be too harsh on him. I need a special list of herbal ingredients and your assistance in working the plants to ease them into dissolving the spell and to kick-start his magic."

My mother handed the crumpled piece of paper over to Bailee. He examined it with a critical eye, scratched his chin, then scraped his fingers across his forehead. "This makes sense, but I suggest swapping out the Black Milfoil with Butterfly Bittercress. It'll make him less nauseous and less likely to throw up the entire mixture."

"But the Bittercress will take hours to absorb. We don't have that kind of time to wait." Ozcar glanced over at my father, whose unusual silence was quite worrisome. He stood there observing with his hands clasped behind his back, taking in the conversation with a greedy smile.

"All right. I guess I'll get to work."

"And I shall help." Ozcar reached into his jacket and pulled out the spatula. Bailee didn't respond with words, but the hatred gleaming in his honey-brown eyes could have bored holes directly through Ozcar's soul and set it on fire. The potted plants surrounding him wriggled and vibrated with magic.

Catching on to his apprehension, Ozcar spoke. "I promise I am here only to release Cole's magic and nothing more. I have no need for anything else from you."

"Your promises are less welcome than gum on the bottom of my shoe." With that, the two of them ambled over to a wooden table and started to work.

My parents stood on opposite sides of the barn, but despite the space between them, they never took their watchful eyes off each other. I could sense their tension, the magic building up in the air. It smothered me like a toxic cloud. My mother's magic smelled similar to Catilda's, a strong sense of summertime sun reminiscent of sitting on a porch, drinking lemonade. My father's magic, on the other hand, reminded me of wet cardboard left out to soak in a salty marsh. Combined, the stench was nauseating, but all I could wonder was if my combined powers reeked in the same way. I couldn't smell my own magic, and it was probably a good thing.

"Cole." Karise pulled over a padded stool and sat down next to the boy. Cole had made himself comfortable in a cozy chair, which looked to be handcrafted by Bailee himself. "This will not be a pleasant experience for you, but I'm here to help you get through it, okay?"

Cole nodded his understanding. His mostly blank expression showed small glimpses of his fear trickling through. He blinked frequently, and his lips trembled ever so slightly. The palms of his hands were rubbing up and down his pant legs.

"I'll feed my magic into you. You'll likely want to push me out. Most people do. The feeling of having someone else's emotions take over your own is like a violation of privacy, but once you accept it, the pain and discomfort will ease. My magic will do its work to keep you calm, and I'll guide you to the memories you need to retrieve."

"It's done." Bailee held up a glass jar filled halfway with a murky green liquid. Ozcar stood next to him, spatula in hand. He wiped off the baking utensil with a towel and tucked it safely back into his jacket.

My parents circled around a set of tables and stopped on either side of Cole. Shiny claws protruded from my mom's fingertips, while my dad licked his sharp fangs. Venomous magic, a different ability than my own, oozed from them as his tongue rolled over the pointed tips.

Anxiety crept down my spine like a spider descending on a trail of silk. If this worked, if Ozcar's potion dissolved the spell, what exactly would Cole remember? I had little faith that my father would just let him go, regardless of what we uncovered, and I knew my mother wouldn't simply accept his demands. But these were my parents. I didn't agree with what my father was doing, but could I really fight my own flesh and blood? I tugged on the thin collar around my neck. Did I even have enough control over my power to confront them?

Bailee handed Cole the jar. "It looks gross, and I'll be honest, it is. I added in a hint of mint to help mask the taste. Good luck, Cole."

"Whenever you're ready, child." Karise took Cole's hand in both of hers and gently stroked it with the pad of her thumb. I couldn't place the smell of her magic, but the sensation it evoked was that of a compassionate hug.

Cole stared at the jar for a moment, his different colored eyes peering down at the cloudy liquid inside as he swirled it. He inhaled a deep breath and tilted his head back. A few gulps later, it was gone.

We waited in anxious agony, all eyes on Cole and what would happen next. My heartbeat quickened and I found myself irritable as I shifted my weight from foot to foot. At first, it seemed like it might not have worked. He burped, rubbing his chest as the nausea set in. Then he slumped in his chair, his head bobbing forward. Karise clasped his hand, but his legs dropped to the side and his other hand slid off his lap, sweeping past his hip.

"Is he falling asleep?" I asked, my voice a hushed whisper. My hand reached for my gun and I pointed it at Ozcar. I wouldn't put it past him to slip something else into that liquid.

"Just wait for it ..." Ozcar replied.

A concussive blast of magic exploded out of Cole. I was thrown back, my gun ripped from my hand and smashed into pieces as it hit a wall. Karise flung off her stool, her grip on Cole's hand lost. His hot magic displaced the cool air around us, sucking the air out of my lungs. It was colorless and odorless, but it rippled through the air in waves, a hazy shimmer scattering and distorting space itself.

"Cole ..." I gasped. The intense magic gushing out of him dragged across my raw skin and kept pushing against me. It buzzed in my ears. Itched my nostrils. Burned in my throat. Choking, slashing, stinging. Pressure built behind my eyes, nearly pushing them out of their sockets. Every time my heart beat, my entire body pulsed with a sharp pang of trepidation.

Cole's body tilted to the side and he collapsed, falling off the chair. His wide eyes swirled with chaos that consumed his rage, grief, and fear. No response came from his open mouth, but his silent screams reached my ears.

24

---◈---

"*CAPTO!*" MY SPELLED boots scraped against the loose dirt on the ground, unable to keep me in place. My claws dug into the soil and my sticky fingertips fought for purchase.

Karise had been knocked out cold, blood matting her thin hair. Bailee ran behind a table, Ozcar hiding right next to him. My mother attempted to shield herself from the force of magic with a raised hand, but my father—his spider magic encased his skin with an invisible, hardened exoskeleton that repelled the scorching heat. Engaging his strength, he just stood there with his arms folded over his chest, one hand scratching the bottom of his chin. A loose strand of his slicked back hair fluttered in the air. His silver eyes assessed Cole while the rest of us struggled to break free from the torrent of magic pummeling into us.

On the outside, Cole was merely lying on the floor. Twitching, jerking, and, every once in a while, blinking. The magic radiating off him continued pouring out. It charged the air with an electric energy that buzzed across my skin. Inside his mind, memories flooded his brain, screeching for release. The pain, the happiness, the sorrow of every single memory returning to him quicker than I could snap my fingers. Tears slipped down his cheeks. A teenage boy should never have to experience something so terrifying.

My newfound strength took over and I inched closer to Cole. His magic whipped at my arms and legs. Heat lashed at my face. The sound, like hundreds of vultures flapping their wings as they swarmed their prey, drowned out everything around me. My protective shirt absorbed some of the impact, but the rest of my body felt like it was pushing against the force of a freight train. Tense and strained, I broke past my limits. My mouth opened, pointed fangs grazing my lips.

"Zulli, don't!" my mom screamed. A wave of magic drowned the words out.

I understood now why my father had feared Cole. Strength might overpower an opponent, but the power of knowledge could easily outwit him. Unfortunately, Cole's magic had been suppressed almost his entire life. The knowledge, the memories … it was too much for his brain to process all at once. I had to help him.

My fangs pierced his wrist, biting deep into his flesh. A jolt of his magic slammed directly into me, paralyzing my muscles, but I held firm. I was taking a gamble, not knowing what might happen when I sucked out Cole's magic with my new abilities.

My heart sped up and thousands of data points processed through my brain at light speed.

Fingers cold. Ice in veins.

Rapid breathing. Dizziness. Chest pain. Confusion.

Cold sweat. Tired, difficult to stay awake. Lungs failing. Brain damage.

Damaged brain cells cannot be repaired.

Sorrow swelled in my chest and heat coiled in my stomach. Cole was processing his own death based on the knowledge he wielded, and now it would seem that same ability had been passed to me. I had somehow copied his magic, and thanks to the potion Bailee had given Cole, all of his memories were being transferred with it.

Heat scorched my tongue as the magic slid down my throat and burned in my chest. My stomach filled with a combustible energy that expanded against my ribs, but I continued drawing out his magic. More memories crashed into me, flashes of long lost moments in time.

Cole, a curious infant, sitting on the floor next to a fireplace. Building blocks formed the shape of a tall, house-like structure. His parents—Herah and Cohlin—joyously watched over him. The carefree couple laughed, smiles laced with love stretched across their youthful faces.

The memory washed away. Cole, maybe a couple of years older, accompanied his mother in the vineyard as she cared for the plants.

"Too much water will rot the leaves," she explained, although the toddler didn't seem interested. *"We spray a waxy substance derived from the stem of a diavac plant to seal the leaves and prevent disease. Bugs also don't like the slick surface."*

Flash forward. Cole was a little taller now. Concern bled through his vision. A cunning man, my father, pulled Cole's parents aside for a private conversation in their office. The door was left ajar, and Cole watched the argument unfold.

"I will pay you handsomely for that magic pesticide. Just as you protect the plants, I can adapt it to protect humans from diseases, as well. Come work with me. I will make you rich." My father locked his eyes on the couple. His features were much younger, his hair black and wrinkles less prominent, but that same voice that commanded obedience blazed through him.

Cohlin's arm swept out in front of his wife to defend her. Her lips were trembling as she cowered in the shadow of my father, but her husband remained fearless. *"Our secret is not for sale, especially to you. We don't want your money."*

"We'll see about that." My father stormed out of the office, knocking Cole over when he thrust the door open. He gave Cole a sinister glower and then disappeared.

"Zulli!" My mother's voice broke the bridge between Cole's memories and reality, momentarily snapping me out of the past. "Zulli, stop!"

Her arms wrapped around my waist, and she yanked hard. My fangs ripped from Cole's wrist as I was pulled away. I crashed into my mother's chest, her arms hugging me tightly and refusing to let go.

Having sucked out a heavy dose of Cole's magic, the intense heat emanating from his body and rippling through the air around us had dampened. Instead, it filled my belly like an overblown balloon about to burst. Bile rose in my throat, my stomach on fire like a pot of boiling acid. I couldn't stop gasping for air, the erratic thump of my heart begging for cool oxygen.

"You wielded his magic, didn't you, my little spider?" My dad approached, his shiny dress shoes pointing at the bottom of my feet as I lay on the ground in my mother's embrace. "What other skills have you been hiding from me?"

Pain flared from my head, traveling to my core and out toward every limb. My heart was pounding furiously with every emotion—fear, grief, panic, desperation. Wincing, I clutched a hand to my chest and wished desperately for my claws to rip out my own heart to stop the ache.

When I didn't answer, my father crouched down beside me. My mother squeezed me tighter, as if he might rip me away from her. "Keep your secrets, my little spider. It doesn't matter. But it seems like Cole can't handle his immense magical power just yet. So, I will get my information from *you*, Zulli."

"What?" I huffed out in between quick gasps of air. "I … can't do … that."

"You're a terrible liar, Zulli. Always have been. I know my own daughter. Even in this depreciated state, you avert your eyes from me and bite your lip. Now tell me. What did you see?"

"Nothing important," I rasped out. My mother helped me up and sat me down in the same chair that Cole had fallen out of. Bailee rushed over to Cole, lifting his head and pouring some herbal concoction down his throat. Cole choked on it as he swallowed. He was conscious, but barely.

"Then I expect you to *find* something important, or I'll have to kill the boy based on insufficient data." He held out his hand and spread his fingers wide. Thin silky strands shot out of his fingertips, weaving an intricate braided rope that coiled around Cole's feet and legs, clenched around his torso. It spiraled around his neck, up to his lips, and around his head. With a quick flick of his hand, the strands of my father's magic pulled tight around Cole's body and squeezed.

"Stop!" Bailee exclaimed. "You'll suffocate him!" He tried to poke a hole through the webbing where Cole's lips were, but every time he managed a small slit, the webbing healed itself and resealed.

My head flopped to the side. Cole's magic still burned strong within me, but I could already feel its effects waning. Ozcar handed me a glass of cold water that I painfully swallowed as he spoke. "If what I suspect is true, your fangs have drawn out Cole's magic, and for a limited time, will grant you the same powers as the person you stole them from. You currently have both Cole's power and memories in your mind. So I added a little Bliss into the water for extra encouragement to recover what we came here for."

I dropped the glass and spat on the floor, but from the moment I'd taken my first sip, it was already too late. "Ozcar, you backstabbing piece of scum!"

He shrugged. "Maybe I am. I'm just keeping my promise to retrieve Cole's memories. I never promised who they'd come from. And if I'm being honest, I'd rather be on your father's good side and take a chance with your mother's bad side."

"Wise choice, Mr. Thorne." My father leaned in toward me, his silver eyes glinting with an edge of darkness. "Now tell me, Zulli. Tell me *everything* about Colton Meyers' memories."

Full of power, force, and intensity, his words demanded obedience, but it was the magic that made me comply. Heat rushed into the pit of my stomach and a sudden tide of fiery energy burned to consume my body, mind, and soul. Something snapped inside my mind, the magic tugging on the strands of each thought. I pushed against it, refusing to give into his command, but ultimately I lost the fight.

The dam opened and Cole's memories flooded within me, full force. My skull was a fragile eggshell, cracking under the pressure.

"Zavyr, don't do this! You'll kill your own daughter!" My mom's words rang out as if from a distance, but she was right next to me. I barely registered her stroking my hand with her thumb. "Zulli, remember what I told you. The more you fight against it, the more it'll consume you. There's nothing you can do now but embrace your magic."

"Be quiet, Tabatha!" My father held out an open palm, and a wad of shimmery webbing splat right across my mother's mouth. With a single claw, she attempted to delicately cut through it without slicing herself open while my father continued. "Zulli, dig through Cole's memories. Tell me about the vineyard. The pesticide. What did Cole see?"

Pain like a thousand needles stabbed behind my eyes, and I squeezed them shut.

Memory after memory played through my mind like a movie reel, moving so fast I could barely make anything out. A flash of Cole's smile. A glimpse of Cole's tears. A flicker of Cole's fear.

"Cohlin ... he's arguing with Herah about giving you the formula."

"Yes, Zulli. Tell me more."

I listened to the conversation inside my head.

"We have to give him something, Cohlin. The business isn't worth our lives or our son's." Cole's mom, a fragile woman with ash blonde hair, stood across from her husband in the vineyard's storage facility. Cole was hiding in the shadows behind a stack of oak barrels. The room was dark, and I got the sense it was late at night. It didn't appear that his parents knew he was there.

"You know we have to keep it a secret." Cohlin ran a hand through his cropped blond hair, then dragged it down the stubble on his face. *"Since when do magiceutical companies ever want to cure people from their ailments? He only wants it so that he can exploit the sick and control the market."*

Cohlin stalked past the barrels and opened a thick door at the end of the aisle. Both he and Herah stepped inside but didn't bother closing the door behind them. Cole followed, staying hidden. He watched from behind another barrel as his father handled a few different jars of dried herbs and liquids. He placed them down on a small table in the private tasting room.

"What are you doing?" Herah wrapped her hand around his wrist to stop him.

"He unleashed some disease on our vineyard. You know he did. It's taking more and more of the formula to protect the plants. He's testing us to make it stronger, better, more powerful. He knows we'll need extra resources to keep this place running, and he wants us to grovel at his feet and beg him for help. He'll get the secret one way or another. I refuse to let him do that."

My father's voice cut into the memory. "Zulli, tell me what you're seeing."

Cohlin uncapped a bottle of dried green herbs. Cole squinted to read the name on the label.

"He's opening a jar of Western Goldenglow and putting it into a large metal bowl."

"Yes, yes. Go on," my father encouraged.

I watched through Cole's eyes as Cohlin mixed the other ingredients. "Belladoris. Milfade. Pollen from a flower. I don't know what kind though."

"Describe it." Curiosity came from Ozcar's words.

Cole's description came to mind. "It's large, about the size of Cohlin's palm. Six petal-like segments form the shape of a bell. It's bright yellow, streaked with red veins. There's a long stem in the middle, and Cohlin is using both the pollen and leaves in the mixture."

Both Ozcar and my father shot their gazes at Bailee, still attending to Cole. His eyes widened and terror grasped his throat as he sputtered to get his words out. "I will tell you what that flower is but only if you let Cole go."

My father regarded him with a look of disinterest. The webbing binding Cole loosened slightly, although didn't fully release him, and a small opening formed between his lips. Cole's head jerked as he gasped and filled his lungs with a full breath of air. At least he was still alive, but there was no telling how much longer my father would allow him to live.

"It's called the Liliflora. Very temperamental plant. Requires a specific nutrient in the soil to grow, an exact amount of water and sunlight to flourish, and just the right humidity to bloom. Its pollen is said to have a special property that bonds well to other magic. When boiling its petals, an enzyme is released that, when mixed within a spell, can prolong its intended effects."

"Prolong magic, you say?" My father scratched his chin and hummed. "Of course. With this plant, I can intensify the effects of Bliss and make it last longer! Zulli, what else can you tell me?"

My mother, having freed herself from my father's gag, spoke with a tongue fierce enough to sting. "Zavyr, you got what you came for. *Now leave!*"

Her threat hung in the air. With claws flashing, she made a move toward Zavyr when Ozcar stepped in front of her to block her. "Let the man do his work, Tabatha."

My mother's gaze flitted around the barn. Cole, still wrapped in webbing, was on the floor next to Bailee. I was under my father's control with Bliss, and there was no way she could rely on

Ozcar for any help. She was a fierce fighter, but by engaging now, she'd put the rest of us at risk.

A scream burst out of my throat, followed by nervous, rapid-fire breathing. Tension ratcheted through my body, winding my muscles tighter and tighter. Cole's magic stretched like a piece of taffy, trying to separate itself from my own.

"It's wearing off," Ozcar observed. "Unless she draws more of Cole's magic, there's not much time left before it disappears and she can no longer access the memories."

"Then have her take more of his magic," my father scoffed.

Ozcar shook his head. "I'm not sure the boy can handle it. I know you're not particularly fond of him living, but if he dies before you get your answers, the information will be gone forever if you can't extract it from Zulli before the magic permanently wears off."

Heat. Insufferable heat devoured my body as a vision of flames rose into the air. I couldn't physically feel it, but Cole remembered exactly how it felt when the vicious blaze burned his home to ash. From above, a wooden beam dropped from the ceiling. It hit a dresser, splintering into several pieces. A chunk broke off, and as Cole looked up, the fiery piece of timber struck him in the face. He wailed in pain, his hand cupping his right eye. Through his frightened sobs, a five-year-old Cole cried out desperately for his parents. "*Mommy! Daddy!*"

My heart sank to my toes, and tears of my own sprung from my eyes. Outside his window, a nighttime sky was lit with a glowing orange aura. The flames raced across the vineyard, consuming everything in its path. This was Cole's memory of the night his home burned to the ground. The night his parents died. The night he lost everything.

Both Herah and Cohlin stumbled through the bedroom door, dropping to their knees as they crawled toward Cole. Soot was smeared across their skin, and Herah couldn't stop coughing. Cohlin threw an arm around both his wife and son, pulling them in for a tight embrace.

Despite Herah's discomfort, she snatched a blanket off the bed and wrapped it around her son. *"Contego."* Magic rippled around Cole, an invisible shield that protected him from falling debris and the raging inferno surrounding him.

"Whatever happens, Cole, I know you'll remember that we will always love you very, very much." She kissed him on the forehead and whispered something in his ear. Sharp needles pierced behind my eyes, and the memory fizzled away, along with the rest of Cole's magic flowing inside me.

Her words lingered in my ears. It would be the last time Cole ever heard his mother's voice. It took me a moment before I could speak.

"Serenity rose." My voice was almost silent, full of regret as I fed my father the information I so desperately wanted to withhold. Blinking the barn back into focus, everyone was standing still, evaluating me slumped in the chair.

"Serenity rose," my father repeated, glancing over to Bailee for answers. "I've never heard of that plant."

Bailee, having made his way over to tend to Karise, shook his head. "That's because it doesn't exist. It's a myth. The serenity rose grows on a tree, and supposedly, when the petals are steeped into tea, the healing properties are unparalleled to any synthetic drug or herbal potion ever made, so much so that it can bring someone back from the dead. But the thorns on its vines are so poisonous it can kill with one prick, and if anyone manages to get close enough to snip off a flower, the tree screams so loud it kills anyone who hears it. It's said that the roots then absorb the human life it claims and it continues to grow its power each time."

My father rubbed his chin, pondering Bailee's statement. "Perhaps some form of it does exist if Herah mentioned it. It must be the key ingredient to complete the spell that protected the plants in the vineyard. And it's the last ingredient I need to perfect Bliss. If I could remake their original spell, I could alter it to fortify the mind and make the effects of Bliss permanent."

A wave of dizziness washed over me. My head rolled to the side, my limbs pliant like limp noodles. All the energy had been drained from my body, and I barely had enough stamina left to blink.

"So, what are you going to do now, Zavyr? Kill your own daughter?" My mom positioned herself in between me and Cole, fingers curled with sharp claws ready for slicing.

"Kill her? No need. Cole's magic has worn off. She won't remember a thing. But the boy ... well, when he comes to, his full powers will have awakened. I contemplated taking him with me, but I have what I want. I know you'll be a nuisance and come after him anyway. And I surely can't let him stay with you, not with all that priceless information in that brain of his. The boy has to die to protect this information from falling into the wrong hands."

"It already *is* in the wrong hands." My mother crouched down low, magic flowing over her skin. In addition to her claws, pointed ears and a furry tail sprouted from her head and lower back. "If you want to get to Cole, then you'll have to go through me first."

"Splendid." A slippery smile tugged at the corner of my father's lips. "I'll get to finish what Davian failed to do all those years ago."

25

---◈---

WITH HER SWIFT speed and agility, my mother lunged into action. Claws sliced across my father's chest, shredding his white dress shirt, but he jumped back a step before she reached his flesh.

"I see your skills haven't diminished with age, Tabatha." He peered down and frowned at his torn shirt.

"Stop!" I choked out. My distress was just enough to make my mother flinch, and my father took that opportunity to drive her directly into a work table with the full force of his strength.

I pushed off the chair onto my unstable feet. Steadying myself, I charged at my father. My feet dragged across the dirt, my vision slightly blurry. He didn't even bother defending himself. When his head twisted toward me, amusement was woven into his intense silver eyes. My clawed fingers stopped an inch from his throat.

"And what do you plan on doing with those?" he asked, a sly smile creeping up his mouth.

My hands shook uncontrollably. Air sucked into my lungs in urgent gasps. Fury and fear raged against each other, fighting for control. Despite the disgust I harbored for everything my father was doing, he was still family.

"That's what I thought. Why don't you put those powers to good use and attack your mother instead? She abandoned you for all these years, left you to grow up without a mother. She doesn't deserve your love." He snatched my wrist and flung me back into the side of the chair. I awkwardly crashed into it, my arm draping over the side and my knees scraping the hard dirt floor. My mother came running over. Fresh cuts and swollen bruises, thanks to Cole's explosion of magic, marred her face and neck.

"Zulli, kiddo, are you okay?"

When she was close enough to place a hand on my arm, I swung mine outward and narrowly missed slicing her throat. Fury coursed through me, boiling the blood and magic running through my veins. My father's demand took control of my limbs and the thoughts in my head. *Attack my mother.*

"You are stronger than this, Zulli. Fight the Bliss!" She stepped back.

Emotions poured out of me in a maelstrom of violent turmoil. Tears streamed from my eyes, anger infused in my words. "You left me! Do you know how lonely it was growing up without you? I was devastated! Broken! They told me you were dead! I didn't want to believe it, but the more I thought about it, the more I wanted it to be true. Because the alternative meant you made the conscious choice to abandon your family!"

"Zulli, we've been through this. I didn't have a choice." She held up her hands, expecting me to attack.

A menacing snicker came from my father. My mom flinched, and I charged toward her. She dodged my swinging fist, my claws hacking through the stalk of a plant instead. My mom dropped and went for my legs. With the dexterity only a cat could have, I leaped into the air, avoiding her foot and landed back on my feet. Magic pumped into me, the collar around my neck pulsing, trying to contain it. A throbbing ache spasmed through my lower back, and when I looked down, a long black tail was coiled around my waist. A second set of pointed ears twitched on the top of my head.

"Zavyr, stop this! This is our fight. Leave Zulli out of it!"

My tail whipped from side to side, my claws longer, sharper, and ready for dealing punishment. I wanted nothing more than to use them to strangle my mother, then tear out her throat.

My father's laugh grew darker, evil laced into every cruel note. I drew on my power, welcoming it to take control. Adrenaline surged through my core, blossomed in my middle, and blasted outward, replenishing my previously stolen energy.

Ozcar and Bailee stood nearby, keeping their distance from the fight and tending to Cole and Karise. I eyed them, and in that brief moment, a tinge of regret flashed through my mind. My mother must have caught the subtle display of emotion.

"You were never alone growing up, Zulli. You had Catilda and the Harpers looking out for you. Your brothers. And you're not alone now, either. You have Ryker and Kasra. Not just teammates, but your best friends, who would do anything to protect you. You have new friends, like Salynn, waiting for you to return. People relying on you to keep them safe, like Cole and Karise. You have every right to hate me for what I did, but you didn't need me. You're a strong, fierce woman, Zulli. I need that fighter to come out now. You need to make a choice. What do you really want, Zulli?"

The question left a confusing thought in my head. In this moment, I loathed every single thing about my mother. But was it not a day ago that she had vouched for me in front of numerous strangers and touted about how proud she was of my accomplishments? Did she not come to my aid to save me and Kasra from nearly dying ... by the hands of the people my father had sent after me? The Bliss brought forth a lifetime of emotions I had stuffed away, far into the depths of my aching soul.

My hardened gaze slowly traveled toward my father. The urge to attack my mother was strong, but the impulse to stop my dad outweighed it. "What Mom did is unforgivable. But what you're currently doing is even worse. You are controlling people against their will, warping their personalities, their memories, and changing them into people they aren't. You might be right, that I don't have the strength to hurt you, but that doesn't mean I can't find other ways to make you suffer. I *will* end this."

My father's hand reached for a pair of pruning shears from a worktable next to him. He ripped the two blades apart and drew back both of his hands.

Fingers shaking, I threw out my hand and webbing spurted from the tips. I caught one of his wrists, but not before both blades sailed directly toward my mother a few feet away.

"No!" My flimsy, silky strands snapped easily under my father's strength. The first blade missed its intended target, striking my mom in her shoulder. She bent forward, hissing as she ripped the sharp object out of her flesh. Blood gushed from her wound, the dark, shiny liquid blossoming like the red flower patterns on her silky blouse.

Panic flared inside my chest at the sight of the second blade aimed directly at my mother's head. I raced toward her, knowing I would never make it to her in time. My hand reached out in front of me, hoping by some miracle my magic would stop the blade and save her.

The assault unfolded as if time had slowed. My mother threw up her hands to shield herself, but her reaction wouldn't be quick enough. Terror screeched along my nerves and icy dread touched my spine. I wouldn't make it. The lethal weapon had been thrown with enough force to embed itself into my mother's skull. It would end her life.

A spicy scent tickled my senses and I sneezed. Its warmth was a little nutty and slightly peppery. Notes of vanilla danced delightfully within it.

The blade disappeared a mere centimeter from my mother's head and reappeared to stab my father's leg. A howl of unendurable pain ripped from his throat, his hand clutching his thigh as he collapsed to one knee.

Something dark briefly flashed through Ryker's expression. He was huffing like an angry bull, so much anger and rage etched in his eyes. He rushed over to my mom, checking to make sure she was okay. Then the hard lines on his face melted into a satisfied smile. A surge of warm joy and happiness, mixed with chittering glee, enticed a laugh to come out of my mouth.

"Zulli!" Ryker dashed toward me with open arms, then wrapped them around me in a tight embrace. I melted under the comfort, surrendering the rest of my strength. "I needed to make sure you were okay."

The moment of relief didn't last long. "My dad!"

I ripped away from Ryker's arms to see a thick ivy vine coiling around my father's ankles. Bailee, offering his payback, was moving his hands to control his pet plants. Magic vibrated angrily from the leaves, steam rising into the air as the acid emitting from them began eating through the fabric of my father's pants. He tried to kick out his feet, then tugged at the thick vines with his hands, but Bailee only willed the plants to squeeze tighter.

"Doesn't feel so nice to have your limbs crushed, does it?" he berated.

My father held out his hand toward Bailee. Before the webbing left his fingertips, someone snuck up behind him and roundhouse kicked him in the side. He pitched sideways, but the vines prevented him from falling over.

A satisfied breath came from his attacker. Her long, glossy black hair was braided behind her back. She had lost her gloves, beanie, and, for probably the first time in her life, exposed her skin with a stylish t-shirt and capris.

"Salynn?" My heart danced heavily with excitement. She was alive, awake, and looked full of energy. But what was she doing here?

246

She took a moment to adjust her prosthetic limb, the metal creaking with her touch. Her attention then turned to me.

"Hey, Zulli. Give me a minute. I'll settle this."

She raised her hands to place her palms on either side of my father's head. He snarled and flashed his pointed fangs.

"Salynn, his teeth!"

It was too late. My father sunk his venomous fangs into Salynn's arm. He laughed quietly, relishing in his easy victory over her.

Salynn didn't even flinch. "You don't remember me, do you, Mr. Taracula?"

My father growled, biting down harder. Blood rolled down her arm and dripped to her feet.

"About twenty years ago, my aunt brought me to you, looking for help. My magic was killing me, poisoning me from the inside out. You experimented on me for months, painful and torturous tests that only sped up the production of my deadly magic." A cunning smile creased her thin lips when my father's eyes widened. "Yeah, that's right. My body has been producing poison since the day I was born. Whatever weak magic is in those fangs of yours will have absolutely no effect on me. But my magic on the other hand ..."

Salynn crushed her hands against his head. A sinister, ominous magic emanated from her skin and the smell of ... vinegar? ... overpowered the floral scent in the barn. Her poisonous magic vibrated at a savage intensity as she pumped it into my father's body. Salynn's smile took on a razor's edge.

"Salynn ..." I warned.

My father started heaving, choking on the toxin being absorbed through his skin. His silver eyes turned dull with detachment.

"Salynn!" I shouted again. Wary faces watched her. No one dared get close enough to touch her, knowing what her magic was capable of. No one except me.

Before Ryker could stop me, I ran toward Salynn. Coating my own arms with my webbing, I plowed into her and pushed her out of the way. She tripped over her own two feet and fell to the ground.

"What the hell, Zulli? I wasn't trying to kill him. I've been training my whole life to control my magic. Now, I finally can. I only slipped him enough poison to make him violently ill for a few days."

My father bent over as vomit spewed out of his mouth and splattered onto his shoes. He gasped, trying to suck in air before he gagged again and another round of his stomach juices came forth. He wiped his face with his shirtsleeve.

"Rusl!" my father called out in a croaky voice.

I sensed Rusl's earthy magic before the man appeared.

"Are you all right, sir?" he questioned, raising an eyebrow at my father.

"Let's go." My father clutched his chest, sweat beading on his brow. He heaved in and out, his face turning bright red.

"What about the boy? And the others at the prison?" Rusl asked.

"Forget them! Just get me out of here!"

My father's gaze lingered on me, a predatory warning that promised this wasn't the end. He didn't have to say a word. I knew he had been hunting my mother, and now he would hunt me.

Rusl placed a hand on my father's shoulder, and with a loud pop, my father and his transporter disappeared.

My attention turned to Ozcar, pouring something over Cole to dissolve the webbing that encased him. It would eventually disintegrate on its own, but without my father releasing his hold on the magic, it would take quite some time.

Karise had stirred awake, dizzy and confused but only suffering from a bump on her head. Ozcar helped her into a chair, giving her a tube of some floral-scented healing ointment to rub onto the wound. Bailee and my mom were tending to Cole while

Ryker and Salynn remained on high alert, as if expecting someone else to return to the barn and finish the fight.

"This place is pretty cool," Salynn remarked. "It's very ... jungley." She brushed a finger along a thick leaf the size of her palm. I expected it to shrivel up and die, but it didn't. She saw me smiling and gave me a hearty grin back. She rushed over and embraced me with a hug.

"You're the first person I've physically touched in twenty years." Her voice cracked and she sniffled. "Except for your father just now. I don't count that."

Bailee coughed loudly to grab our attention. His gaze scanned the mess that had taken over the barn. Dirt was upturned, ceramic pots shattered. Most of his precious plants had been trampled on or sliced by claws. His worktables, along with all the equipment on top of them, had been overturned and broken. Jars filled with his herbal mixtures were shattered into pieces, the various colored liquids staining the ground.

"Sorry, Bailee." The words rang sincere. This was the second time I'd brought chaos to him. "I can help clean up if you want."

He flashed me an annoyed but friendly smile. "I think it goes without saying, but the next time you need my help, I'm coming to *you*."

26

---◈---

As IT TURNED out, Reeva and the goons from the Black Mark hadn't kept their promise to burn the prison to the ground, even though Ryker and Salynn defied their orders to escape. My father's lackeys locked everyone else in cells and, once receiving word of his retreat, made themselves scarce as well.

After freeing everyone, Lana went to work in the infirmary, tending to those in need of medical attention. She examined Cole, bandaged the cut on Karise's head, and used some fancy magic contraption to seal up my mother's stomach wound and encourage its healing. With a little rest, everyone would recover just fine. Almost everyone.

"We lost two people." Despair was heavy in Dr. Fischer's words. "An elderly couple too brave for their own good. They saw one of the Black Mark members about to hit a young child because she wouldn't stop crying. They sprung into action to make sure they wouldn't lay a finger on her."

My gaze found fascination with the tile floor under my feet, my heart sinking to my toes. They had died honorably, but their deaths shouldn't have been necessary. I should have been there to do something. We should have been more careful to prevent my father from attacking in the first place.

"I've finished the roll call. Everyone is accounted for, except one. Ethin Henderson," my mother growled. "They took the mayor from us."

My thoughts returned to when I'd seen Ethin in the lab at NightFly Technologies. Bliss had been pumping through his veins. The last time I saw him in his cell, he was completely out of it. What would my father do with him now?

"Are you okay?" Ryker stood next to me while I sat on an exam bed and waited for Lana to release me. He was violently rubbing his fingertips against his temples, his eyes closed and brows scrunched in discomfort. His headaches seemed to be getting more frequent and the pain more intense, but Ryker never complained about it.

"I'm fine. Just exhausted. How are—"

"It seems like I missed out on some serious fun," Kasra complained as she jostled her crutches and propped them up against the side table. She took a seat in a chair beside me and stretched out her leg. "I did get to ram the end of my crutch into some sleazeball's nuts, though. He learned his lesson not to get too close to me, or any woman for that matter."

"I'm not sure I'd call any of this fun." Kasra caught the detachment in my voice and immediately regretted her words.

"I'm so sorry, Zulli. I didn't mean to—"

Dr. Fischer appeared by my side and cut her off mid-sentence. "You're good to go, Zulli. Just take it easy for the next few days."

"Thanks. I think I'm going to bed. I'll meet up with you guys tomorrow."

Neither Kasra nor Ryker argued with me and let me escape the infirmary without a fight. Ryker, usually the first in line to comfort me, didn't even follow. He stayed behind to check on Maycee and a few others.

I was halfway to my bedroom prison cell when I heard Ozcar scolding my mother. The door was closed, but with my hearing, it was easy to decipher what they were bickering about. I pressed my ear to the door and listened.

"I held true to our agreement, Ms. Taracula. I unlocked Cole's magic and you retrieved his memories. It's not my fault it didn't play out as smoothly as you had hoped."

"You drugged my daughter, and Zavyr now has all the information I was trying to keep from him in the first place." A rumble came from inside the room. Judging from the sound and vibration, I suspected it was her hand slamming down on a metal desk.

"Keeping it from him was never in our agreement. I did what I had to do to get the job done, and now I expect my payment. You already have your husband coming after you. I highly doubt you want to add me to that list as well."

A few choice words came from my mother's mouth before she sighed and finally agreed. "Fine. I will get you what you requested. Do you still promise that everything I provide you will only remain in your possession? That you're not planning to blow up half the planet?"

"That part has not changed. This is for my own personal use and will remain only in my hands. I have told no one of my plans."

"Then give me a few days. I have to make a few calls, set up a few meetings, and arrange a secure drop off of the materials."

"I will return in a week. That should be plenty of time."

Footsteps grew louder as they traveled in my direction. I jumped back, trying my best to pretend like I had been casually walking by when Ozcar opened the door and filed into the hallway.

"Zulli. Looks like you're feeling much better." His hazel eyes flickered with something halfway between teasing and actual concern. I clenched my hands into fists and pressed my lips into

252

a thin line. "By all means, if you have something to tell me, just spit it out."

"The only payment you deserve is a hearty dose of Salynn's poison after that stunt you just pulled."

He laughed, and the wide smile on his face looked more than a little manic. "What I did had to be done, Zulli. I knew what I was doing. I dosed the Bliss perfectly so that it would affect you only briefly. That rage was all yours, and if you want to lead these people here then you really have to work out your family issues."

"Like I need a backstabbing criminal telling me how to live my life," I scoffed at him.

"I ran a powerful drug empire, and now I'm running an even more lucrative business trafficking weapons, drugs, and sometimes even people."

"*People?*" It took all my strength to not flay the skin off his face. Instead, I settled for childishly flipping off his ball cap.

"Rude," he intoned, picking up his hat and placing it back on his head. "Especially after all I did to help you."

"You made everything worse, Ozcar!" My words carried down the hallway, and a few people walking nearby stopped to check out what was going on.

"I beg to differ, Zulli. Just like Cole, you needed help to unleash your full power. But unlike Cole, who embraced his magic, perhaps a bit too much, you push yours away. You're a protector at heart, and I know you don't enjoy hurting people. If you want to prevent yourself from doing that, you need to accept your magic and learn to control it. And I have to say, I think you learned some new moves today, no?"

My mouth dropped open and confusion rushed in. "W-Wait a minute. You're trying to say that by sabotaging the whole plan, you were actually *helping* me?"

"It worked, didn't it? That was very clever what you did with your webbing to protect your arms from Salynn. You should also have the same hardened skin abilities as your father, but for now, the webbing is a sufficient alternative. And I'm gathering you noticed the ears and tail? Was that the first time you were able to partially shift into a cat?"

My hands reached for my scalp and scratched where the pointed ears had once appeared. I shook my head, sputtering off a bunch of incoherent sounds before I finally got something out that made sense. "Why would you even want to help me? Aren't we enemies?"

"Enemies?" He threw his head back and chuckled. "We are not friends, but we are hardly enemies either. You have helped me just as much as I have helped you." He patted a hand right above his beach ball gut, gesturing to the spatula hidden underneath his jacket.

"Not like you left me much of a choice." I crossed my arms and frowned at him.

"Your choices are your own, Zulli. You had enough time to come up with a way to use the spatula against me, but you didn't. Instead, you used that time hoping to counteract Bliss and save the world from becoming a hoard of detached, mindless zombies under your father's command. You have your father's drive, but your mother's compassion. Combined, those are powerful traits, but if you're not careful, they can also bite you in the ass. Your mother was right about one thing. You need to figure out what *you* want to do and, whatever it is, make it happen on your own terms."

No response formed on my tongue. I stared at Ozcar with a blank expression. He was a cold, hardened criminal, who had only ever looked out for himself, but somehow, his words had resonated with me. It was time I did what was best for me. My father and mother had pinned themselves against each other, but I was stuck in the middle—the voice of reason. If anyone could end this war between them, it had to be me.

Ozcar tipped his cap and smiled slyly. "Until next time, Zulli. I expect to see you rise to the occasion."

254

He strolled down the hallway, his hands in his jacket pockets and humming a triumphant tune to himself. I didn't bother to retort because I had a feeling he was right this time. This wouldn't be the last I'd see of him.

"What was that all about?" My mother emerged from the office, slipping her arms through the sleeves of her heavy coat, embroidered with a stylish pattern made from golden threads.

"Nothing. Just Ozcar being Ozcar, I guess." I raised an eyebrow as she bundled herself up. "Where are you going?"

"Grab your coat. It gets cold at night in the mountains."

I hurried to my bedroom cell and grabbed my leather jacket. Seeing the way my mom was dressed, it probably wouldn't be warm enough, but it was the only coat I had.

Outside, the bitter cold of the oncoming night was approaching. Following my mom, we climbed up into a watchtower that overlooked the vast expanse beyond us. The sun had mostly set across the horizon, leaving behind a dull glow that stained the clouds pink and orange. I knew little about Clathe other than that it was a mountain city surrounded by wilderness. The prison sat on top of the mountain, buildings circling around its base.

"Beautiful, isn't it?" my mom mused. The watchtower soared above the prison and was one of four that lined the crumbling brick wall that barricaded the entire compound. Glass windows surrounded the tower, and inside was a control panel with a multitude of buttons and monitors for surveillance. Wrapping around the control station was a balcony with a rusty metal railing. My mom leaned against it, peering out into the distance.

"What you said back at the barn, Zulli ..."

"I meant it." I held onto the railing, the cold metal rough against my palms. "Dad was never Father of the Year. He buried himself in his work, and with Brodin and Maeck being older than me, they joined him at NightFly Technologies as soon as they could. I really did feel alone. It's true, I had Catilda and her family, but the person I really wanted to be with was you. I couldn't talk to Dad about my first boyfriend or even share my excitement in joining the military. He didn't get me like you did, and I always felt like a failure in his eyes."

"Kiddo, just because you didn't rise to meet his unrealistic expectations doesn't mean you're a failure. His disappointment stemmed from the fact that, by joining the military, he knew you'd be a threat to him."

"I know that *now*." A chilly breeze bit through my leather jacket, the tips of my ears numb with cold. "But I didn't back then. From the day you left, I spent every waking moment trying to prove to him I deserved his love. And even now, with everything he's doing, I can't help but still want it."

"That's completely understandable, Zulli. Your world was turned upside down practically overnight. You learned who your father really was and that the mother you lost was actually still alive. It's a lot to process, and it'll take time to heal. But in the meantime, you have to remain strong. Your father won't back down. Events have been set in motion. He *will* make a move, and we have to be ready for it." A knowing smile stretched her lips and deepened the lines around her mouth.

"Why are you smiling? We just got our asses handed to us by Dad. He not only knows where we're hiding out, but he's going to use that formula to strengthen Bliss. He's going to administer it to everyone, to mold the personalities and minds of the most influential people to get whatever he wants. They'll basically lose their free will."

"Yes, your father got some very helpful information. But I know something he doesn't." She turned to face me, her green eyes reflecting the last rays of the setting sun.

"And that would be ...?"

"Serenity Rose." The silence stretched for a tense moment before she explained. "It's not just a mythical flower from a fairy tale. It's the name of an old acquaintance. And I'm pretty sure I know where to find her."

"An acquaintance?" My hands clenched tighter around the railing. "Then she's in danger. If Dad finds out ..."

"He will eventually, I'm sure. But for once, we're one step ahead of him. So, what do you wanna do, kiddo?"

"You're asking me?" My lips parted, a white cloud of breath escaping from my mouth. Ozcar's words still echoed through my mind. This was my chance to take ownership of the mission that my mother had put me in charge of. To do things *my* way. "Well, we obviously have to find her. And then we need to perfect Bliss before Dad does."

My mom's eyebrows knitted together, her eyes narrowing. "And why is that? You just said that controlling people is wrong."

I let out a heavy sigh, releasing every last ounce of conviction within me. "Because we're not using it to erase his memories and control him. Instead, we can use Bliss to help him remember who he once was—a devoted father and loving husband. To bring back the man he was before power corrupted him."

"And you think by reminding him about this past that it will make him just stop what he's doing and change his ways?" My mother's tone was curious, but not exactly convincing.

"It has to," I exhaled a long breath. "Because I fear what the alternative might come to."

Author's Note

Whoo! You made it to the end. Zulli's got a lot to think about. Zulli returns for another adventure in Fury of a Phantom.

Did you know that every time you leave a review, my dog gets to celebrate with a piece of cheese? Okay, sometimes I save some for myself, but you can help a pug out by leaving a review and supporting our cheese addiction. You can find me on Amazon, Goodreads, Barns & Noble, or BookBub.

I encourage you to follow me on Instagram, Facebook, and TikTok (@CSchulzWrites). I share contests, merch giveaways, updates, and of course adorable pictures of my pug eating cheese.

Ever wonder where that magical spatula came from? Check out my website at www.christineschulzwrites.com to download Mixing Magic & Mayhem, a free short story that takes place right before Dawn of a Demon begins. You'll learn more about Ozcar and how Zulli got involved in his business.

Made in the USA
Middletown, DE
25 August 2023